THE BIG SWITCH

Keeping his gaze locked with hers, David dragged something from one of the burlap sacks and held it out to Hannah.

"Oh, no." She was already shaking her head, backing away several inches for good measure.

"Please, Hannah." He took a step toward her, boxing her in. "Our lives depend on this."

For long seconds, she stood stock-still, scowling and wishing ten thousand plagues on this devious, manipulative man.

"You'll owe me for this, Walker," she bit out. "This had better work. And for this, you'll owe me forever. And I mean *forever*."

With that, she yanked the repugnant purple dress from his hands and marched toward the closet to transform herself from an innocent young schoolmarm to a practiced courtesan.

And then she was going to strangle David with a strip of lace from this Jezebel dress he loved so much.

HANNAH'S HALF-BREED

HEIDI BETTS

LEISURE BOOKS 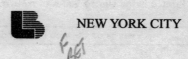 NEW YORK CITY

A LEISURE BOOK®

January 2003

Published by

Dorchester Publishing Co., Inc.
276 Fifth Avenue
New York, NY 10001

ISBN 0-8439-5073-0

The name "Leisure Books" and the stylized "L" with design are
trademarks of Dorchester Publishing Co., Inc.

Printed in the United States of America.

Visit us on the web at www.dorchesterpub.com.

To Joanne Emrick—

Isn't it funny how people come into our lives just when we need them most? We'd traveled in the same circles for years without realizing how much we had in common or that we would hold each other up when earlier moorings began to crumble.

Thank you for the long talks, brainstorming sessions, and your unwavering support. For both the slow, leisurely critiques and the more frantic, last-minute ones when I think the only place a story might make sense is in my head. For the laughter and for being another member of the Suzanne Sugarbaker Fan Club. Most of all, thank you for being a true and loyal friend.

You know I wish you the best of luck with your own endeavors. My scream will be the loudest you hear when your dream finally comes true.

ACKNOWLEDGMENTS

I would like to offer a super-size thank you to Theresa Leskovansky Hutton at the Holt Memorial Library in Philipsburg, PA, for not only tracking down an out-of-print copy of *Comanche Dictionary and Grammar*, which I needed desperately for the writing of this book, but for helping me to renew it month . . . after month . . . after month.

My added appreciation is extended to Dan Tingue at the Penn State University Library, who let Theresa renew this book month . . . after month . . . after month . . . and told me he would only take it away if a professor needed it for classes, thereby saving me from clutching the volume to my bosom and crying out, "You can have this book when you pry it from my cold, dead hands!"—which I was fully prepared to do.

Librarians . . . they make the world a better place. Thank you.

HANNAH'S
HALF-BREED

Chapter One

"There's no *s* in encyclopedia, Frederick," Hannah mumbled disgustedly to herself as she corrected her students' weekly spelling exams at the small oaken table in the middle of what passed as the dining room of her tiny cabin.

With a sigh, she rose to her feet and crossed to the cast-iron cookstove where a pot of water was just beginning to boil. She poured the steaming liquid over a spoonful of loose tea leaves in the bottom of her earthenware mug and carried it back to the table.

She was about to sit down, ready to continue grading papers, when she heard a low sort of scuffling noise outside the cabin door. At first she thought it might be leaves blowing

1

across the ground, or a stray raccoon sniffing around for something to eat. But a moment later, she heard the sound again, followed by what was almost certainly the nicker of a horse.

Cautiously, Hannah moved to one of the small windows on either side of the front cabin door, lifting the gingham curtain just a hair to glance out.

It was dark, the tall trees surrounding her small house obscuring any moonlight that might otherwise illuminate the yard. But even so, Hannah thought she saw something. Slight, shadowed, but a movement nonetheless.

For one panicked moment, she thought about hiding or escaping out the back. But then reason returned and she reminded herself that she had always been safe here—just a few minutes' walk from the main street of Purgatory, Texas—and that it was unlikely anyone would want to hurt her, anyway.

Just then, the horse nickered again, and even though her heart stuttered in her chest, she let the curtain fall and moved to the door. She opened it in one quick, smooth motion, without hesitation.

"Hello?" she called, not loudly but with enough force to be heard by whoever was lurking about.

A pale arc of light shone from inside the cabin and illuminated several feet in front of her. A large piebald stallion sidestepped into that shaft of light and Hannah's breath caught in her lungs.

Mounted astride that horse were a man and a child. Both wore buckskin shirts and leggings, and leather moccasins on their feet. Both had straight black hair that fell to their shoulders and beyond. And both stared at her as though *she* were the one out of place in this quiet little spot outside her cabin.

But it was the man who made Hannah's mouth go dry. Not only was he towering and intense, but she found him handsome beyond belief.

If any of the citizens of Purgatory who had hired her to educate their children could have read her thoughts at that moment, they would surely have thrown her out on her ear.

More than his dark skin and penetrating gaze, however, she couldn't help feeling that his strong features were somehow familiar to her.

Which was impossible, of course. There were any number of Indian villages in the areas surrounding Purgatory, but she had certainly never visited any of them. And the members of those tribes rarely, if ever, set foot in town; they likely would have been stared at, mocked, or run off if they had.

Before she had a chance to speak—indeed, her mouth was still too parched to form a single word—the man reached in front of him,

3

wrapped a hand around the boy's arm, and lowered him carefully to the ground. She thought she saw the man wince, his lips thinned and nostrils flared . . . and then decided she must be imagining things.

"*Miartu,*" he told the child. The word, whatever it meant, was said in a low, harsh tone.

The boy, six or seven years of age, Hannah guessed, tilted his head slowly in her direction. He studied her for a long moment, his eyes narrow and distrustful, before turning back to the man still sitting astride the black and white mount.

"She's a good woman," the man told the child. "Stay with her; she'll take care of you."

And then his gaze shifted to her. "Take care of him, Hannah. He needs your protection."

A shiver rippled through Hannah's body, and she finally found her voice. "How . . . how do you know my name? Who are you?"

The stranger—a stranger who knew her name and knew where she lived—shook his head, looking grim. "Take care of him," he said again, even more roughly this time.

And without another word, he turned his mount and started away. The horse's black tail flicked, drawing her attention to the child left in her care by a man she didn't know . . . but who apparently knew her.

The poor boy, she thought. Abandoned by someone he obviously cared about, judging by the way he watched after the stranger's retreating back. With a woman he knew not at all.

Though he stood ramrod straight, Hannah didn't miss the slight tremor that shook the child's shoulders, or the diamondlike glint of tears as the light from the house reflected off his damp eyes.

She started forward, thinking to comfort him, possibly lure him inside for a warm cup of milk.

But just as she reached the young boy, she heard a grunt of pain not far off in the direction in which the stranger had disappeared. That muffled sound was followed by the horse's low neigh and a hard, solid thud.

The boy, whose eyes were apparently better adjusted to the dark than Hannah's, rushed forward, but she followed close behind. They found the man lying on his side on the ground, unmoving.

"*Ara?! Ara?!*" the child cried out, shaking the man's leather-clad shoulder.

Hannah came up behind him. "It's all right," she assured him calmly. "He'll be all right." She hoped.

Shifting the boy a step out of the way, she rolled the man to his back. She could barely see anything, not even the outline of his face. Going by feel, she ran her hands over his arms, his ribs, wondering if he'd broken any bones in his fall from the horse.

Or perhaps he'd hit his head. She stroked

5

her fingers over his temples and through the silky black of his long hair but found not the slightest bump or abrasion.

Moving back to where she'd left off, she ran her hands over his torso, around a set of revolvers strapped to his waist . . . and stopped. Her fingers came away from the left side of his abdomen wet, and she highly suspected that if she walked into the light, it would reveal the red of blood.

She needed to get him inside, but how she was going to accomplish such a thing she had no idea. He had to be nearly two hundred pounds of pure muscle, while she often had to take in the seams of even the smallest-sized dresses sold at the Purgatory General Store.

Taking a deep breath, she squared her shoulders determinedly. She had no choice. She couldn't leave him out here on the ground to bleed to death.

Hooking her hands beneath the man's arms, she began to tug, throwing her entire bulk backward in an attempt to drag him to the cabin.

After a few short minutes, her chest heaved and her breath hissed through her teeth. And she'd managed to move him only two insignificant inches.

"Well, this certainly isn't working," she muttered to herself, knowing the child at her side—glowering at her—wouldn't care, even if he could understand her words.

"Wait here," she said. "I'll be right back." She darted into the house. A moment later, she returned with the sheet from her bed.

It took some doing, but she managed to spread the material on the ground and then roll the man's unconscious form onto it. Twisting the hem of the sheet around her fists, she once again started dragging him toward the cabin, surprised when the boy's hands appeared next to hers.

It still took longer than she'd hoped, and they were both breathing quite heavily by the time they reached the house. Perspiration pooled between her breasts and made the thin cotton of her calico dress cling to her back, but at least the injured stranger was inside where she could tend to him.

She pulled him across the coarse plank floor to the corner of the cabin where her bed stood. It wasn't large, but it was slightly wider and sturdier than a cot, having needed to support Purgatory's last schoolmarm, a rather hefty, beefy woman. It should hold this man's well-muscled bulk.

But if dragging him into the house had made her sweat, getting him onto the bed nearly killed her. Inch by inch, she moved him up and over, using her body as a lever.

When he was finally flat on his back on the mattress, she sat down beside him to catch her breath and took a closer look at his face.

Eyes narrowed, she hurried across the

room to retrieve the lamp she'd been using to grade papers and returned to his side. Flickering yellow light illuminated his features, showing the shallow creases at the corners of his eyes and the white line of pain that ringed his slack lips.

My God. It couldn't be.

She lifted the lantern higher, leaned closer, and studied him all the more intensely.

"David," she breathed, the air rushing from her lungs as though someone had punched her square in the stomach.

She didn't know how it could be, and yet she was certain it was he. She hadn't seen him in years, not since he'd left the Purgatory Home for Unwanted Children to go live with the Walkers.

She'd often wondered about him, wished he'd come back to visit her. And even though she hadn't thought much about him while they'd both been wards of the orphanage, she'd missed him after he'd gone. The way he'd always seemed to be there, like a shadow, watching over her and keeping her company.

He'd also been the only one to chase away the horrors when she woke, screaming, in the middle of the night. It wasn't until he'd moved away that she realized he'd always been there the minute the nightmares began, even though the boys weren't allowed in the girls' sleeping quarters.

And now here he was, once again coming to her in the middle of the night. Only this time, he needed her help.

Setting the lamp safely aside on the nightstand, she began to remove his clothing, searching for wounds. Ignoring the heat emanating from his smooth flesh, the stark white of her skin against the dark tan of his own.

Sure enough, his side was still oozing deep red blood, seeping into the tanned leather of his fringed shirt.

As she looked closer, prodding the area with a gentle finger, she realized what had most likely made the hole in the otherwise flawless flesh of his abdomen.

"A bullet," she whispered, aghast, and then craned her neck to look at the boy who stood silently a few paces from her hip.

"Did someone shoot at you?" she asked him. "*Who* shot at you?"

She didn't expect an answer from this child who had so far refused to speak a single word to her, and she didn't get one. But it frightened her to think of someone trying to kill the man lying unconscious before her, let alone the small, vulnerable boy with him.

The first thing she needed to do was clean and bandage this wound . . . and find out whether the bullet was still in there. Letting her fingers drift to his back, she felt an equally

9

ragged, sickening hole opposite the one in front.

She swallowed hard and pulled her hand away, averting her eyes from the stickiness coating her skin. Careful to keep from getting blood on her dress, she skirted the child standing only a few feet away and moved into the kitchen area at the back of the cabin.

Using the indoor pump, she quickly washed her hands and then filled a copper kettle to put on the stove. While she waited for the water to boil, Hannah began bustling around, looking for as many clothes, towels, and bedsheets as she could find to use for cleaning and bandages. An old petticoat or two and a pillowcase that already had a hole in it anyway would serve nicely.

She carried them all to the small bedside table and began tearing them into long, thin strips. When the kettle began to whistle, she ran back to the stove to retrieve it and returned with a basin full of steaming water.

Ideally, she wished for a bottle of whiskey or some other type of strong libation to properly cleanse David's wound. But, of course, she didn't drink. Even if she'd wanted to, the Purgatory school board would never allow it. If they suspected she had so much as a bottle of spirits tucked away at the bottom of the linen closet for medicinal purposes, they would discharge her immediately. She would have to settle for water hot enough to peel the whitewash off the schoolhouse and a bit of homemade soap.

Dropping the round cake into the water, she let it build up a bit of lather and then dipped one of the clean pieces of cloth into the basin and squeezed out most of the excess moisture.

She was glad David was unconscious as she started to wipe away blood, both dried and fresh, and bits of ragged, ravaged skin. The very sight of it made her stomach clench, and it was all she could do not to turn away in disgust. She purposely breathed slow and shallow through her mouth to keep from getting sick.

When both the front and back of the wound were as clean as she thought she could get them, she mixed a bit of the leftover hot water with some herbs she kept on hand for minor injuries to create two small poultices that she hoped would keep him from developing an infection. Once those thick pads were in place, she used several of the long strips of material to wrap around David's entire waist, and tied them tight.

She sat back with a sigh, thinking she had done all she could . . . and praying it was enough.

Chapter Two

His head hurt and his side ached like a son of a bitch. For a moment after waking, he kept his eyes closed and remained still, trying to figure out where he was and what had caused his body to throb as though he'd been run over by a locomotive.

From somewhere nearby, he heard voices. Or rather, one voice. A woman's. He didn't recognize it, but the tone was soft and cajoling and laced with enough femininity to make him think of well-worn calico and lace, and soft, supple skin.

"I know you must be frightened," she said gently. "I'm a stranger to you, and your . . . father—or whoever that man is to you—is hurt. But he's going to be all right, and I want to help you. Won't you please tell me your name?"

Walker cracked open one eye to see what was going on. He saw Little Bear sitting on the bench of a rough oaken table, his small features—almost identical to his mother's—sharp and unyielding. His mouth was a firm, straight line, and it didn't look like he intended to open it anytime soon.

Across from him, with her back to Walker, sat a woman in blue. Her blond hair, left loose and falling to the middle of her back, looked almost brown in the dim lamplight. Her delicate hands rested on the table's flat surface and the sky blue of her dress tapered at her narrow waist before flaring out over attractively curved hips.

That's when he remembered where he must be. Hannah's house. After rescuing Little Bear from that bastard Ambrose Lynch—and taking a bullet in the side for his troubles—he'd brought the boy to Hannah, knowing she would protect the child until Walker could finish the rest of his business and come back for him.

Apparently he hadn't gotten very far.

Letting one hand drift down his chest, he carefully tested the place on his torso that throbbed so mercilessly and found it swathed in bandages.

Thanks to Hannah, he might not die after all. No matter how much it felt as if he would.

13

"At least eat something," Hannah said almost desperately, gesturing toward the bowl and spoon at the place in front of Little Bear.

If possible, Little Bear's lips thinned even more, his posture going rigid.

"Eat, *ara?*." The words came out scratchy and broken, but they were enough to bring both heads swiveling in his direction.

"*Ara?*." Little Bear jumped up and raced to his side, with Hannah trailing close behind. She stopped only long enough to pour a cup of water and carry it with her.

"I'm all right," he told the boy, running a hand over his dark, ruffled hair.

Hannah leaned over, placing the back of her fingers to his brow and putting the curve of her breasts directly in his line of vision.

"You feel warm," she murmured.

With the enticing view she offered and the caress of her skin on his arm, she had no idea just how warm.

"You're probably fighting off an infection." She held the heavy earthenware cup to his lips and whispered, "Drink."

The cool water rolled past his lips and quenched his parched mouth and throat.

When the cup was empty, Walker let his gaze meet hers. She was as beautiful as he remembered. Maybe more so, with her long, corn-silk hair and eyes that reminded him of bluebonnets in spring.

"How have you been, Hannah?" he asked

14

quietly, letting his fingers slip down and brush the back of her hand where it rested on the mattress beside his bandaged waist.

For a moment, she remained still beneath his touch. And then she carefully pulled away, letting her arm fall to her side, well out of his reach.

She cleared her throat. "I should be asking you that question, don't you think? What did you do to make someone shoot you, David?"

"Walker."

"Yes, I know your last name is Walker."

"No," he corrected. "I go by just Walker now."

Her brows knit. "Why?"

This wasn't the conversation he'd pictured them having at this point, but he didn't suppose he had much choice. "I took a new name when I returned to my Comanche mother's village. Spirit Walker . . . because Clay and Regan had adopted me and given me their name, and because—due to my mixed blood—I walk in both the Indian and the white man's world."

"So no one calls you David anymore?"

"Only Clay and Regan." One side of his mouth lifted in an amused grin. "You know my ma."

She did, though Hannah mostly saw Mrs. Walker after Sunday services or to discuss how one of her younger children was doing in school. By the time Hannah left the or-

15

phanage and started teaching, David had already been full-grown and off on his own. He didn't attend church, he didn't spend much time in town, and eventually she'd learned that he'd left Purgatory altogether.

She remembered that day distinctly. Her heart had slammed painfully against her rib cage when she'd heard the news, and Hannah feared the battered organ still bore a deep purple bruise.

And yet she hadn't realized until this very moment how much David was in her thoughts, how she'd longed to see him again. How many times she'd looked for him in a crowd or thought of him late at night when she couldn't sleep. Or worse, how often thoughts of him kept her awake.

Seeming to sense her sudden discomfort, David—or Walker, as he preferred to be called—turned his attention to the child between them.

"I take it you've been giving Miss Hannah a rough time."

His voice was more patient than chastising, but still Hannah rushed to defend the boy. "Oh, no, he's been fine. Very well behaved. He's exceptionally quiet, but I think that's because he doesn't understand what I'm saying. And I, of course, don't understand whatever language it is that he speaks."

"Comanche. He's half-Comanche, half-white, same as I am. But he understands English well enough." With a pointed glance at the child, he said, "Why don't you introduce yourself?"

The boy, looking only moderately less stern than before, turned to her and held out a hand, his arm ramrod stiff. She took it and he gave a sharp shake.

"My name is Little Bear. Who are you?"

"English, he knows," David said with a wry smile. "We're still working on manners."

Hannah didn't return his grin. She couldn't. She was already two steps ahead and too nervous.

"My name is Hannah Blake," she told Little Bear. "I'm very pleased to meet you." And then she turned her gaze on David. "Is this . . . your son?"

One coal-dark brow winged upward. "My son? No, he's my nephew, my Comanche sister's son. And since when do you go by the name Blake? You were just plain Hannah when we were growing up."

Just plain Hannah. Yes, that description suited her even now.

Setting the empty cup on the nearby nightstand, she busied herself fussing with the unused bandages to avoid meeting his eyes.

"Are you hungry?" she asked, bustling across the cabin to retrieve another bowl and spoon.

17

"I could eat," David responded agreeably, well aware that she had avoided his question. "You should finish your meal as well, Little Bear," he told his nephew, and gave him a gentle push toward the table and benches.

The boy went without argument, and now that his uncle was awake to reassure him, he gulped down his soup as though he hadn't eaten in several days. Of course, knowing Lynch's mean streak, it was possible he hadn't.

Once Little Bear was busy slurping down his dinner, Walker turned his attention back to Hannah. He found her discomfort and need for distraction intriguing. He didn't see why a simple inquiry about her surname should make her nervous, but it was interesting all the same.

She returned to his side with a bowl of light-colored broth and sat on the very edge of the bed, keeping her attention firmly focused on her actions as she held the spoon to his mouth.

His side might have a hole the size of Austin in it, but his arms were working just fine. But far be it for him to share that fact with Hannah. Instead, he let her feed him, just to keep her close by.

"You never answered my question, Hannah," he pointed out between spoonfuls.

She didn't pretend not to remember. She merely shrugged one slim shoulder, still refusing to look at his face, and said, "You know how it is at the Home. I remembered some things from before my parents were killed, but not everything. When it came time to leave, I needed a last name. I've always been fond of William Blake's work, so . . ." She shrugged again, trailing off.

" 'The sun descending in the west, The evening star does shine; The birds are silent in their nest, And I must seek for mine.' "

Her eyes widened at his recitation and finally met his own.

His lips twisted in self-derision. "Not bad for a worthless half-breed, huh?"

For the first time since he'd known her, her expression blazed with fury. "I've never thought of you that way, and you know it."

She slapped the spoon down in the bowl, sending yellow chicken broth flying. Fat drops of the hot liquid hit his bare chest. He ignored them.

"Clay and Regan Walker have never treated you that way, either. And if anyone in this town has, they deserve to be horsewhipped. *You* deserve to be horsewhipped for propagating such nonsense."

Walker bit the inside of his mouth to keep from grinning. The situation wasn't the least bit amusing, and yet *she* amused him. Her

19

spirit, and her fire, and her beautiful corn-flower eyes.

But if she thought he was laughing at her, she'd be likely to dump the bowl of scalding soup in his lap, so he kept biting until his cheek muscles no longer quivered and his lips no longer threatened to curl upward.

"You're different than I remember, Hannah," he said when his features were finally schooled. "You used to be quiet and shy. Wouldn't say 'Excuse me' if a body tramped on your toe. Now you look about ready to slug someone."

He almost expected her to retort with a sharp, *Not someone—you*. Instead, she lowered her eyes to the bowl in her lap and started stirring the spoon around and around until the broth inside threatened to shoot over the edge of the dish.

"I grew up," she said simply.

She certainly had. He remembered when she'd been a gangly, awkward, still-growing adolescent. He'd been an adult by then—or at least he'd thought of himself that way—and concluded it was wrong to be mooning after someone he considered still a child. That was when he'd decided to leave Purgatory and return to his Comanche mother's village to learn more about his people and his heritage.

But now he was back. And Hannah was all grown up.

While mooning over her was still out of the

question, he couldn't help noticing all the hows and wheres and ways she'd . . . developed. The soft roundness of her breasts. The tall column of her neck. The flowing length of her silky hair.

And those were only half of the attributes playing around in his head. They caused him to break out in a sweat that had nothing to do with his building fever.

"That's why I brought him to you," he said, forcing his mind away from her delicious curves and back to his reason for coming here in the first place.

Grasping his meaning immediately, Hannah glanced over her shoulder at Little Bear. He'd finished his dinner, pushed the empty bowl out of the way, and now sat with his chin resting on top of his folded arms, staring across the room at them.

"I don't understand," she said, returning her attention to Walker.

She offered him another spoonful of broth, which kept him from speaking for several long seconds.

"I knew you would take care of him," he told her. "Protect him."

"Protect him? From the same trouble that put that hole in your side?" She inclined her head toward the bandaged wound, her eyes growing cloudy.

"That was an unfortunate offshoot of the

21

problem. Little Bear needs protection from
something far worse than a bullet."

"And that would be?"

"His father."

Chapter Three

His father.

How could a child need protection from his own father? What kind of parent would put his own child in danger?

Hannah had wanted to ask those and a hundred other questions. But before she'd gotten a chance, she'd noticed the thin layer of sweat beading David's brow and the tight set of his lips, attesting to the pain he refused to voice.

Tamping down on her curiosity, she'd helped him finish a bit more broth, then made him drink a glass of water mixed with some special herbs to help him sleep. Soon enough, he'd drifted off and had now been sleeping peacefully for nearly an hour.

Heidi Betts

To keep her hands busy and her mind occupied, Hannah bustled about the cabin. Cleaning up, gathering a few items she thought she might need when David awoke, making sure Little Bear wasn't still hungry.

Of course, that was none too easy, considering that the child continued to refuse to speak to her. But at least he'd graduated to nodding or shaking his head in response to direct questions. Hannah considered this a step in the right direction and tried to think of even more personal questions she could ask to draw him out.

"Are you sure you've had enough to eat?" She ladled a scoop of reheated soup into a bowl for herself.

He nodded, but toyed with what remained of the slice of bread in front of him.

She took her dish and sat down across from him, testing the temperature of the soup and then dipping a bit of bread into the broth.

"Your uncle didn't get a chance to tell me much about you before he fell asleep." She wanted to ask him how old he was, where they'd come from, why David had been shot. But since she didn't expect Little Bear to answer her verbally, she had to make sure he could respond to anything she asked with a firm yes or no movement of his head.

As compassionately as she could—because she simply couldn't think of any other way to phrase it—she asked, "Are your mother and father still alive?"

Yes.

"Do you live with them?"

Yes.

"Did you want to come with your uncle when he brought you here?" She didn't think David had abducted the child, of course, but with a bullet wound in his side, she could only assume the circumstances surrounding the boy's departure had been less than perfect.

And sure enough, though his eyes grew dark and pensive, Little Bear didn't respond.

"Do you know who shot your uncle?" she asked quietly, and then wondered why she bothered, since he certainly wouldn't tell her.

The boy nodded, but that was all.

"He's going to be all right, you know," she tried to reassure him. "The wound will hurt for a while, and he may run a fever, but he'll be fine."

The only sign of relief she saw was a slight softening of his tight jaw and stiff posture.

"Your uncle told me you speak English," she said. "And you obviously understand me. Is there a reason you won't talk to me?"

He inclined his head.

"Don't you like me?"

A slight hesitation, and then a quick shake.

"Are you afraid of me?"

His eyes darted toward the bed where his

uncle lay before returning his gaze to her—
though not directly. He nodded.

Her heart lurched at that. She'd never
frightened a child in her life. In fact, she'd
spent most of her adult years helping children, teaching them, comforting them. She
couldn't recall doing anything to scare Little
Bear, but he'd been taken from his parents,
seen his uncle shot, and then deposited at the
house of a stranger. She supposed that was
enough to make anyone ill at ease, let alone
a young boy.

"There's no reason to be scared of me, Little
Bear," she said softly. "I'm actually a very nice
person. Or at least I try to be," she added,
casting him a sly glance and a small smile.

"Did your uncle tell you anything about
me?"

Yes. But with no elaboration, of course.

"Did he tell you I was a good woman?" she
asked, remembering David's words when he'd
first shown up outside the cabin with Little
Bear. Before he'd collapsed. "And that I
would take care of you?"

A nod.

"Did he tell you that I'm a schoolteacher?"

No.

"I am." She took a bite of bread and a
mouthful of warm chicken broth. "I teach at
the small schoolhouse in town and have eigh-
teen students in all. I teach them reading and
arithmetic, and we study about great battles

and distant lands. Do you go to school?"

He shook his head.

"Do you know how to read?"

No.

"Do you know your numbers?"

No.

"I could teach you," she offered casually. "If you'd like."

He didn't respond, but Hannah thought she saw a slight glitter in his eyes, a lift to his narrow lips.

She ate a few more bites and let the silence fold around them before trying once again to make conversation with the little boy.

"Did your uncle tell you that he and I have known each other since we were about your age?"

The child's eyes definitely widened at that and he looked suddenly alert, interested.

"Oh, yes. We both grew up in the local orphanage. It was called the Purgatory Home for Unwanted Children then. Isn't that a terrible name for an orphanage? As though any child could truly be unwanted. Just because mothers and fathers sometimes die, or can't care for their children properly, that doesn't mean a child is unwanted. Thankfully, they've renamed it the Purgatory Home for *Adoptive* Children.

"And that's exactly what it is now. I was never adopted by a new family, but your uncle was. He went to live with a wonderful cou-

27

ple." She noticed the keen interest on the child's face. "Did he ever tell you about that?"

Little Bear shook his head fervently.

"Would you like to hear what your uncle was like when he was a boy?"

This time his nod was eager and he leaned forward on the table, straining to hear every word.

"How about this," she said carefully. "I'll tell you about growing up with your uncle if you start talking to me. With actual words," she qualified.

His face darkened and he began to look away.

"We can start small," she offered, not wanting to scare him off by asking too much too soon. "Instead of nodding or shaking your head, you could say 'yes' or 'no.' That doesn't sound too hard, does it?"

He studied her, his eyes narrowed, then slowly moved his head back and forth.

"All right. Now how about answering the same question, only with the word 'no.' That doesn't sound too hard, does it, Little Bear?"

"N-no."

The single word was low, tentative, but Hannah acted as though he'd just recited the Emancipation Proclamation from memory.

"Excellent, Little Bear. Thank you. Having someone to talk with makes me feel less alone in this tiny cabin. I don't get visitors very often."

Finishing the last of her supper, she pushed her bowl away and lifted the napkin from her lap. "Would you like to help me wash these dishes?" she asked the boy. "And while we do, I'll tell you what your uncle was like as a child."

Little Bear began to nod, then seemed to recall their deal and, a bit more confidently than before, said, "Yes."

"Come on, then."

Hannah stood and collected their dirty bowls and utensils. She led Little Bear to the kitchen area, set their dishes in the cast iron sink, and poured water over them from the metal pail she kept heated on the back of the cookstove. Adding a dash of strong powdered soap, she worked it into suds and started scrubbing, casting a sidelong glance at Little Bear where he stood on tiptoe to stare into the deep sink basin.

"I hate to admit this," she began, "and I don't want to give you ideas, but your uncle was quite a troublemaker growing up. He was forever running away from the Home and doing things to infuriate the adults."

She was surprised when Little Bear's voice—uttering something other than "yes" or "no"—reached her ears.

"Why?" he wanted to know.

She lowered her gaze to study him, noting the way the pale light reflected in his deep brown eyes as she debated how much to reveal to this child. Because he seemed far wiser than his years, she decided to be honest with him.

"Most people back then considered your uncle a half-breed. Do you know what that means?"

"Yes." Little Bear's face grew shuttered. "That's what my father calls me."

My lord, Hannah thought, not just a one-syllable response, but an entire sentence. She would have been ecstatic if the child's words hadn't made her want to weep.

"That isn't a very nice thing for your father to call you," she told him, letting her derision show clearly through her words. "It's not a very nice term to use at all, especially when people make it sound like a negative quality. But just remember that *half-breed* simply means you have two types of blood running through your veins. And when you think of it, that's true of every single person who walks this earth."

She'd nearly rubbed the spots off the blue-and-white speckled bowl in her hands and made a conscious effort to slow her movements and set the dish aside.

"I carry the blood of both my mother and father, as do you. It's not your fault—any more than it was David's . . . I mean Walker's—that one of your parents was white and the other was Indian." She ran the back of her damp hand over his bronze cheek. "And just

30

because a goodly number of the people in this world are ignorant and narrow-minded enough to believe that makes you somehow less deserving than they are doesn't mean you have anything to be ashamed of."

Hannah took a deep breath, suddenly aware that her voice had risen and her fingers were clamped like a vise around the edge of the cast iron sink. Heat suffused her face as she remembered all the times David had been treated as less than human simply because of his Indian blood, simply because his skin was darker and his hair was straighter than the other townspeople's. Even some of the other children in the orphanage had treated him differently . . . taking their cue from the actions of adults, she was sure.

Hannah had never seen the differences. Oh, she'd known his hair was longer than most boys', and that his skin was several shades darker than her own, which was extremely pale and often seemed nearly translucent.

But to her, he'd been the boy who watched her out of intense brown eyes. Who mysteriously appeared at her bedside in the middle of the night to chase away the terrible dreams that haunted her. Who seemed to always be close by, ready to step in and offer his protection if she needed it.

He'd acted almost like an older brother, though she'd certainly never thought of him that way. Casting a lingering glance over her

31

shoulder at the man dozing comfortably in her bed, she realized she didn't think of him that way now, either. Looking at him set off too many tingles and heart palpitations for her to consider him any kind of relation.

Tearing her attention away from her memories of the past, Hannah realized Little Bear was watching her intently, waiting for her to continue.

"Until the Walkers took your uncle in and showed him what it was like to belong to a real family, he got into his fair share of trouble. But the thing I remember most about your uncle," she said quietly, "is the way he held me when I cried."

Chapter Four

Walker kept his eyes tightly closed, feigning sleep. He didn't know why Hannah was revealing such personal emotions, such private moments, but hearing her tell Little Bear about the nightmares she'd suffered as a child made his heart twist in his chest. Listening to her describe how she'd felt when he'd comforted her caused his breath to catch in his throat.

He remembered those nights. He remembered the first time he'd heard her shrieks of absolute terror all the way across the orphanage, in the boys' sleeping quarters. He remembered sneaking in to see what was going on and seeing the nuns attempting to calm the light-haired, light-skinned newcomer with terror leaping in her eyes.

He also remembered later, hearing the nuns whispering about what caused those nightmares—the violent death of her parents on the trip west, when their wagon had overturned and been swept downriver. Six-year-old Hannah had witnessed the episode from another wagon that had crossed safely only moments before.

Something about her plight had touched him as a boy, and from that day on, he'd made a point of staying close to the little girl. Of shadowing her, protecting her, sneaking out of his bed at night and sleeping on the floor beside her cot in case she needed him.

And she had, so many times. She tossed and turned and awoke in tears, and he was right there to hold her, comfort her, tell her everything would be all right. He also remembered, even at the ripe old age of fourteen, being determined to see that everything *was* all right for her. No one would harm a hair on her sun-blond head as long as he was around.

And no one ever had.

Walker felt the peculiar urge to renew his childhood vow. To stick by Hannah's side and see that she was taken care of, even though she was all grown up now and could likely take care of herself. Hell, she'd even taken care of him, and it looked like she was well on the way to winning over Little Bear as well.

At the sound of feminine laughter, he opened his eyes and let his vision clear. He saw Hannah standing at the sink with a white apron wrapped around her waist and a towel in her hand. Little Bear stood at her side, grinning from ear to ear and laughing at something Hannah had just confided.

"You weren't supposed to tell anyone what a hellion I was as a kid," he chastised from across the room. "Least of all my impressionable young nephew."

His comment brought Hannah around to look at him with a startled expression on her face. She clutched the dish towel to her breast.

"I'm explaining how much trouble you used to get into so he won't be foolish enough to attempt any of the same stunts," she told him. And then she set the towel aside, removed her apron, and started toward him.

"How are you feeling?" she asked, touching his brow.

Her cool fingers felt like pure silk, and he had to fight the temptation to reach out for her wrist, to draw her closer.

"I'm all right." He was warm and a little clammy, but he didn't think that had anything to do with the hole in his side.

"*Ara?,*" Little Bear said, coming to his side and leaning on the edge of the mattress.

35

"Hannah Blake told me about growing up with you in the orph'nage, and how you used to run away. Where did you go when you runned, *ara?* Did you go far away like when you brung me here?"

Walker cast Hannah a falsely reproachful glance, ignoring her cringe at Little Bear's less than proper grammar. "See what you've done?"

She lifted a brow. "Aren't you going to answer him? Where did you run off to all those times . . . David?"

Cornered. Getting it from both guns. He shifted his gaze to his nephew and smiled gently. "I ran to where I most wanted to be," he answered simply, if somewhat cryptically, thinking of all the times he'd escaped from the Purgatory Home for Unwanted Children to visit Widow Regan Doyle. She'd baked cookies and let him sleep in a room by himself, and treated him like a real person instead of some parentless half-breed. And then Widow Doyle had married and become Mrs. Regan Walker. She and her new husband had adopted him, treated him like family, and he'd never had to run away again.

He didn't tell Little Bear—or Hannah—all that, though. A man was deserving of some privacy, after all.

"Happy?" he asked, turning his attention back to Hannah. He could tell by her expression that she wasn't. His answer hadn't quite satisfied her.

"Had you been trying to convince him you were a saint? Because I'm not sure anyone who knows you could believe that."

His mind raced to come up with a proper response, but all he could think of was, "True enough. You're nothing if not honest, Hannah."

And then he grew serious, catching her eye. "That's why I'm leaving Little Bear with you. You'll take care of him. You'll protect him. And you'll stand up to anyone who tries to take him from you."

Her eyes narrowed and her gaze bored into him. "How do you know I'll do any of those things? We haven't seen each other in ten years. And what do you mean 'leaving' him with me?"

She was wrong. She might not have seen him in the past ten years, but he'd seen her. Seen her, watched her, kept track of what she was up to.

The only time he hadn't known where she was or what she was doing was when she'd gone away to school. He'd spent most of those years in his Comanche mother's village, too torn up and distracted by Hannah's absence to remain for very long in Purgatory.

Thankfully, she'd come back. Even though his visits were never very long, he'd remained in close contact with his parents, and they'd inadvertently informed him that Hannah was coming back to town to take over as Purgatory's schoolmarm. After that he'd stayed with Regan and Clay for more extended periods and caught glimpses of Hannah when he could.

He decided not to answer the first part of her question. He knew she would do all that he'd said and more. He'd watched a kind and caring little girl develop into a smart and generous woman. But he certainly didn't intend to reveal his decade-long obsession with her, so he focused on the second half of her query instead.

"I'll be leaving in the morning, Hannah." He reached out to take his nephew's hand, knowing the child would be nervous about being left with a stranger, even if Hannah had begun to win him over. "I appreciate your patching me up and thank you for taking in Little Bear, but I have to go."

"Where? Why would you bring Little Bear all the way here only to leave again? You're not well enough to ride or even walk very far."

"I'll be well enough by morning. I don't have any choice."

Lines of confusion and concern etched Hannah's otherwise smooth brow. "Why not? What's going on, David?"

"Walker," he corrected her. "People call me Walker now."

"Anyone who would drag himself off with

a hole in his belly, I would call stupid. Or crazy. Or looking to die."

He couldn't help it; he grinned. After all the time he'd spent observing her from afar, he'd known she had a backbone. He just hadn't realized her tongue was so sharp.

"I still prefer Walker," he replied blandly, ignoring her increased annoyance.

"My sister—Little Bear's mother—is in trouble. I have to go back to help her." He didn't give Hannah any more details than that. He wasn't sure how much he was ready to share with her, and he didn't want to worry Little Bear about his mother's condition, more questionable the longer Walker left her in harm's way.

Hannah watched him closely for a minute, studying his eyes, his mouth, his bandaged abdomen.

And then, without a word, she rose to her feet, placed a hand on Little Bear's back, and led him away.

"I think it's about time we got you ready for bed," she said easily. She shot a glance over her shoulder. *"We'll* continue our conversation in a moment."

He watched from the bed as she gathered sheets and blankets and folded them into a pallet on the floor. On the far side of the room, he noticed, likely to give them more privacy when she finally returned to quiz him for information.

39

Hannah saw Little Bear settled and then blew out the lantern in the middle of the table, casting the room into darkness save for the small glow the lamp beside the bed offered.

She took her time, doing this or that to stay busy until a small snore sounded from Little Bear's corner. Then she made a beeline for Walker.

Hands on hips, voice low so as not to carry across the room, she demanded, "All right. Now tell me exactly what's going on."

"I'm not sure it's in your best interest to know, Hannah," he hedged, even though he realized she would have none of it.

"You should have thought of that before you arrived on my doorstep with a little boy and a bullet in your side. Best interest or not, I have a right to know what you've gotten me into."

For several long seconds, he remained silent. Then he nodded. "Fair enough. You know I divide my time between Purgatory and my mother's Comanche village."

It was a statement, but Hannah inclined her head all the same.

"I have a sister, Bright Eyes. She's full-blooded Comanche, born to my mother and her first husband, before he was killed in a raid. A few years after that, my mother met Nolan Updike and got pregnant with me." His teeth clenched at the mere mention of his father, the white man who had seduced his Comanche mother and then left her with a child to raise. A half-breed child.

"Bright Eyes left the village with a white man named Ambrose Lynch. He'd been coming to visit her for years. She even had a child with him—Little Bear—and I knew she fancied herself in love with him. When he lured her away from the village last year with promises of marriage and becoming a real family, I didn't say anything because I didn't want my feelings about my own father to tarnish her happiness. And I hoped Lynch was a good man." His jaw tightened at the thought of just how wrong he'd been. "But he's only kept her as his mistress, and I just found out he's been abusing her."

Glancing in his nephew's direction to be sure the boy was still sleeping, he continued. "Little Bear is his son, but you wouldn't know it by the way he acts toward him. He beats Bright Eyes, treats her no better than a slave. And he's hit Little Bear, too, I'm sure."

Hannah's breathing, he noticed, had sped up, causing her breasts to rise and fall rapidly beneath the blue calico of her dress. He told himself not to stare, but . . . well, certain parts of his body weren't listening.

A healthy dose of color bloomed in her cheeks and the hands that had slipped from her hips while he spoke rose back up as her anger grew. "Well, I'm glad you did bring

41

Little Bear here, then. No child—or woman, either, for that matter—should have to live like that. I assume you're going to help your sister leave him. I mean, she doesn't actually want to stay there with that awful man?"

Walker felt a muscle tick in his jaw and his hands fisted in the sheets at his waist. "I don't plan to give her a choice. I told her when I took Little Bear that I'd be back for her. She's expecting another child with that bastard, and if I don't get her away from him soon, I'm not sure she or the baby will survive."

Hannah gasped in shock, her mouth forming a small, open oval. "You don't mean . . . he'd kill her," she gasped.

As much as it pained him to say the words, he told her the truth. "I do. He's come close to it already, and I'll be damned if I'll let him succeed."

"So this Lynch person," Hannah began, "he's the one who shot you."

Walker shifted uncomfortably on the tick mattress. "He or one of his men. I was riding away at the time, so I didn't see the shooter. I just count myself lucky whoever it was didn't wing Little Bear. I'd have turned around and murdered them all if they had."

A strange light took over Hannah's sky blue eyes and she took a step closer to the bed. "And what will you do if Ambrose Lynch hurts your sister before you can get to her?" she wanted to know.

That was easy, and for the first time since he'd begun confiding in Hannah about his sister and nephew's situation, he let out a relaxed breath and the tension in his muscles disappeared.

"I'll kill him."

Chapter Five

Something, some small noise or movement, awakened Hannah. When she opened her eyes to slits, it was still dark out.

She turned her head on the hard pillow of the pallet she'd made on the floor near Little Bear, trying to figure out what had stirred her from her deep, comfortable sleep.

"Hannah," she heard softly just above her ear as a warm hand curved around her nape and into the hair at the back of her head. It took less than a fraction of a second for her to recognize both the voice and the touch as belonging to David.

"I'm going now, Hannah," he whispered in her ear, his lips brushing softly against her

44

temple. "Thank you again for watching after Little Bear. And for nursing me."

Hannah fought against exhaustion. This was important; she really wanted to be awake to listen to every word. But she was so tired, and the feel of his fingers in her hair and his lips on her skin lulled her as easily as a mother's touch.

"I've missed you, Hannah. It was good to see you again."

His mouth moved from her temple to her lips. And then he was kissing her. All she remembered after that was lifting her arms to his shoulders, opening her mouth beneath his, and falling backward into the most wonderful sensations she'd ever experienced.

The next time she opened her eyes, the sun was just coming over the horizon, casting a pale lavender-orange light through the open doorway and into the cabin.

She rolled to her stomach on the hard floor beneath the blankets and lifted her head, blinking drowsily. It took a moment for her to identify the figure slowly creeping out the door, but as soon as she did, she was across the room in a flash.

"Wait," she called, breathless from her sudden, fast-as-lightning movements. "Where do you think you're going?" she asked, grabbing Little Bear by the arm. Her fingers wrapped

---

Heidi Betts

around soft, tanned buckskin as she turned the boy to face her.

"Where are you going?" she asked again when he didn't immediately answer.

"I'm going with *ara?*. He needs me."

"*Ara?*. Does that mean uncle?"

Holding his body stiffly against her unwelcome grasp, he nodded. "He went after my *pia*, and I'm going, too. He might need me."

"Your uncle wanted you to stay here," Hannah told him, loosening her grip on his arm but careful not to let go altogether for fear he might bolt. "He told me so. He risked his life to bring you here and asked me to look after you."

Little Bear stuck out his chin in a manner that reminded her almost painfully of David's obstinacy as a child. When he'd thought he was in a battle against the entire world.

"He might need me," the boy said again. "*Pia* might need me."

"*Pia*. That must mean mother." Hannah was beginning to catch on, and wondered how much Comanche she would be able to learn before this was over. "Your mother will be fine; I'm sure your uncle will see to that."

At the derisive curve of his lips, Hannah belatedly realized she'd said exactly the wrong thing.

"I can find him," he bit out, his shoulders going back with seven-year-old confidence. "I paid attention to how we got here, and *ara?*

46

taught me how to follow a trail. He says I'll be the best tracker in the village when he takes *pia* and me back."

Wonderful. David had taught his nephew to track game and now the child wanted to follow his uncle into the face of she didn't know what kind of danger.

"I still think it would be best if you remained here. It's what your uncle wanted, and this is where he'll come once he's rescued your mother. You wouldn't want him to return only to find you missing, would you?"

The determined light in his eyes didn't waiver. Without a word, he turned back toward the cabin, shook off her hold, and marched to the oaken table in the middle of the room. Taking a seat on the edge of one of the benches, he sat with his back straight as a pin.

"I will wait until you are busy or have fallen asleep again," he told her. "And then I will follow my *ara?* and help to save my *pia*. You will not know I have gone until it is already too late. My *ara?* taught me this."

"Did he also teach you to be as stubborn as a two-headed mule?" she muttered.

But he heard and turned his head to look at her.

Heat bloomed on her cheeks and breast at being caught giving voice to her frustrations. She worked with children who tested her patience every day. She even dealt with her stu-

47

dents' parents on a fairly regular basis, which sometimes seemed like a study in sainthood. But rarely, if ever, did she find herself snapping at them or mumbling less than polite comments beneath her breath.

"I'm sorry," she apologized to Little Bear. "It's just that you . . . remind me of your uncle when he was a boy."

The child beamed, infinitely pleased by the comparison. He never considered that she might not have meant it as a compliment.

And knowing what David had been like at his age, she also knew Little Bear wasn't going to change his mind. Just as he'd said, he would wait for her to turn her back or fall asleep and take off without her. Then she would have not only David to worry about, but Little Bear as well.

For several long moments, she considered her position within the community. Purgatory's townspeople relied on her. They trusted her with the education of their children. And that trust hadn't been instantaneous, either. Oh, no. She'd had to go away to school and then come back to prove that a former orphan with no parents of her own and a questionable upbringing could have a positive impact on Purgatory's young minds.

But she'd done that, and for the past few years, her position had been more than secure.

Until David Walker showed up on her doorstep.

The people of Purgatory might like her and even look up to her in many ways, but as far as they were concerned, some things were unforgivable. Letting a man into her cabin was one of them.

Never mind that she'd known him since childhood. Never mind that even if a half-breed would normally be scorned simply for the color of his skin, *this* particular half-breed had long ago been accepted by the town—well, most of the town, at any rate—simply because he was Clay and Regan Walker's adopted son. And never mind that he'd been injured and in serious need of medical attention.

The fact of the matter was, he was a man and she was an unmarried woman. He'd spent the night in her house, and Little Bear didn't prove an adequate chaperone.

Even if she weren't responsible for a number of impressionable young minds on a daily basis, Hannah's reputation would sustain irreparable damage if anyone found out about David's visit. She would likely be fired on the spot.

And yet . . . Hannah couldn't seem to work up a proper amount of concern. If she lost her position teaching at Purgatory's one-room schoolhouse, she had no idea where she would go or what she would do. She would lose everything, including her house, since even the very cabin she'd called home these past several years belonged to the town.

But—and a shiver of some unexplainable emotion went through her at the thought— maybe David was worth it. Maybe he was worth the risk and deserved her help, whatever it cost her. He had certainly come to her rescue often enough when she was a child.

"You're determined to do this, then," she remarked to Little Bear. "And you're sure you can find your uncle even though it's been several hours since he started out?"

His head, with its tousled dark hair parted straight down the middle, bobbed up and down eagerly.

"All right, but I'm going with you."

He seemed less sure of that and gave her a quizzical glance.

"It's the only way I'm letting you go," she told him in her sternest tone of voice. "I'll tie you to a chair if you don't agree."

And then, without giving him time to comment, she went on. "I'll need a few minutes to change. Why don't you get a bite to eat while you wait, and *don't* take so much as a step outside of this house without me. Is that understood?"

He'd moved to the kitchen for what remained of the loaf of bread from last night's supper and answered her question in the affirmative around the huge chunk that filled his mouth.

As quickly as she could, Hannah changed from the light blue calico dress she'd worn yesterday and through the night to a pale pink gown better suited to traveling. Of course, nothing she owned really lent itself to the type of traveling she was about to do. She wasn't sure where they were going, how long it would take to get there, or what the terrain would be like. She suspected, however, that much of the journey would be spent walking . . . in the hot Texas sun.

She laced up her most comfortable walking shoes and grabbed the wide-brimmed straw hat she used in the summer or while gardening. It was the best she could do, and yet she knew that by the end of the day, her light and sensitive skin would be red and raw, burned like a roast left too long in the oven.

Tying the hat's ribbon beneath her chin, she took a deep breath and decided to just do what needed to be done. She found a sheet of paper and wrote a few quick lines for anyone who might happen to stop by the cabin— likely a member of the Purgatory school board wanting to know why she hadn't shown up for class in the morning. She informed them only that she'd been called away suddenly and would be back as soon as possible. Let them deduce from that what they would.

51

She'd deal with the consequences when she returned.

She tacked the note to the door with a small nail before turning back toward the kitchen. "All right, I'm ready."

Little Bear was just wolfing down the last bit of bread crust.

"I hope you're right about being able to find your uncle."

"I am," he said as he chewed.

Hannah let him pass before her, closing the door firmly behind them both. And then she followed the trail of crumbs the boy left behind him.

Walker had been moving slowly on account of his injury, not wanting to tear open the wound or expend all of his energy before he got to the Bar L. And only a few miles out of town, he decided to start covering his tracks in case he came back this way and had someone on his tail. Even if he didn't, even if he took another route, this path was fairly deserted and little traveled, and Walker didn't want to leave the slightest evidence of his passage should Lynch attempt to follow him back to Purgatory.

With a large, leafy branch he found on the ground near a copse of trees, he blotted out a good stretch of marks his horse's hooves had left in the dirt. He was tying the branch to the horn of his saddle when he heard something moving several yards away. Or rather, he heard something moving, and panting, and . . . complaining.

He stepped back into the tree line, leading Thunder with him.

"You're doing a very good job of this tracking business," he heard a woman speak breathlessly. "But I'm not as young as you are . . . and I'm obviously not as used to marching at this pace," she finished with a disgusted mutter.

I'll be damned, Walker thought, stepping out of the trees just as Little Bear and Hannah rounded the bend.

Little Bear was indeed marching, taking long, fast, certain steps as he kept an eye to the ground. A bedraggled Hannah stumbled behind, looking much the worse for wear.

Her gown, once flower-petal pink, was covered in a coat of trail dust. The supposedly white lace at the wrists, hem, and modest neckline was now dirt brown. Her equally dusty straw hat flopped over her brow with every step, and the porcelain skin of her lovely, innocent face was splotched red with exertion and streaked with grime from where she'd apparently wiped sweat from her cheeks and forehead.

Little Bear saw Walker standing in the middle of the path almost immediately and simply stopped, teeth gleaming in a wide smile at having achieved his goal of tracking down

his uncle. It took a few moments longer for
Hannah to spot him, however, and when she
did, she gave a shriek of alarm and stumbled
back a step.

"Lord, David," she huffed, slapping a hand
to her heart, "you scared ten years off my life.
Why can't you make noise when you walk like
a normal person?"

Walker chuckled at her wheezing admon-
ishment. "Like you, you mean? Every critter
within ten miles heard you coming and hied
off to the next county."

She didn't respond to that, but pursed her
lips in annoyance.

"What the hell are you doing here, anyway?" he demanded, his amusement vanish-
ing as he began to consider the consequences
of their sudden appearance.

"Don't look at me. It was your nephew's
idea, and he's just as mule-stubborn as you've
ever been."

"Is this true, *ara??*" he asked, lowering his
gaze to Little Bear.

The boy looked a little sheepish, but raised
his chin proudly. "*Haa.* I wanted to be with
you, in case you need my help. And I knew I
could find you . . . you taught me how."

Walker returned his gaze to Hannah, only
to see one blond brow arching upward as if
to say *I told you so*.

"One child, Hannah," he said without in-
flection, retrieving a canteen from the side of

54

his saddle and twisting off the cap. "I ask you to watch after one seven-year-old boy, and you let him run roughshod over you. How is it that you manage to control an entire classroom of students?"

Although their following him did annoy him, he was teasing, and he suspected she realized it because she took a long, *looooong* drink of water before lowering the canteen, wiping her mouth with the back of her arm, and fixing him with a less than heated glare.

"Most of my students are quiet, decorous children and not related to you in any manner. They are quite biddable, unlike some people I might mention." She cast a meaningful look from Walker to Little Bear and back again. "Can you believe he actually threatened to wait until I turned my back or fell asleep to run away? And I honestly believe he'd have done it."

"You let him manipulate you into coming after me?"

She took exception to the word *manipulate*, if the angry spark in her eye was any indication.

"On the contrary," she said in her best I'm-the-teacher-that's-why tone. "I weighed Little Bear's . . ."

"Threat?" he offered helpfully.

She scowled. "*Convictions,*" she emphasized, "against what I knew of you and your sister's situation, as well as the risk to my reputation as Purgatory's sole schoolteacher, and made an educated decision."

"Uh-huh. And just how did you expect to help me? I was hoping to sneak in, grab Bright Eyes, and sneak out again." He tilted his head to indicate her frilly, if neglected, dress. "You stick out like a posy on a fence post."

Hannah glanced down at herself, and then back at him and Little Bear. "Perhaps I didn't think that far ahead," she admitted, "but even if I had, I'm afraid I don't own anything made out of buffalo hide."

"Deer hide," he corrected.

"Any kind of hide," she snapped, clearly exasperated.

Walker studied her for a moment, half thinking of turning them around and sending them back home. But knowing Little Bear—and Hannah, too—it wouldn't be long before he found them tripping at his heels yet again. And he didn't want to take the time or effort to *escort* them back. Not when he needed every minute and ounce of strength he could spare to rescue Bright Eyes.

It appeared he had little choice. He would have to take them with him.

"All right. If you're coming along, we'd better get moving. Hannah, you ride for a while. Little Bear and I will walk."

A light of undiluted relief flashed in her eyes and she eagerly stepped forward to let him help her into the saddle. His large hands spanned her tiny waist and he found himself running his thumbs over the soft material, wishing it were her bare flesh.

"We've got to get you out of this dress, *notsa?ka?*," he said for her ears only, in no hurry to release her. "You're a mess."

She scowled at him, and he chuckled before stepping back.

"I want to make one thing very clear," he told them both sternly as she arranged her legs and skirts. "I'm in charge from here on out. I don't care how smart or stubborn either one of you think you are . . . you do what I say when I say it. Got that?"

Hannah nodded, likely willing to agree to anything as long as she didn't have to walk again for the next several hours. When Walker turned his head toward Little Bear, it took the boy a minute to decide, but then he nodded and they started off.

He had no idea how he was going to deal with having Hannah and his nephew along on this venture, but he did know one thing: Some small part of him—surely his more reckless side—was thrilled to have Hannah's company.

Chapter Six

"Where are we?" Hannah asked, not sure her harshly spoken words would reach any ears but her own.

"Hell," Walker responded over his shoulder. Little Bear tagged along beside him, neither of them missing a step as David led the horse she was riding down the main street of town. If this could indeed be considered a town.

Several large buildings, connected by a weathered boardwalk, resembled the buildings that might be found in most Texas towns. But she didn't see a mercantile, a post office, a bank, or any of the other types of businesses one would expect to find.

Instead, what would normally be several

buildings seemed to mold together to comprise one single business . . . a very large, very loud saloon and brothel. Bright light, raucous laughter, and off-key piano music poured from the first floor of the establishment. Upstairs, vividly dressed women with too much flesh showing under their gowns and too much paint covering their faces called down lurid invitations to the street below.

Straightening her spine and pretending her clothes weren't covered with an inch of trail dust, Hannah kept an eagle eye on David as they passed the women, watching to see if he would respond to their hoots and whistles. She planned to smack him soundly with her hat—and later with something much more formidable—if he so much as glanced in their direction. Thankfully, he didn't.

And as though the mile-long bordello on her right, boiling over with loose women, wasn't intimidating enough, the opposite side of the street was made up of run-down, surely vermin-infested shacks.

"It certainly looks like hell," she muttered with distaste, unable to fathom the idea of someone actually living in the dilapidated buildings.

At that, David did turn his head to take in the ample-bosomed women leaning over the saloon balustrade, and Hannah began untying the ribbon of her hat.

She might not be a woman of low morals,

and her appearance might not be particularly eye-catching at the moment, but she'd be a speckle-winged titmouse before she'd let the only man currently in her company accept the offer of a hurdy-gurdy girl. Or worse yet, many of them.

"It does possess a personality all its own," he agreed.

Then he turned his attention straight ahead, so she didn't actually need to whack him. It had been tempting, though.

"But this hole-in-the-wall town is actually named Hell," he went on, speaking over his shoulder in low, moderate tones. "It's an outlaw hideout of sorts. Men come here when they don't want to be found, and the law rarely comes calling because they know they'll be outnumbered about three to one."

"Lovely." A town made up entirely of robbers, murderers, and . . . she cast a sidelong glance toward the saloon once again . . . prostitutes. With no one to maintain order or keep them from killing each other. If what she was seeing now was an example of Hell on a sunny Sunday afternoon, she hated to think how these ruffians behaved on a Friday or Saturday night.

"Why did you bring us here?" Hell wasn't an appropriate place for her to be, let alone a small child. Although Little Bear had barely spared a glance for the scantily clad women hanging from the second story balcony and didn't seem the least bit bothered by the noises wafting out of the Devil's Den saloon.

"I need a place for you two to stay. Somewhere no one will ask questions or come looking."

He stopped in front of one of the shacks, close to the edge of what David called a town. If she wasn't mistaken, this particular building looked even more run-down than some of the others. The door, hanging crooked on its hinges, stood open, and Hannah was almost afraid to see what was inside.

"Here?" She gulped. "You want us to stay here?"

David dropped the reins and came around to her side. "You have a problem with dirt, Hannah?" He wrapped two fingers around the hem of her skirt, shooting her a cocky half-smile. "Doesn't look that way from where I'm standing."

She shifted slightly on the saddle, trying to avoid the long, fringed leather pouch that held his rifle, and fell unceremoniously to the ground, not even caring if the whole world got a scandalous glimpse of her petticoats as she did so.

Her legs felt like jelly, but she locked her knees and managed to stay on her feet, looking David squarely in the eye. "It's not dirt I have an aversion to," she informed him. "It's snakes and spiders and mice. And if you make me sleep with any one of them, David, I promise you'll be sorry."

For a moment, he said nothing. And then his half-smile turned into a full-fledged grin. "I'm never sorry when you're around, *notsa?ka?*."

Hannah narrowed her eyes. "What does that mean, that word you just used?"

He shrugged one loose shoulder beneath his doeskin shirt. "It's Comanche for . . . Hannah."

Somehow she didn't believe him, but before she could question him further, he turned and ushered Little Bear into the shack, then placed a hand at the small of her back and let her go ahead of him.

"Don't worry," he told her. "I promise to kill anything that tries to crawl into the blankets with you."

She tilted her head at a coy angle and cast a pointed look back at him, brow lifted. "Good idea. I think I'll do the same."

Her meaning couldn't have been more clear if she'd written it in the sand. But David's only response was to throw his head back and laugh, so loudly he drowned out the noises from the saloon.

One thing about Hannah, she sure knew what to say to a man to get his blood pumping. Granted, she could do that just by standing still, but he hadn't been able to stop thinking about crawling under the blankets with her since she'd all but threatened to clobber him if he so much as tried.

If Little Bear hadn't been with them, he'd have probably given it a shot, just to see what she would do.

He took a sip of the dark brown, nearly flat ale sitting in front of him and pondered the possibilities. Most of them amused him. A few made him hard.

Not good, Walker. It was not good to start thinking things, feeling things about Hannah. He'd always had a soft spot for her, sure. But having a soft spot and lusting were two entirely different things. Especially when Hannah was light-skinned, light-haired, and blue-eyed . . . and he was her opposite in every way. A mixed breed who, standing next to angelic little Hannah, stuck out like a man with two noses.

And that was something that was never going to change.

"Can I get you another beer?"

Still scowling, Walker lifted his head to look at the ox of a man standing before him. The bartender's long handlebar mustache twitched as he waited for Walker's response.

Walker shook his head. "No. Thanks. I'll just finish off this one." He swirled what was left of the warming amber liquid at the bottom of the glass. "You could tell me where I can find a few changes of clothes, though.

Women's clothes. You don't seem to have a mercantile around here."

The man's entire body jiggled as he laughed, from the jowls that hung around his chin to the belly that hung over his belt. "Nope, you're right on that count. Fella tried to open one a few months back, but folks around here generally steal what they want, so stores don't tend to be too successful."

That was nice to hear. Walker shifted uncomfortably, lowering one boot from the foot rail of the bar and lifting the other to take its place. He hoped Hannah and Little Bear were all right by themselves in the cabin where he'd left them, and decided not to waste too much more time on his errand before getting back to them.

"You can buy or trade for most of what you need around here, though," the man behind the bar continued. "And if you're lookin' for ladies' duds, your best bet would be talking to Cora." He hitched his almost bald head toward the other side of the room, and Walker turned to follow the movement. "She's the gal in red, holding court with all them drooling idiots over by the pi-ana."

"I can see why they're drooling," Walker returned, zeroing in on the woman in question.

She was tall and shapely, with sleek black hair pulled into a tight twist at the nape of her neck and crowned by a large red flower that perfectly matched her dress. She smiled broadly and laughed often, making each of the patrons surrounding her feel like he was the only man in the room. And that was really saying something, considering the type of people who frequented the Devil's Den—all outlaws avoiding capture or rowdy sorts who didn't fit in well with regular society.

Hell was a town where a man could remain nameless and blend into the background. No one asked questions and no one looked too closely at faces.

Even so, there were unwritten rules that governed the town, a certain honor among thieves. Minor arguments and the occasional knifefight broke out but were ended quickly if both parties wished to remain in Hell. And men didn't turn other men in to the law, no matter how high the bounty might be. If they did, they could easily find themselves bleeding to death in an alley with a bullet in their backs, or waking up with their throats slit.

It was the ideal place for Walker to hide because no one would ask questions about his presence and, even better, no one would care.

But as nice as all that might sound, Hell was no Garden of Eden. That was why the name Heaven had been reserved for the more pleasant, God-fearing town located on the other side of Purgatory.

And regardless of the honor-among-thieves aspect that made Hell appealing to Walker, he didn't find it reassuring enough to leave Hannah alone here for long.

With that in mind, he made his way across the crowded saloon to Cora's side. The loud, boisterous conversation taking place within the circle of her admirers came to a screeching halt as soon as Walker stepped past the men and stopped directly in front of Cora.

The woman, waving a lacy black fan in front of her exposed and heaving bosom, gave him an appraising look, running her gaze from the top of his head to the toes of his boots and up again.

"Is there something I can help you with, handsome?" she all but purred.

Walker gave a silent nod. "I was hoping I might have a moment of your time, ma'am."

When he heard a snarl from somewhere behind him—he swore he did—he turned and smiled reassuringly at Cora's admirers. "Nothing too personal, fellas, I swear. I'll have her back to you in two shakes."

He heard definite teeth-grinding and saw a few fists clench, but no one tried to pound his face in. A fact Walker much appreciated.

"Over here, sugar," Cora drawled, wrapping her long-fingered hand with its painted nails around his elbow. When they were several feet away from the potential lynch mob, she said, "Now what can I do you for?"

Wanting to make it out of the Devil's Den in one piece, he got right to the point. "The man behind the bar told me you might be able to help me find some women's clothes. For a lady friend of mine."

"What kind of clothes are we talking about, honey?" The black fan snapped closed and she tapped it gently against the palm of her other hand.

"Trousers, mainly. She needs something easier than a dress and petticoats to travel in, and I'd like her to pass as a man, if at all possible."

"And I trust you know this lady friend's size?"

Oh, yeah, he knew Hannah's size. Right down to how much of her breasts he could cover with his hands and how well her bottom would fit into the vee of his thighs. He'd had ten long years to measure every inch of her incredible figure in his mind.

Instead of letting Cora in on his wayward thoughts, he merely nodded.

"It'll cost you," she warned.

"I've got money."

"All right, then. Come with me. I'll be right back, boys," she called over his shoulder, and Walker cast a cautious glance in the same direction to make sure a knife wasn't hurtling at his head.

Cora led him around the bar to a back room, and Walker's eyes widened when she opened the door. The room looked to be used for storage, but not for the usual things he'd expect to find in a bar. He didn't see any bottles of whiskey or barrels of ale. No glasses or even extra chairs and tables.

Instead, it was filled from floor to ceiling, wall to wall, with what Walker could only think to describe as pirate's booty. Silver candelabra and assorted gold figurines filled the shelves. Brass-framed cheval glasses reflected his and Cora's likenesses. And battered leather trunks that looked as if they might have spent a few years at sea littered the floor.

"I don't get much call for putting my girls in pants, but we do a lot of trading with folks around here for all kinds of things." She lifted the rounded lid of one of the chests that sat in a corner. "And you never know what you might be able to use down the road."

Pushing aside a layer of what appeared to be shifts or camisoles or some other type of ladies' unmentionables, she came up with a pair of thickly woven, dark brown trousers. They were a bit worn around the cuffs and at the seat, and might be a little big for small-boned Hannah, but they would do.

Handing them over her shoulder, Cora asked, "That what you're looking for, honey?"

"Those'll work just fine," he told her, stuffing the folded pants under one arm as he dug in the tiny leather pouch at his waist for payment. "Got any shirts to go with them, and maybe a hat?"

"Does a cowpoke pine for his herd?" she

retorted, and flipped him a blur of red plaid that looked almost new, followed by a battered black hat.

"Thank you. How much do I owe you?"

"Normally I'd ask you to give up something in exchange, but it don't look like you have much to part with, handsome. And since my clientele is mostly menfolk, it wouldn't do me much good to ask for a few hours of your time. So let's say . . . three dollars."

He handed her five.

She lifted a brow and gave him a smile, small lines forming like half-circles at the corners of her mouth. "Now that deserves a little something extra, sugar. Here." She pulled one last item from the trunk before letting the lid fall shut, then thrust it into his open arms. "Give your lady friend this . . . and tell her to come by with it on if she's looking for work."

Walker gave Cora a nod and backed slowly out of the room. Sure, he'd pass along the message to Hannah. The next time he was looking to lose a couple of teeth.

Chapter Seven

A few minutes later, Walker left the Devil's Den and headed back to the cabin with a pillowcase full of garments for Hannah. His stride was long and purposeful, eager to return and see that she and Little Bear were all right.

He pulled the crooked door open on its rusty hinges, letting a shaft of sunlight into the dim room. Dust floated in the yellowed air.

He'd expected to find any number of things upon his return . . . Hannah and Little Bear huddled in a corner, being accosted by some drunken stranger, or—God forbid—missing. What he didn't expect was to find Hannah cleaning, with Little Bear recruited to help.

She had the soiled linens off the tick mattress, part of them balled up in her hand to dust every surface in the room. On his hands and knees, and looking none too happy about it, Little Bear used the other sheet to sweep the loose debris covering the dirt floor into manageable piles.

With a grin, Walker slung the sack of clothing over one shoulder and leaned his full weight against the doorjamb, hoping the creaky wood would hold him. "I should have known you wouldn't waste any time getting this place in order."

She straightened from dusting a small square table in one corner that wobbled on a short leg whenever she touched it. "If we have to stay in this . . . *hovel*—" She shot him a disparaging glance. "Then it's going to be clean. Or as clean as I can get it," she qualified, her nose wrinkling.

"And you're going to help. I need you to flip the mattress and decide which side is less disgusting, then find us some new sheets and blankets. These were positively revolting," she said, indicating the dirt-covered fabric in her hand. "I debated about even using them this much, for fear they'd get the floor dirty."

He chuckled. "I'll be happy to turn over the whole bed for you, if you want, but first I have a surprise for you."

He reached into the pillowcase and pulled out the trousers.

"What are these?"

"Pants," he said as she fingered the rough material. "For you. You stand out too much in that pretty pink dress, and it's not a good idea to stick out in a place like this. I'd feel more comfortable if you were dressed like a man." He gave her the plaid shirt and felt hat to go with the trousers. "At least then we might have a chance of making people think you are one. If they don't look too close."

She raised one eyebrow and studied him carefully. "You want me to dress like a man."

She said it as though he'd asked her to drop her drawers and dance on the tabletop. Not that he should be surprised. Hannah wasn't the trousers-wearing type.

But in this case, she needed to be. It was for her own good.

"I know it will feel really strange at first, but it really is necessary, Hannah. There are too many reprobates in Hell to believe you'd be safe if someone found out an innocent woman was here practically alone. If you're dressed like a man, and no one looks too closely, then they'll be more apt not even to come near you." His voice lowered and he fixed her with a solemn expression. "Please, Hannah."

She sighed. "Fine, I'll wear the pants. But you have to finish sweeping the floor. And find us something to sleep on so we don't have to spend the night on the bare ground.

Heaven only knows what crawls around this place when it's dark."

"Fair enough," Walker agreed.

Leaving the pillowcase just inside the door, he stepped forward to start on her growing list of tasks. He wanted to see Hannah and Little Bear settled and safe before he took off after Bright Eyes, anyway. Might as well see them settled to Hannah's specifications.

He crouched down, helping Little Bear transfer the small piles of litter he'd accumulated onto one of the sheets to be taken out and shaken.

"What's this?"

Still resting on the balls of his feet, he raised his head in Hannah's direction. She'd moved near the door and was rifling around in the pillowcase he'd used as a sack.

Uh-oh. She'd found the dress.

"What's what?" he asked, playing dumb.

It didn't work. She quirked a brow and pulled out a fistful of the purple, ruffly, just-this-side-of-sinful creation.

"Oh. That."

"Yes. This."

She smiled, but the expression reminded him more of the look on a rattlesnake's face right before it strikes than of a beautiful woman pleased by the gift of a new dress.

Of course, considering the dress . . .

"Would this be for me?" she asked sweetly.

Walker got that rattler feeling again, skit-

73

tering right down his spine. He'd planned to simply tell her about the gown. How Cora had slipped it in as an extra, free of charge. That he'd only bought the shirt and trousers with the intention of asking her to wear them, not the gaudy saloon girl getup.

But with her standing there, all puffed up and indignant, waiting for an explanation, he suddenly didn't want to give her one. Suddenly, he wanted to yank her chain, see how she would react if she thought he'd brought the dress specifically for her . . . and expected her to wear it.

Schooling his features, he continued with the business of scooping up the grit from the floor and depositing it in the center of the sheet Little Bear held. The boy did his job well, standing at the ready in case Walker needed him. But the boy's eyes were riveted on the bright purple material, edged in black lace, sticking out of the white sack.

"It is for you," Walker said smoothly. "Do you like it?"

"It's . . ."

"Pretty," he supplied for her. "Don't you think it's pretty? Go ahead, pull it out so you can see the whole thing."

Her eyes narrowed and she seemed no more eager to see the entire dress than to dance with a grizzly bear. Still, she dragged the garment out, letting the pillowcase fall to the earthen floor as she shook open the folds of the dress and held it up in front of her.

Hannah's sky blue eyes glittered like diamonds in the sun, snapping with disapproval that he'd so much as *think* she would ever wear such atrocious apparel.

The problem was, Walker thought she'd look damn good in the thing. Although he was careful not to let on that the sight had any effect on him whatsoever, watching her stand there with that dress held against her shapely form had him wishing he were wearing something a little less constricting than doeskin breeches.

"It's pretty," Little Bear offered from over Walker's shoulder, startling him out of his sensual reverie.

"It sure is," he agreed, wondering if the low noise he thought he heard could actually be Hannah's teeth grinding together in fury.

The gown that had her so worked up was purple like the startling hue of a Texas sunset, and made out of a shiny material that begged a man to stroke its folds. The bright panels of the form-fitting bodice were interspersed with rows of black lace. The arm straps were nothing more than thin braids of the same black lace that could either loop over her shoulders or fall loosely around her upper arms. And the skirt . . . well, the skirt was nothing a true lady would wear. Full and rustling, with black lace bordering the hem, it rose a good two feet off the ground, which would leave Hannah's calves, knees, and a small portion of her thighs visible.

What Walker wouldn't give for a healthy glimpse of Hannah's legs. . . . And this dress would certainly fulfill that particular fantasy.

"Why don't you try it on?" he suggested, knowing that was the last thing she wanted to hear. "Little Bear and I can step out for a minute. We have to dump this sheet, anyway."

"I'm not trying this on. It's disgraceful. I'd look like a . . . a . . ." She sputtered, searching for the right word. "Like one of the women over *there*." Her head hitched toward the door, where the Devil's Den sat across the street.

No. Hannah could never be mistaken for a soiled dove. She was too lovely, too soft, too innocent. But that didn't mean she wouldn't look amazing in that dress.

Rising to his feet, he took the sheet from Little Bear and brought the corners together to keep from spilling the dirt cocooned inside.

"Maybe you can put it on later," he offered, heading for the door. As he passed, he paused and whispered in her ear, "Just for me."

What was he thinking?

The dress. Those eyes. That suggestive remark.

Maybe you can put it on later. . . . Just for me.

What was the man *thinking*?

It wasn't like David to say such . . . salacious things.

Not that she really knew what David was like nowadays. She hadn't seen him in over ten years. Maybe it was *exactly* like him to whisper insinuating comments in young women's ears. Maybe he hadn't gone out *only* to find her a change of clothes, but with the sole intention of buying her that dress. If such a scandalous garment could indeed be called a dress.

Maybe when he'd gone across the street, it hadn't only been in search of trousers, either. Maybe while he was over there, he'd spent time with one of those women who had been hanging over the balcony—whistling, hooting, calling out—as they'd passed by earlier.

And maybe she was overreacting just a trifle. What David did privately, and with whom, was none of her business. Even if that last thought did rankle more than a little.

The idea of him being with one of those women. Of removing from a stranger's body a gown similar to the one he'd brought for her.

Oh, lovely. Now she didn't know which transgression to be more upset about—the dress or the harlot.

With a frown puckering her brow, Hannah

let out a frustrated sigh and fell backward onto the rickety bed. The iron frame creaked loudly in protest and the straw of the mattress poked uncomfortably through the cotton of her pink traveling dress to scratch at her bottom.

At least she knew David wasn't with one of those loose-moraled girls now. Not with Little Bear tagging along.

Thank goodness for small favors.

Hannah rose from the scratchy mattress and crossed to the crooked table, where her new canvas trousers and masculine shirt were resting in a neatly folded pile. She might as well change into them, if David expected her to dress like a man while she was here.

Unfortunately, there was nowhere private in which to change. No separate room, or even a screen or curtain to slip behind.

Crossing to the door, she pushed it open a crack, using her foot to help move the sagging bottom across the ground where it stuck. Popping her head out, she looked in both directions down the street. When it appeared that no one was around or headed toward the small shack, she closed the door and darted to the far side of the room, stripping out of her dirt-streaked dress as quickly as she could.

She shed her petticoats first, leaving the camisole to act as a minimal cover while she struggled to drag the stiff pants over her shoes and up the length of her legs. They were a little loose around the hips and calves, but the thick material still hung more closely to her skin than a dress and would take some getting used to.

Instead of shedding her old clothes completely, she left her camisole on and put the plaid shirt over it, tucking the tails into the waistband of the trousers.

All in all, she thought she looked pretty darn manly. At least from what she could see by staring down at herself.

"Very nice."

Hannah's head jerked up at the low-spoken words. She hadn't heard the door, but there he stood, just inside the cabin, raking his gaze up and down her body.

"How long have you been standing there?" she demanded.

"Not long enough." One corner of David's soft mouth curved upward. "You look good, though. And you'll look even better after you put these on."

He held a pair of boots in one hand, his other thumb hitched into the belt of his double sidearms.

"Where's Little Bear?" she asked.

"Out taking care of Thunder," David answered as he stalked toward her. "He'll be in in a minute. He's got our dinner with him."

Hannah opened her mouth, but hardly more than a squeak came out.

79

David set the boots down on the tabletop, sending the rickety piece of furniture wobbling. Reaching out a hand, he wrapped it into her hair and lifted the mass atop her head. He tugged the hat down over it, covering her to her ears.

"I'm not sure this is going to work," he said quietly, standing so close, she could feel his breath on her cheek. His woodsy, masculine scent enveloped her.

"You're too pretty. Your features are too soft, your skin too smooth. Even from a mile away, a man would know you were a woman."

"What are we going to do?" she asked past the lump in her throat.

"I guess we'll just have to keep you inside and out of sight."

His gaze went to her lips and she felt her heart hammer against her rib cage.

"That way I can have you all to myself."

When his face tipped forward and her vision blurred, Hannah knew he was going to kiss her.

And all she could think was, *Finally.*

Chapter Eight

Finally. Thank God.

She'd been wanting this forever, even if she had never before admitted any such desire— not to herself and certainly not to David.

But now that his mouth was brushing against hers, his tall, hard frame pressed so snugly against her own, his hands ever so gently spanning her back . . . now she realized that this was all she'd ever wanted.

From the time she'd been nothing more than a young girl, clinging to an older boy for comfort from the terrible nightmares that plagued her, she'd known there was something special about David. Her feelings had been innocent then, but they weren't innocent now.

81

They hadn't been for some time, she admitted.

Without conscious thought, her arms swept up to hook around his neck, her fingers tangling in the long, luxurious fall of his straight black hair. She parted her lips and his tongue immediately took refuge in her mouth, twining with her own and drawing a low moan of pleasure from deep in her solar plexus.

The sound seemed to startle David, and he lifted his head, wrapping his hands around her waist to push her away.

She touched the shaking fingers of one hand to her lips in awe, staring at him, dazed and confused. "David," she choked out, her voice raspy. "What—"

Lines formed between his eyes as he scowled. "My name is Walker. Spirit Walker. You'd be wise to remember that, Hannah. I'm not a man you should be messing with. I'm not even a man you should have patched up and let sleep in your bed."

His frown deepened. Running a hand over his face, he turned his back to her. "I'm an Indian, in case you've forgotten. Worse, a half-breed. If anyone in Purgatory knew I'd touched you, they'd string me up from the nearest tree and cheer my demise."

"David—"

"My name isn't David, dammit. I'm not that boy anymore. That boy who held you when you cried and kept the other children at the orphanage from teasing you for it. I'm not sure I ever was. The nuns gave me that name. They tried to make me white. But look at me, Hannah."

He swung around, his eyes flaring with anger, his hand tugging at the long strands of his dark, shoulder-length hair. "I'm not white, I'm Comanche. And no one is ever going to mistake me for being white."

His chin dropped to his chest as he blew out a tired breath. "I'm sorry I touched you. I know better. I know what the penalty is for an Indian touching a white woman, and I never should have done it."

"Then why did you?" The words came out whipcord sharp. She was angry. Furious. Brimming with rage. But not because David had kissed her—because he was apologizing for it. And if he didn't stop demeaning himself with all this Indian versus white rubbish, she thought she would scream. She definitely wanted to throw something at him for being so thick-skulled.

And yet, when she finally spoke, it wasn't to voice any of the responses, the arguments, the chastisements roiling about in her brain. It was to ask him *why*. If he was so aware of his heritage and all the problems he claimed it created, why had he kissed her? Why had he even brought Little Bear to her in the first place?

83

Heidi Betts

"Tell me, David," she demanded when he didn't immediately respond, purposely using his *white* name. "If you're so ashamed of kissing me, then why did you do it?"

His lips twisted into the mockery of a smile. "I never said I was ashamed of kissing you, *notsa?ka?*. And I guess I did it because I've been wanting to since I was sixteen years old. I shouldn't have. I never intended to. But a decade is a hell of a long time to pine for something. I promise you, it won't happen again."

With that, he turned on his heel and strode out of the tiny, confining building.

Hannah crossed her arms beneath her breasts and leaned back against the feeble table.

"We'll just see about that," she breathed. "We'll just see about that."

Well, now I've done it, Walker thought with derision. He'd gone and kissed Hannah, and he was going straight to hell . . . if a posse didn't draw and quarter him first.

And worse—so, so much worse—was that he now knew how she tasted.

Before walking into that shack and touching Hannah, he'd only had to deal with his imagination creating the scents and tastes and textures that made up the delectable Hannah Blake. Now he knew the reality, and he didn't think he'd ever recover.

84

His buckskin breeches cramped uncomfortably at the crotch, forcing him to walk more slowly than usual and stop upon occasion to discreetly adjust himself. This wasn't good. And it couldn't continue.

There was only one thing to do: *Stay away from Hannah*. The sooner he did that, the better, so it was a good thing he'd be taking off after Bright Eyes soon, anyway.

He rounded the corner of the cabin and saw Little Bear stroking Thunder's black and white mane while the piebald stallion buried his nose in a bucket of oats.

"You're doing a fine job with him, *ara?*," he said.

His nephew lifted his head and met Walker's eyes under the horse's neck. He smiled cautiously and then moved a bucket of water closer to the pail of oats so both were within easy reach for Thunder.

Knowing that bastard Ambrose Lynch's disposition, Little Bear had been encouraged seldom enough in his short life. The boy had the disposition of a scared rabbit, always hunch-shouldered and jumping at the littlest thing.

Surprisingly, Walker hadn't noticed that kind of behavior as much lately, which gave him hope. Bit by bit, ever since he'd tracked down his sister and nephew and stuck around the Bar L to keep an eye on them, Little Bear had begun to open up. To talk more, to be

85

more animated, to tell stories and climb trees the way normal children did.

Perhaps Lynch's treatment of the boy wouldn't leave scars after all. At least not deep ones, or as many as Walker had first feared. Thank *Ta?ahpʉ*.

His sister, however, was a different story. Her condition was questionable and, he feared, possibly deteriorating by the day. He needed to get her out of there.

"Little Bear," he said slowly, running his palm along Thunder's broad back, "I'll be leaving before first light to go after your *pia*. I need you to stay here and keep an eye on Hannah. Can you do that?"

The boy studied him for a minute in the fading shades of dusk. "I'd rather go with you," he mumbled, lowering his gaze to the ground.

Lynch, Walker knew, would backhand the child for such a remark. Walker simply considered himself lucky that Little Bear trusted him enough to state his honest opinion without fear of being punished.

"I know you would. And I wish I could take you along."

He let his hand fall from Thunder's rump and moved around to the horse's other side so he could better address his young nephew. Perching carefully on the edge of a discarded wooden crate, he continued.

"You would be a good warrior to go into

battle with. But Hannah isn't like us, Little Bear. She's a woman, and she's white. She isn't strong and self-reliant the way our people are."

That might be only partly true, but he needed Little Bear to stay behind, and he needed his nephew to understand how important it was to protect Hannah. Of course, if she heard so much as a word of what he was saying through the hide-thin walls of the shack at his back, she'd come outside and flatten him with one—or both—of the boots he'd just given her.

"I don't anticipate a problem getting your mother away from the Bar L, and Hannah is very important to me." *Too important*, but he tried not to notice the slide of his stomach as that thought raced through his brain.

"Since I can't be in two places at the same time, I need you to stay here with Hannah until I return." He reached out to squeeze Little Bear's shoulder. "Can you do that for me?"

The child continued to stroke Thunder's neck for a moment, then glanced back at Walker and nodded.

"Thank you." Walker braced his hands on his thighs and pushed to his feet.

"*Ara?.*" Little Bear's soft voice stopped him before he could move away.

"*Haa?*"

The child didn't look at him as he continued

87

petting Thunder and asked, "Are you going to kill my father?"

Oh, boy.

Walker barely repressed a sigh. The truth was, he'd like to strangle the bastard with his bare hands. But a child didn't need to hear such things about his father, and no matter how much Walker might despise the man, no matter how badly he might have treated his "wife" and son, he knew Little Bear didn't want anything bad to happen to Ambrose Lynch.

"Not if I can help it," he answered honestly. "I only want to get you and your mother away from him. If I can do that without ever setting eyes on the man, all the better."

He curled his fingers over one of Little Bear's tiny, buckskin-clad shoulders and gave it a gentle squeeze. "I'll only fight him if he comes after us, *ara?*. And even then, I'll only do what I must to get us all away safely. You have my word on that."

Relinquishing his hold on the horse, Little Bear turned and raised his eyes to meet Walker's, studying him for several long seconds. Then, with a solemn, entirely too grown-up expression on his face, he inclined his head.

Walker smiled with a reassurance he wasn't sure he felt, and bent to retrieve the burlap sack lying on the ground. "Hannah and I will set up for supper. Come in when you're ready."

With that, Walker moved around behind Thunder, patting the stallion's flank as he went, and headed inside.

He'd dealt with Little Bear and cooled his ardor at least by a few degrees. Now all he had to do was step back into the cabin and tell Hannah he was leaving in the morning, without giving in to the temptation to kiss her again.

He'd rather face a pack of rabid wolves.

Chapter Nine

Although she didn't like his going at all, Hannah didn't worry about David when he left before sunup and was gone all the next day. And she wasn't terribly concerned when he remained away through the following night, even if the raucous noises from the saloon across the street kept her tossing and turning into the wee hours.

She started worrying when a second day dawned bright and warm, and David still hadn't returned.

By noon, she'd begun pacing the small floor space of the dilapidated shack and peeking her nose out the door every few minutes in hopes of spotting David.

Little Bear didn't seem the least concerned

about his uncle or mother and calmly sat on the floor playing a string game she'd long ago given up trying to learn.

He'd wanted to go out for fresh meals at both breakfast and lunchtime, but she wouldn't allow him. He was only a boy, and she didn't want him wandering around this outlaw hideout of a town by himself. Not when they still had plenty to eat from the supplies David had left them.

Hannah didn't know why she was so worked up. It wasn't that she was afraid to be left alone in Hell with Little Bear. The town was rowdy, yes, but no one had bothered them so far. And she'd remained dressed in the trousers and hat David had bought to cut down on the chances of anyone taking special notice of their presence.

She was worried about David; that was it. But David was a grown man, she reminded herself over and over. He could take care of himself.

Of course, the last time he'd tried to take someone away from the Bar L, he'd been shot. He might have caught an infection and died if she hadn't taken him in when she did. Imagine how much worse it could be this time, when he tried to steal away with his sister, especially if Ambrose Lynch was expecting him.

Afternoon came and went, the stifling heat giving way to cooler temperatures as the sun set. Little Bear grew bored with the length of string and started playing with a deck of cards that had been left in the cabin by its previous occupant. To make conversation and fill the almost deafening quiet of the room, he also attempted to teach her a few words of Comanche.

For being a teacher herself, she didn't think she made a very good student. She had trouble with the nuances of the language and the subtle differences in the sounds of certain words and meanings.

She did manage to remember *ara?*, meaning both uncle and nephew, which she'd heard him and David call each other frequently. *Haa* meant yes, *kee* no, and *pia* mother.

These were all short and fairly easy to recall, but everything else went right over her head. Hannah chose to believe she was too distracted to retain more of the language, not that she wasn't capable of learning it. In fact, she was determined to do just that . . . as soon as she knew David was safe and out of harm's way.

The merriment across the street started in earnest again, and Hannah judged it to be somewhere between ten o'clock and midnight. Peak hours for revelry in Hell, the time each evening when the cowboys got really loud, the tinny piano played ceaselessly, and the women laughed like braying donkeys at every little thing.

She was about to check outside again when a sharp, insistent banging sounded at the door. Hannah jumped and took two steps toward Little Bear to protect him when she heard David's voice.

"Hannah. Open up, it's me."

With her heart in her throat and the blood pounding in her veins faster than the fingers on the piano keys over at the Devil's Den, she raced to the door and pushed it open.

He stood just outside the entryway, lights from behind drawing shadows on his dark skin. Though she couldn't tell exactly what he was carrying, she saw that his arms were full. Only as he turned sideways to step inside did she realize he was holding a person. His sister.

She looked terrible. If Hannah hadn't known better, she would have thought the woman no more than a girl. She seemed to be small in stature but was also painfully thin, her arms like narrow tree branches, her eyes and cheeks sunken.

And she'd been beaten. Purple, black, and yellow swelled one cheek and lined her face along the opposite temple. The scarlet line of a cut bisected her upper lip, and Hannah thought her nose, bulging and slightly crooked, might be broken.

"Did everything go all right?" she asked, barely above a whisper.

With a sharp, affirmative motion, David brushed past Hannah and deposited his sister on the low cot. The lumpy, straw-filled mattress was covered with a thin white sheet, and Hannah immediately stepped forward to cover the poor woman with one of the extra blankets David had provided for her and Little Bear before he'd left.

As soon as David laid Bright Eyes down, Little Bear raced forward. *"Pia!"* He leaned over his mother's prone form, linking one of his small hands with her own and using the other to pat an unblemished spot on her cheek.

"Pia. Tubunitu, pia."

Hannah cast a questioning glance toward David, who stood on the opposite side of the bed, hovering over his sister.

"He wants her to wake up." He explained the boy's words in little more than a whisper.

Hannah's gaze went back to Bright Eyes, who was either unconscious or so exhausted and relieved at being away from the man who beat and mistreated her that she had fallen into a deep, deep sleep.

Now that the woman was lying down, Hannah's eyes were drawn to her stomach, the only round part of her body. Of course, David had told her his first night at her house that his sister was expecting another child, but only now did Hannah realize how far along in the pregnancy she was, and just how dangerous Bright Eyes's condition could be for the unborn infant.

"He hit her again." Little Bear's words were soft but savage, and filled the cabin with the heat of his fury. Raising his eyes to his uncle, he said again, "He hit her again."

"Haa," David agreed, fists clenching where he rested them at his hips. "But he'll never do it again. Neither of you are ever going back there."

Hannah swallowed hard and turned away to keep them from noticing the sheen of tears in her eyes. They both loved Bright Eyes so much. She only hoped it was enough to help the woman recover fully.

Once she had her emotions back under control, she moved to David's side and spoke softly in his ear. "She's going to need to eat when she wakes up. Can you find me the ingredients for a good soup or broth?"

"I'll get them," he said firmly.

"And something to treat those cuts and bruises."

Tilting his head, he studied her for a long minute. Hannah wasn't sure what to make of the bright, intense flare of his coffee-brown eyes.

"Just tell me what you need," he told her finally. "I'll make sure you get it."

There was a small *chiminea* in one corner

for a fire, with a hole cut in the roof above to take away the smoke. Because the weather had been quite hot during the day and not too chilly at night, and the meals she'd prepared had been cold, they hadn't felt the necessity to build a fire. But now, as Hannah read off a mental list of items to David that she'd require to tend Bright Eyes, she knew the Mexican fireplace would come in handy.

"We'll also need plenty of water and kindling," she added.

"Little Bear can help you with those things." His glance darted to where the child still hovered over his mother. "He knows where to get water, and I'm sure he can find some sticks and leaves to start the fire. I can find more wood to keep it going after I've gotten the rest of your supplies."

He turned to his nephew. *"Ara?."*

Little Bear craned his neck from where he stood next to his mother to look over his shoulder at David, tears glossing his dark eyes.

"Can you help Hannah gather some things, please? She's going to take care of your *pia.*"

The boy hesitated a moment, studying his mother's pale, blotched countenance and trying to decide whether to leave her side. Then his tiny fingers loosened their hold on Bright Eyes's hand and he stepped away, turning to offer his assistance to Hannah and his uncle.

"I'll be back in a bit," David told her, guiding Little Bear out the door and closing it behind them.

Once they'd gone, Hannah moved closer to the unconscious Bright Eyes and began removing her clothes. She wore a doeskin sheath, similar to the tuniclike shirts both David and Little Bear wore, but longer. The garment was ragged, though, with worn patches and most of the colored design at the neck scratched off. The dress looked to be something Hannah would expect to find on a beggar rather than a woman with a son and a man who was supposed to be taking care of her.

The rest of her body was as mottled with bruises and minor abrasions as her face. Even her taut-skinned, distended belly.

Not for the first time, a touch of nausea rolled through Hannah's stomach at the image her brain formed of Ambrose Lynch. She'd never met him, but from the way David had described him and what she was seeing now, she thought the man deserved to be horsewhipped. Drawn and quartered. Dropped into a pit of snakes.

Hannah re-covered the now naked Bright Eyes with the thick woolen blanket, tucking it up to her chin. She would ask David later to buy his sister a new nightgown or some such. For now, it was more important to keep her warm, tend her wounds, and get some food into her so she could gain weight and recover more quickly.

An hour later, the cabin was filled with the scent of meat and vegetable broth as the soup boiled in a dented copper pot over the blazing fire Little Bear had built. Hannah had also mixed together several herbs and had a number of soothing poultices on Bright Eyes's more serious bruises.

Little Bear stood close beside the bed, worriedly watching over his mother. David did the same, between bouts of pacing and low, furious curses. And every time he swore or stalked across the room, Hannah watched Little Bear's concern increase by the deepening of shadows in his eyes and the tightening of the straight line of his lips.

Deciding something had to be done before he sent the child into hysterics, Hannah put a hand on David's arm and drew his attention away from his sister.

She pretended not to notice the rock hardness of the corded sinew beneath his fringed leather shirt. Or the way the feel of those muscles sent tingles through her fingertips and up the length of her arm.

And yet she didn't let him go. Didn't yank her hand away or betray the unique sensation by gasping aloud the way she wanted to. Instead, she maintained the contact and even moved her fingers higher along his arm in a light, stroking motion.

When she lifted her gaze to David's, she found him staring down at her, his eyes burning with something more than mere fury at his sister's condition.

Swallowing past the lump of anxiety that lodged in her throat, she gestured toward the door and said in a low voice, "Let's go outside for a minute."

She picked up the battered black Stetson and stuffed it on her head, not forgetting David's warning about making the residents of Hell think she was a man. Then she led him outside and around the corner of the tiny shack.

As soon as they stopped walking, he looked at her quizzically. "Did you need something, Hannah?" He hitched a thumb in the direction of the cabin. "I really should be inside—"

She cut him off by placing the soft side of her index finger against his lips. His words stopped dead and he looked at her as though she'd just sprouted horns and a tail.

"You're making Little Bear nervous," she told him gently. "He's frightened enough about his mother without having you stomping around, filling the air with expletives. We need to remain calm and assure him that she's going to be all right."

One hand, large and warm and dark against her own light flesh, wrapped around the smallest part of her arm. He pulled her

99

finger away from his mouth but didn't release her.

"Will she be all right, do you think?" he asked, visibly concerned about his sister's welfare even as his thumb drew lazy circles on the underside of her wrist.

It was hard to concentrate, hard not to block out everything but the sensations he was creating and lean forward into his body to experience even more. But she tried to keep her mind clear and focus on David's question.

"I think she will be," she answered honestly. "She's terribly thin, and the baby is probably sapping much of her strength. But none of her injuries are that serious, and I think once she's gotten some rest and nourishment into her, she'll start feeling better."

"And will the baby be okay?"

That, she wasn't so sure about. "I certainly hope so. Do you know how far along she is?"

He shook his head, a frown marring his otherwise smooth brow.

"The longer she has to fully recover before giving birth, the better, I would imagine." She felt his fingers flex nervously. "I hope you understand that I'm only guessing about all of this, David. I'm doing the best I can because I want to help. But I'm not a doctor; I don't know anything for sure."

His smile was as welcome as it was unexpected. "You're a miracle," he murmured quietly. "I didn't plan for you to be here, that's for sure, but now I honestly don't know what I'd do if you weren't. I'm very grateful you came along, Hannah."

Her heart filled with pleasure at that and her blood seemed to swell in her veins. "I'm glad I came along, too," she admitted, licking her suddenly dry lips.

His smoldering gaze zeroed in on that action, driving the temperature around them up by several notches.

"You know this is a mistake, Hannah. We shouldn't be here like this."

But even as he spoke the words, his grip tightened on her wrist and his other arm reached up to brush a thumb over the line of her jaw.

"I'm not afraid of you, David, or of anything we do together. And I don't care about the color of your skin."

His movements ceased, but he didn't let go of her. He simply stood perfectly still, watching her with those intensely dark eyes.

"I wanted you to kiss me the day before you left to rescue your sister," she went on, encouraged by his silence. "I wish you would kiss me again. And anything else you might want to show me along those same lines . . . well, I'm as good a student as I am a teacher, and I think I'd really like to learn more about whatever this delicious sensation is that seems to be running between us."

Heidi Betts

David opened his mouth, exhaling a breath of air on a harsh laugh. His grip on her arm tightened, drawing her nearer by a fraction of an inch.

"You have no idea what you're saying, Hannah," he warned in a gravelly voice.

"Yes, I do." She responded without hesitation, because she was speaking from her heart now, not from her head. "I know precisely what I'm saying, precisely what I feel. The question is: How do you feel about me, David?"

Chapter Ten

How did he feel about her? How did he *feel*?

He wanted to lower her hand to the front of his trousers and show her exactly how he felt. He wanted to drag her down to the ground and divest her of those ugly pants and shirt, or back her up against the wall of the cabin and take her standing up.

And wouldn't she just love to be privy to those thoughts as they swirled around in his brain? If she knew that was the kind of thing he longed to teach her, she'd run screaming and never look back. Despite her claims of not caring about the color of his skin, she'd likely stop at the first sheriff's office she got to and tell them a savage had tried to rape her.

103

Not fair, Walker, he castigated himself. Hannah had never said a single derogatory word about his heritage. Not even when they'd been young, and pointing and laughing at the abandoned half-breed boy had been the other children's idea of a good time.

So if Hannah didn't seem to have a problem with his Comanche blood, what was keeping him from doing what his body so desperately desired?

Nothing, apparently. And if he still suffered a stab of guilt at that, he'd deal with it later.

Grabbing her by the elbows, he yanked her forward until they were molded together from chest to thigh. The brim of her hat tipped back as he thrust his face close to hers, tilted his head to the right, and pressed his lips to hers.

A low groan of pleasure and long-suppressed need rolled its way up his throat and he drew her even closer, until the stiff buds of her nipples rubbed against his chest and the hard ridge of his arousal pressed into her belly.

If he never touched another woman in his life, the memory of this moment would be enough to carry him happily through to the hereafter. Her soft, feminine skin going warm beneath his callused fingertips as he gently cradled her cheeks in his hands. Her full, rosy lips moving beneath him, parting slightly to allow him entrance. Her light, delicious scent that reminded him of fresh, yellow lemons and seemed to linger on her skin and in her hair, even after a day of travel and two days in this outlaw-ridden town.

He didn't know how she did it. He didn't know how she did anything. All he knew was that he loved everything about her and counted himself lucky for having known her all these years. For being here with her now.

She was an angel come to earth, and he had no business touching her.

Yet he couldn't seem to stop himself.

Even as the thought crossed his mind to let her go, to walk away, his grip on her tightened. His hands swept down to the swell of her hips, then to her buttocks, where his fingers dug into the soft flesh and rocked her against his straining manhood.

Walker alternated between gently biting and sucking at her luscious mouth and tangling his tongue with her own.

The hat fell off her head completely and bounced to the ground as he brought one hand up to stroke her hair. It fell through his parted fingers like sand and made him think of how beautiful she would be stretched out on a feather bed, those honey-blond tresses spread out behind her.

He might be half-Indian, but he was half-white, too. And as comfortable as he'd always been sleeping in a tipi on a pile of furs while visiting his mother's village, he wanted Hannah in a bed. A big, soft bed with enough room to roll over and over and then stretch full-out afterward.

After making love with Hannah.

Holy hell! The thought nearly brought him to his knees, even as he tilted back her head for better access and slipped his hand down to cup her breast through the thin fabric of the plaid shirt.

Her nipples were pebbled with desire and pressed into his palm. He could feel the moan that purred in her throat in his own lips, and her hands had somehow drifted down his chest, curling in the loose buckskin material at his hips.

There was no feather bed in sight, not even a room where they could go for privacy. And yet, if they didn't cease soon, he *would* make love to her. Here, on the ground, against the side of the building. He didn't care, not anymore. He only wanted. Needed. Knew he would die without her.

Slowing their kisses, drawing back little by little, he finally lifted his head. They both gasped for breath, struggled to fill their lungs with much-needed air.

But they didn't let go of one another. Their bodies were still molded together, hands flitting over firm muscles and cushiony flesh, exploring.

"Hannah, *notsa?ka?*" he said, his chest

heaving. "Before this goes any further, I need to know . . . Are you sure?"

He brushed a strand of silky hair behind her ear, letting his thumb slide leisurely over the gentle curve of her cheek. "Because if you're not, I'll stop. I swear I will."

He would probably have to soak in the horse trough for a week, but he would cut off his own hands—and more—before he'd ever raise a single hand to this beautiful woman against her will.

Hannah's tongue darted out to wet her lips from one corner to the other, and Walker nearly moaned aloud. His pulse pounded in his ears, his erection straining painfully behind the tanned placket of his trousers.

With a hint of rose tinting her cheeks, she raised a soft palm to caress his jaw and whispered the two most wonderful words he'd ever heard: "I'm sure."

He groaned, a strangled, almost desperate sound, and wrapped his arms around her waist. Squeezing her, hugging her, lifting her off her feet and kissing her until the world around them disappeared.

He'd had some nice moments in his life. Being adopted and taken home by the Walkers. Finding out he was going to be a big brother when Clay and Regan had their first child. Returning to his mother's village and learning he had a half sister and a young nephew.

But nothing topped this. Not a single thing

before or in the future could surpass the warm, ecstatic feeling swirling in the pit of his stomach and spreading out to his limbs at the knowledge that Hannah Blake wanted him as much as he wanted her.

Still holding her a few inches off the ground, he half-walked, half-staggered toward the back of the row of cabins, away from the street. It was darker there and they'd be less likely to be seen.

Part of him hated this. Hated that he was about to make love to her outside, in the shadows behind a rickety old shack in an outlaw town like Hell. He wasn't going to let her go or try to change her mind—he wasn't crazy, after all—but he still wished they could be inside a fancy house or hotel, on a clean, comfortable bed.

Another part of him was just . . . damn grateful.

There was nowhere to go, nothing to do except prop her gently against the back wall of the cabin as he kissed her, tasted her skin, reveled in the soft, satiny feel of her womanly form.

While he used his teeth to nibble at her mouth, her ear, the line of her throat, his fingers deftly undid the row of buttons at the front of her shirt. She wore a lacy white camisole beneath.

Hannah was a petite woman, petite all over, including the small, round globes of her breasts. Walker had always gravitated toward more buxom women, though he'd never been quite sure why. Now, he wondered how he ever could have found those full, top-heavy figures attractive when Hannah's tiny stature suited him so much better.

His hand slipped inside the folds of her shirt and gently cupped one of the spheres, no bigger than an overturned teacup. It filled his palm just right.

Keeping one hand locked on her hip, he trailed a line of kisses along her jaw and down the side of her neck, smiling to himself when she let her head fall back and moaned in pleasure as the heat of his mouth neared the shallow dip of her cleavage.

"Ara?! Hannah! Ara?!"

It took a minute for the loud cries to cut through the haze of desire that surrounded Walker. When they did, his head jerked up, his hand slipped out from beneath Hannah's shirt, and he took an abrupt step backward.

Hannah, looking equally dazed by the sudden interruption, ran a hand through her tousled hair and quickly began to straighten her disheveled shirt.

With a mild curse, Walker returned to her side and helped her get the small buttons through the correct holes. He retreated again just as Little Bear rounded the corner at a full run.

Sliding to a halt, chest heaving, he looked

from one adult to the other. *"Pia,* she is awake. *Ara?,* come. Hannah, come, come." He waved for them to follow and raced back to the cabin.

Walker blew out a breath. Though he couldn't deny his happiness at hearing that his sister had regained consciousness, he also suffered more than a little disappointment that his time with Hannah had been cut short.

He held out a hand to her and wrapped it around her elbow when she moved within arm's reach.

"Are you all right?" he asked softly, just above her right ear.

She nodded. Halfway around the cabin, she cocked her head to the side and looked up at him, and Walker suffered a sudden dizziness that caught him by surprise.

It was her eyes. Those ravishing blue eyes. Even in the dark, when he couldn't see their exact color, they shone up at him and drew him into their molten depths like a siren's song.

At the corner of the building, he stopped, pulling her to a halt beside him.

"What?" he asked. He had to know what that look meant.

She smiled gently and curled her fingers into his forearm, nails digging in a fraction. "I was just thinking about what a superb kisser you are. And how much I enjoy the touch of your hands on my body."

Rising up on tiptoe, she pressed a soft kiss to his cheek, and the devil in her eyes sparkled even more. "And how I can't wait until we get the opportunity to finish what we started."

With that, she let go of his arm and continued into the cabin to check on his sister.

Walker stood outside, in the moonlit night, for a short while longer. Trying to absorb the meaning of Hannah's words. Trying to calm the raging of his blood and brain and breeches. Trying to figure out just when he'd fallen so madly, tragically, head over heels in love with her.

Chapter Eleven

Hannah was surprised when David didn't enter the cabin directly behind her. Or even in front of her, as concerned as she knew he was for his sister.

Of course, she had flustered him with that remark about being eager for their next opportunity to make love.

But she couldn't help it; he was so fun to tease, so easy to knock off his guard.

Not that she was joking about wanting him that way. She did. She had for a very long time, regardless of the fact that they weren't married or the threat such an action could pose to her schoolmarm position.

And *that*, she decided, was something she'd have to deal with when the time came. It was too much to contemplate all at once.

She'd already missed a good week of school and was sure the townspeople were wondering where she'd run off to. But she would cross that bridge when she came to it, give them some excuse for her absence that hopefully would not get her fired. What she wouldn't do was tell them anything about being alone with David or kissing him behind a run-down old shack in Hell. The Purgatory school board might pay her and put a roof over her head, but they didn't deserve to know everything about her private life.

Shaking herself out of her woolgathering, she held a cup of cool, fresh water to Bright Eyes's mouth, helping the frail woman to sit up a bit and drink her fill. Little Bear stood at her side, nervously hovering over his now conscious mother.

The door opened and David walked in just as Hannah was propping a pillow behind his sister's head. He looked strong and handsome, even in the dim lamplight filling the small cabin. Only his fingers worrying the brim of Hannah's forgotten felt hat betrayed his nervousness.

Glancing briefly in her direction, he moved to his sister's side and crouched beside the bed. "*Nami?*, it's good to see you awake. You look better."

Bright Eyes smiled faintly and reached out a hand to grip David's arm. Then her gaze

113

flashed questioningly toward Hannah.

"This is Hannah Blake," he explained. "Hannah, this is my half sister, Bright Eyes."

"Hello, Bright Eyes," Hannah greeted her with a kind and what she hoped was a reassuring expression.

"Hannah is an old friend from when I lived at the orphanage in Purgatory. She's been nursing you and watching after Little Bear."

Bright Eyes turned her head on the pillow to look up at Hannah. And then her hand, almost skin and bones, reached out to squeeze her arm the same as she'd done with David. "*Ura*. Thank you," she said softly.

Giving the woman a reassuring nod, Hannah asked, "How are you feeling? Is there anything I can get for you?"

"No. Thank you, I am fine."

Her English was slow and a little stilted but clearly understandable. Hannah knew now how Little Bear had learned the language so well, and Bright Eyes had likely come by her knowledge either from that Lynch fellow or her brother, David.

"Little Bear." Pushing to his feet, David addressed his nephew. "Stay with your mother while Hannah and I talk. Let us know if she needs anything."

Little Bear's black hair bounced as he nodded. From the look on the child's face, Hannah doubted a team of horses could drag him away from his mother's side.

David rounded the end of the cot and dropped Hannah's hat on the lopsided table-top. Catching her elbow, he led her to the opposite side of the room.

"Is she really all right?" he asked, bending close to whisper in her ear.

"I don't know. I told you, I'm not sure of what I'm doing; I'm just . . . trying the best I can."

"And I appreciate it," he rushed to assure her. "I don't know what I'd have done if you weren't here."

His thumb came up to caress the soft swell of her lower lip, and she took a moment to savor the sensation before casting a glance over his shoulder to the woman laying still and battered on the lumpy tick mattress.

"I think she'll be fine. It will take some time to build up her strength, but her eyes are bright and she seems determined to survive. She also has a young child to care for and a baby on the way. I think that's enough to make any mother fight to recover."

"Ura, Ta?ahpɨ."

"What does that mean?" she asked, returning her gaze to David's.

"Thank you, Great Spirit."

"Yes. I couldn't agree more." There was an intensity in his dark brown eyes, something mesmerizing, begging her not to look away. And like trying to pry Little Bear from his mother's side, she didn't think a herd of wild

115

mustangs could tear her attention off David at that moment.

His thumb fell away from her mouth, but his hand remained at her cheek, curving beneath her jaw. "We've got to do something about this, Hannah," he grated.

A vise seemed to clamp about her chest and the air left her lungs in a soundless whoosh. "About what?"

"This." He waved his free hand between their two bodies in a futile, wordless gesture.

"I told you what I wanted to do about it," she said with more courage than she felt.

A wicked, glittering light came into his eyes, and it had nothing to do with the fire burning in the *chiminea* behind them. "You've grown up, Hannah. And I think it's safe to say you've become a little bit dangerous."

She tipped her chin and shot him what she hoped was a saucy grin. "Just a little bit?"

His low chuckle ran like molasses down her spine.

"Make that very dangerous." He dropped his hands and took a step back from her. "I'd better watch myself or you might lure me into your evil web."

Oh, she wanted him in her web, all right. Even if that made her the spider and him the fly. But she merely shrugged a shoulder in nonchalance before moving toward the fire to fill a bowl of broth for his sister.

116

"You know where to find me if you change your mind," she told him softly. And then, turning to fix him with one last, challenging glare, she added, "If you're brave enough to risk getting caught."

The next several days passed uneventfully. Bright Eyes regained some of her strength and started to get the color back in her face, thanks to the excellent care Hannah and Little Bear provided, barely leaving her side for five minutes. The mottled purples and yellows of her bruises were fading, and she was filling out again with the return of her appetite.

Much to Hannah's disappointment, however, she and David found very little time to be alone together. And she suspected David planned it that way, making a point of being outside when she was in, or across the room from wherever she stood.

But she didn't let his behavior discourage her. As hard as he might try, he couldn't hide the spark of attraction that sizzled to life in his eyes every time he looked at her. It made her feel special and set off a series of tiny heat explosions in her belly and lower extremities. She was practically humming with the expectation of what was to come.

And it was coming. She could feel it in her bones.

Just as she was helping Bright Eyes back

into bed after a short walk to relieve herself in the corner chamber pot, the door burst open, startling a small gasp out of both women. David loomed in the opening, his chest heaving as early evening sunlight poured in behind him, casting a long shadow across the earthen floor in front of his tall frame.

"We've got to get out of here," he blurted without preamble.

"What's wrong?"

"I just spotted Lynch and some of his men at the far end of town," he told them as he stepped forward and started gathering their things—any sign that they'd ever occupied the dingy cabin.

Ignoring his sister's gasp and Little Bear's sudden stiff, protective stance, David went on. "They'll no doubt search each and every cabin in Hell, so we have to get out of here. Grab it all; I don't want anything left behind."

With Bright Eyes perched on the edge of the bed, Hannah moved to help him collect their things. Throwing dirt and ashes over the low-burning fire to extinguish the flames, rolling up blankets, tossing every bit of food in sight into an empty burlap bag.

"Where are we going? Your sister shouldn't be riding yet, or traveling a great distance."

"We aren't going far," he answered curtly. "I've got a place set up for us to hide. If we play our cards right, he won't find us even if he searches there."

Hannah wanted to ask more, wanted to know more. But David was distracted—for good reason—and she figured she'd learn about their destination soon enough.

He shoved the burgeoning sacks and piles of bedclothes into her and Little Bear's arms. "You two take these. I'll carry Bright Eyes."

Hurrying to the bed, he swooped his sister into his arms and started out the door. Hannah and Little Bear followed obediently.

Hannah had no idea what Ambrose Lynch looked like, but she found herself scanning the street and sidewalk for him all the same, just as David's gaze darted cautiously from side to side. He led them across the dusty street and down a narrow, darkened alley that bordered the main entrance of the Devil's Den. Rounding the corner, they found a woman holding open a back entrance to the saloon, and David quickly slipped inside.

The woman took a second to look them over, then gave them a quick flick of her fingers. "Come on, sugars. I'll show you upstairs."

Making sure Little Bear was keeping up, Hannah managed to sidle close to David. Bright Eyes had her arms linked about his neck and he was carrying her as carefully as he might a newborn babe.

119

Heidi Betts

"Who is this woman?" she whispered harshly.

"Her name is Cora," he answered, not bothering to lower his voice. "Cora, this is Hannah," he said by way of introduction.

Cora, dressed in a skin-tight gown an ungodly shade of red, turned her head slightly and gave Hannah a nod. "Charmed."

"Are you sure we can trust her?"

Even though Hannah hissed the words as softly as she could, Cora still overheard and answered the question herself. "Your man is paying me plenty not to tell anyone where you are. It'll be your job to keep from being found once you're in the room, though. I can't keep whoever it is you're avoiding from searching this place."

They had traversed an unlit rear stairwell and a long, carpeted hallway with a mahogany balcony that overlooked the main room of the saloon. The walls bore faded satin brocade and gold, glass-covered sconces every few feet to light the way. Cora led them around a corner and threw open the door to one of the four rooms located in this particular wing.

David wasted no time stepping inside and setting Bright Eyes gently on the wide feather mattress. The covers were turned back and the sheets were gleaming white—a far sight better than what she'd been sleeping on at the cabin.

Still standing in the doorway, Cora said, "If you need anything, darlin', you just let me know. It will cost you, of course. . . ." She flashed David a beaming, suggestive grin. "But maybe you'll think it's worth the price."

With that, she left the room, closing the door behind her, and Hannah turned to face David.

"What are we doing here?" she demanded. Her hands seemed to go automatically to her hips, her feminine sensibilities riled by having to set so much as one foot inside a house of ill repute.

David now stood beside Little Bear, digging through the multitude of items they'd brought with them. Shooting her a sidelong glance, he said, "Don't look so scandalized, *notsa?ka?*. This whorehouse may just save our lives."

She ignored his use of the detestable *w* word and cocked her head questioningly. "*May* save our lives?"

He inclined his head in a single, affirmative motion. "You're the only one who can really keep Lynch from finding us."

"And how's that?"

"You won't like it."

"Undoubtedly." Her arms had moved up from her hips to cross beneath her breasts as she awaited his response.

"I need your help, Hannah." He glanced pointedly at first Little Bear, then Bright

121

Eyes, his expression conveying the urgency of his request. "You have to do this."

"Do what?" she asked, growing more and more wary by the moment.

Keeping his gaze locked with hers, he dragged something from one of the burlap sacks and held it out to her.

"Oh, no." She was already shaking her head, backing away several inches for good measure.

"Please, Hannah." He took a step toward her, boxing her in. "Our lives depend on this."

For long seconds she stood stock-still, scowling and wishing 10,000 plagues on this devious, manipulative man.

"You'll owe me for this, Walker," she bit out, calling him by the name he'd been encouraging her to use all along. "This had better work. And for this, you'll owe me forever. And I mean *forever.*"

With that, she yanked the repugnant purple dress from his hands and marched toward the closet to transform herself from an innocent young schoolmarm into a practiced courtesan.

And then she was going to strangle David with a strip of lace from the Jezebel dress he loved so much.

Chapter Twelve

In a matter of minutes, Hannah changed out of her man's shirt and trousers and into the gaudy purple dress. When she stepped out of the darkened closet, David looked her over from head to toe, an appreciative light in his eyes. Hannah's stomach fluttered in response, but she had no intention of letting him know that.

She shot him a quelling glare and stalked across the room, giving him her back. This was *not* the way she'd envisioned herself helping David save his sister and nephew.

While he hid their belongings deep in the closet she'd just vacated, Hannah moved in front of the long chest of drawers, topped by a wide mirror, that lined one wall.

The gown was ghastly; there was no denying it. And certainly nothing a proper woman
should be caught standing anywhere *near*, let
alone *in*.

It had an off-the-shoulder design with one
of the lowest bodices she'd ever witnessed.
And even though she couldn't fill the bust
nearly as well as she knew one of Cora's girls
would, she had to admit that it didn't look
half bad on her. She'd never bared so much
pale skin before, and the early evening air
brought out tiny beads of gooseflesh on her
uncovered shoulders, chest, and the hollow
area between her breasts.

The bright taffeta hugged her form like
scales on a snake, the sewn-in bones—hidden
behind vertical rows of the same material in
black—digging into her ribs and almost cut-
ting off her breath. The skirt flared out
slightly, aided by layers of attached petticoats
that showed beneath the knee-length hem.

She wasn't sure what to be more embarrassed by—the extremely low bodice, showing most of what God had seen fit to gift her
with, or the high-cut skirt that made visible
entirely too much of her legs. She hadn't re-
vealed so much as an ankle in public since
childhood.

Waving a hand in front of her face, she
tried to dispel the heat of a blush from her
cheeks, even as the chickenflesh over her
bosom grew larger.

Taking all of these discomfitures into consideration, Hannah wondered how she could still find the gown almost . . . alluring.

Judging by the number of working girls downstairs dressed similarly to this, and the bevy of cowboys eagerly swarming around them, she gathered men liked women in this type of garment. Which might explain the look David had given her when she'd first appeared in the barely there outfit.

He was attracted to her. He liked seeing her dressed this way. Or maybe the sight of so much of her bosom would cause any man to stare. It certainly had her bug-eyed. •

She tugged ineffectually at the dipping dress front and then turned to face David as he finished clearing the room of any sign of their presence.

"What do we do now?" she asked.

His gaze skimmed her getup once more and she hitched a hip seductively. At least she hoped the pose came across as seductive. She'd never really attempted to attract a man before, so she couldn't be sure.

"We're going to hide Bright Eyes and Little Bear behind the bed, and then you and I are going to pretend to be conducting business."

Hannah felt her brows shoot up. *Conducting business?* She looked down at the dress she was wearing and wondered why she hadn't figured out this portion of his plan sooner.

The room, decorated in gold and burgundy, seemed to spin around her, and a high-pitched squeal sounded in her ears. Just how far would he expect her to go to play out this particular charade? With other people in the room.

The thought made her palms turn sweaty.

David moved to his sister's side and helped her round the bed, then waited for Little Bear to slither beneath the frame of the four-poster before lowering Bright Eyes down beside him. Because of her burgeoning belly, she couldn't fit all the way under like her son, but would be adequately hidden in the small space between bed and wall. Provided no one searched the room too closely, of course.

And Hannah assumed she was the one they were relying on to keep that from happening.

"Oh, mercy," she breathed, slapping a hand to her forehead in despair.

When she raised her head, David stood towering above her. A completely inappropriate grin split his face.

"Ready?"

She pinned him with a wry glance. "Do I have a choice?"

"Not anymore. Although, if you'd chosen to keep Little Bear back in Purgatory with you, you might not be in this mess now."

She didn't miss the pointed look he cast at her shiny purple gown.

"Thank you. I'll remember that for the next

126

time I'm able to set the clocks back and relive my life. Unfortunately, your nephew is as stubborn and thickheaded as you are." Her demeanor wasn't the least bit kind, and she didn't apologize for it.

Then she sighed, resigned to her leg-baring, cleavage-exposing, purple-dressed fate. "What do you want me to do?"

"Sit on the bed and look like you've just finished servicing me."

"Excuse me?"

Her mouth fell open and her eyes all but popped out. And David—blast his hide—had the nerve to chuckle.

"You're too innocent for your own good, *notsa?ka?*. And normally I'd do my best to protect you from this sort of thing. But this time, I'm afraid we don't have much choice in the matter."

Unbuckling his gun belt, he set it carefully on the bedside table. Then he crossed his arms over his midriff and pulled off his buck-skin shirt.

Catching sight of the shocked expression she knew must be gracing her face, his lips lifted. "Don't worry, Hannah, I'm not actually going to make love to you. Not yet, anyway," he added in a whisper meant for her ears only. "We just need to make it look like you work here and I'm a paying customer."

"Won't Lynch recognize you?" she found the presence of mind to ask, still riveted by

127

the bronze flesh and sculpted muscles of his bare chest.

"Hopefully not, if I'm under the covers with my back turned." He threw his shirt to the far side of the room and began kicking off his boots. "Your appearance is going to need a little work, though. Come here."

He crooked a finger, beckoning her close. At first she hesitated; then she took a step forward.

His hands wrapped around the back of her head and he gave her hair a great tousle. Then his fingers moved to the buttons at the front of her dress.

She immediately threw her arms up to block his movements, but he merely pushed them aside and slipped two or three tiny metal hooks from their eyes.

"You need to look well-loved, *notsa?ka?*." Moving to the bed, he started to shuck his pants. "And you may want to turn around if you don't want to see me in the altogether."

Was it just her imagination, or did it take her an exceptionally long time to avert her gaze? Facing the other direction, she kept her eyes tightly closed, too afraid she might be tempted to glimpse his nakedness in the dresser mirror.

She heard the bed frame creak, and then David called out, "All right, I'm decent."

Without thinking or knowing what to expect, she spun around . . . and sucked in a deep breath of air.

Decent was definitely in the eye of the beholder.

Covered to the waist by a thin, white sheet, David reclined against the mahogany headboard. His long black hair fell like a shroud over the pillow at his back.

"Your turn," he said gently.

Step by slow step, she made her way to the edge of the bed. She was supposed to climb in with him? Under the covers? Without him wearing a stitch of clothes?

Because she definitely didn't believe he was the sort of man to wear something as civilized as drawers beneath his well-worn leather trousers.

"You don't need to lie down," he said, unwittingly putting her mind at ease. "I think it would look better if you just sat down, rumpled your skirts a bit, and waited for Lynch or one of his men to come in. If you can take off your stockings and pretend to be rolling one back up when he opens the door, all the better. Like I said, we need to make it look as if we just . . ."

"Did the deed," she supplied flatly. "Yes, I understand that part. And what will you be doing while I'm rolling my stockings up and down?"

She heard the amusement in his voice when he replied, "Sleeping, of course. That

sort of thing always wears me out. I'll have
my back turned. Hopefully they won't notice
the length of my hair behind you and under
the pillow. If they suspect I'm an Indian,
they'll want to have a closer look, and there's
no doubt they'll recognize me. Try to keep
them from seeing too much of what's behind
you, if you can."

Her tongue held a sharp retort on its tip.
Something about her new dress making it
hard to hide much of anything, let alone a
full-grown, naked man, stretched lengthwise
at her back. Instead of giving voice to that
thought, however, she swallowed hard and
gave a slight nod.

She was one woman, four-and-twenty
years old. Five and a half feet tall, coming
only to David's chin. She'd been told that with
her slight build, she looked as though a strong
breeze would blow her over.

Yet she was supposed to use her body, her
feminine wiles, and a painted-on purple
gown to protect three other people from a
large, looming, very bad man.

The mattress bounced beneath her and
Hannah bounced with it as David got situ-
ated.

"Can you hand me my gunbelt?" he asked
her, the words muffled as they hit the wall
before him and ricocheted back to her.

Her gaze went to the reddish-brown holster

resting on the nightstand. Reaching out, she slowly wrapped her hand around the smooth leather that held his six-shooters.

She twisted around to pass him the weapons, and the warm, callused pads of his tan fingers brushed the top of her hand as he rolled toward her to take it. A spark of sheer awareness rocked through her flesh, through her blood, through her bones. It beat a staccato rhythm to the very center of her being and warmed her from the inside out.

Without taking his eyes off her, David placed the Peacemakers and all their trappings on the stark white sheet near his stomach and then lifted the same hand to cup her cheek.

She'd gone pale, she knew, even if it felt as though steam was about to seep out of her pores.

"Soon, *notsaʔkaʔ*. This will all be over soon. And then we'll see about . . . the rest."

His meaning was clear, and she didn't pretend not to understand. It almost comforted her to know she wasn't alone in feeling as though a thunderstorm was brewing in her belly.

Almost, but not quite.

She started to turn away, but he caught her wrist, holding her in place.

"There's just one more thing," he murmured softly.

131

The coffee brown of his eyes riveted her, created the sensation of floating, being swept downstream and not caring enough to fight the current.

"What's that?" she heard herself ask in a husky, breathy voice she scarcely recognized as her own.

Rather than answering verbally, his palm slid from the side of her face to the back of her head, tangling in the loose fall of her hair. His mouth came down on hers unexpectedly, causing her to gasp. But the sound was lost as he molded his lips to hers, pressing and licking and smoldering her into acquiescence.

The kiss was hot and hard, their teeth and tongues scraping. She thought her lips might be bruised by the end but wasn't sure she cared.

She certainly didn't attempt to pull away. Instead, she leaned closer, brought up her arm to touch his bare shoulder. His skin burned like fire beneath her fingers and a muscle in his biceps spasmed.

When he finally released her they were both breathing heavily, sucking oxygen into their deprived lungs. Without conscious thought, her fingertips went to her lips, tracing the love-swollen ridges. She considered swearing off food and drink so nothing would wash away the delicious taste of David and his kisses.

"Well-loved," he said, carefully removing his hand from the long strands of her hair. "No one could ever doubt it."

133

Chapter Thirteen

He never should have kissed her. It was necessary, however—or at least it made her look more appropriate to the part she was about to play.

Unfortunately, aiding her to come across like she'd just made love only made him want to do exactly that. Gaudy dress or worn trousers, lives in jeopardy or not, he wanted Hannah. Only covering his torso with the thin sheet and lying with his face to the wall kept that fact from being patently obvious.

And as soon as they got out of this—*if* they got out of this—he was going to see that she knew it.

He only hoped she was amenable, even if it meant burning in hell or swinging at the end of a rope for ever touching her. At this point, it would be well worth the gamble. Whatever his punishment.

Turning away from her before he started something he couldn't finish—or before she saw something in his face he wouldn't have time to explain—he unsnapped the safety strap of his holster and slid one of the revolvers out just a fraction for easy access.

He didn't want to use it. There were too many innocents in the room who could catch a stray bullet. And Hannah would be right in the line of fire.

But if worse came to worst, he was more than willing to shoot Ambrose Lynch straight between the eyes, and would do everything he could to keep Hannah safe in the process. Not to mention Bright Eyes and Little Bear.

Tugging the sheet to his waist and twisting his hair beneath his body and the pillow so it would appear shorter than it was, he wrapped his hand around the grip of the gun and prepared himself for Lynch's—or one of his men's—impending arrival.

Over his shoulder, he asked Hannah, "Are you all right? Are you ready for this?"

"I'm rolling."

"What?" He almost bent back around but knew that would disrupt the pose he'd worked so hard to make look authentic. Instead, he merely cocked his head a fraction and strained to see her in his peripheral vision.

135

"You told me to make it look like I'm getting dressed again after . . ."

She trailed off, unwilling to put a word to what she was supposed to look like she'd been doing. Walker grinned and was glad she couldn't see it.

"So I'm rolling my stockings up and down. First one, then the other, up and down, up and down. . . ." She sounded bored and far from happy with the situation she'd been forced into.

Her tone had little effect on Walker, however; he was too busy picturing Hannah's every slow, erotic movement. Perched on the edge of the bed, legs crossed, skirts hiked to her thighs. The tight bodice he'd unbuttoned himself gaping open in a wide vee. The small, white globes of her breasts straining against the black stays and purple material, possibly coming close to popping free as she leaned forward to roll and unroll these sheer, silky stockings that had come with the gown.

And he didn't even want to think about her legs. Thanks to the short skirt of the saloon-girl dress, he now knew exactly what they looked like, down to the smallest detail. Long and shapely and seeming to go on forever before they disappeared beneath the hem of her gown. The image of her running her hands continuously over those attractively curved limbs had the sheet tenting around his groin and his grasp tightening on the butt of the pistol.

How likely was it that Lynch and his men would believe he was another of Cora's satisfied customers if he was still sustaining an El Paso–size arousal?

He shifted restlessly beneath the bedclothes and tried to slow his racing pulse by taking slow, deep breaths.

Somewhere down the hall, he heard a muffled female shriek. Then angry male expletives and a door slamming shut. A few seconds later, the scene played itself out again. And again, growing closer to the room they occupied.

Walker's gut clenched, his muscles tensing. "Get ready," he warned Hannah in a whisper. Below him, he heard his sister's breathing hitch in alarm, then grow silent.

He tried to relax, told himself he needed to appear completely sated and deeply asleep. He just hoped whoever checked this room wouldn't look too closely at the scene within.

When the door finally burst open, Hannah gasped and rocked back on the bed. He felt the mattress lurch with the motion. She couldn't have been surprised by the stranger's sudden entrance, and Walker found himself both astounded and proud of her excellent acting skills. His own body was frozen, poised to react.

"Pardon me, ma'am," Walker heard a man

greet her from the doorway. He couldn't tell if the low voice belonged to Lynch or not; he hadn't been in contact with the bastard enough to be familiar with his speech patterns.

"I'm lookin' for someone," he went on. "A stinkin' half-breed Injun what kidnapped the woman of a friend of mine."

"I'm afraid I can't help you," Hannah replied, her tone taking on something between a drawl and a slur. "There are no Indians in here. And there ain't nobody in there, I can promise you," she said when the man's gaze apparently strayed to the closet. "I get extra when folks wanna watch, and this fella—"

Walker imagined her cocking her head in his direction and hoped the gesture didn't draw too much attention to his supposedly sleeping form.

"He hardly had enough for one quick tumble, let alone bringing an audience."

For a couple of minutes that felt to Walker like years, the man didn't say anything. And then he heard a floorboard creak and the stranger mumbled, "Sorry to bother you, ma'am. I'll let you get back to your . . . um, business."

"No problem," Hannah told him, uninterested. Just before the door clicked shut, she called out, "And, mister . . . stop back sometime when you aren't in such a hurry."

Walker's teeth ground together at that, and

his trigger finger flexed reflexively at the amusement in the man's voice when he responded.

"I'll do that."

Two seconds after the door closed, just as Walker was thinking they were home free, Hannah lost it.

"Oh my God. Oh my God. *Ohmigod, ohmigod, ohmigod.*"

Jumping off the bed, she waved her hands frantically in front of her face and hopped from foot to foot in a little panic dance. Her bodice still gaped open, revealing a fair amount of the porcelain flesh of her chest, and one silky stocking had fallen, bunched now about her left ankle.

Walker bit his tongue, hard, to keep from laughing aloud. She'd probably clobber him if he did, but she looked so damn adorable with her cheeks flushed, her breasts bobbing, and her lips moving in a constant stream of distraught mumbles.

"Hannah, sweetheart." Since he was naked as a jaybird, he couldn't jump up and go to her the way he wanted. Letting go of his revolver and leaving it on the mattress, he tugged the corners of the sheet free and wrapped it around his waist as he threw his legs over the edge of the bed.

"*Notsa?ka?.*" With one fist at his hip holding the sheet in place, he used his other hand

139

to grab her elbow and try to calm her frantic movements.

"It's all right, it's over now. You were amazing."

"Ohmigod, ohmigod, ohmigod. Did you hear me? Did you see him? Did you hear what I said?" Her hummingbird movements were slowing, but she still bounced on the balls of her stockinged feet, fingernails digging tiny half-moons into his forearms.

"I heard you." And he still didn't know whether to be furious or amused. "You were wonderful. You saved our lives."

"I sounded like a trollop. A real, honest-to-goodness hurdy-gurdy girl. I've never been so petrified in my life."

This time, he did chuckle. Her eyes were too bright and she looked too pleased with herself not to. "You were great. I believed every word you said. Are you all right now?"

She nodded, and even though her entire body was still vibrating with unspent energy, he believed her.

Releasing her arm, he rounded the end of the bed and leaned down to help his sister to her feet. "You can come out now, too, *ara?*," he called out to his nephew.

Little Bear shimmied out from beneath the bed, glancing anxiously around the room before moving to his mother's side.

"How are you two doing?" Walker asked.

They both nodded and looked infinitely relieved at having escaped Lynch's clutches . . . until a knock sounded on the other side of the door.

Walker's wasn't the only face that blanched, and he didn't give his nudity a single thought as he waved Bright Eyes and Little Bear back under the bed with one hand and reached for his pistol with the other.

But before they had a chance to do much of anything, the door opened a crack and Cora stuck her head in. "It's just me," she singsonged. "I thought you might like to know your friends are gone. Finished searching the place and rode out of town a few minutes ago."

She flicked a wrist at Walker, who stood on the other side of the bed, the sheet in a forgotten puddle at his feet. "You might want to put on some pants there. It doesn't bother me, mind you, but your lady friend appears about to swoon."

Walker glanced toward Hannah to see that she was, indeed, quite wan. She was staring at him, her eyes round as flapjacks and locked on a very low portion of his rather private anatomy.

"Jesus," he grumbled and made a grab for the sheet.

Any other time, he'd welcome a perusal like that from Hannah. He would even be encouraged by where it might lead. But with three other people standing around, watching them, he could only think to cover himself before they noticed the reaction her reaction had on him. Which he did by draping the bunched-up material around his torso and holding it there in a vicelike grip.

"Thanks for keeping an eye out for us, Cora. It's much appreciated."

"Think nothing of it, honey. You paid me well for the trouble." She opened the door behind her once again and gave them all a friendly smile. "I'll leave y'all alone now, but if you need anything else, just give a whistle."

After she disappeared, Walker turned to his sister, his knuckles still tightly wrapped about a hunk of sheet to keep it in place.

"You feeling okay?" he asked.

She nodded, absently running a palm over her growing stomach.

Turning his attention to Little Bear, he said, "Do you think you can take your mother back over to the cabin? I want to stay here with Hannah until she's changed clothes and calmed down a little more. Would that be all right with you two?"

Both agreed and started out of the room.

As they passed Hannah, Bright Eyes paused and reached out a hand to squeeze her arm. "*Ura,*" she whispered. Thank you.

Hannah inclined her head, though Walker wasn't sure she understood his sister.

Bright Eyes moved slowly as she and Little Bear continued on their way, but she was do-

ing much better now that she'd had some
time to recover from Lynch's brutal treatment.

Again, thanks to Hannah. The woman was
a wonder. An angel from heaven sent down
to earth.

The thought was a bit saccharine for Walker's tastes, but he almost didn't care. What
he did care about was the woman standing
before him, still wearing that out-of-her-
element dress and looking positively stunned
at what had occurred over the past half hour.

He wanted to go to her, draw her into his
arms, and kiss her senseless. He wanted to
drop the sheet from his waist, tear the rest of
that purple gown from her body, and lay her
down on the worn carpeting at their feet. And
when they were finished on the floor, he
wanted to carry her to the bed and start pleasuring her all over again.

But if he did any of those things, made so
much as a move toward her to carry out his
erotic fantasies, he would regret it.

Well, maybe not. He could never bemoan
making love to Hannah when it was all he'd
wanted for nearly a decade.

But *she* would regret it. When she woke up
and realized she'd given her virginity to an
Indian. When she started to understand that
if anyone else ever found out, they'd look at
and treat her differently for ever letting a half-
breed touch her. She was bound to be ostra-

cized if the people of Purgatory learned she'd been lying with him, no matter what they thought of their sweet-spoken schoolmarm.

No. Making love with Hannah might fulfill every wish his heart had ever held, but it would make her life a living hell.

He wouldn't do that to her, not even to quell the desire throbbing so blatantly beneath the crumpled sheet.

He cleared his throat and hiked the protective covering even higher over his abdomen. "Would you . . . um, hand me my pants, please?" He gestured toward the chair where he'd thrown the trousers, swallowing hard when his voice came out sounding like a plow blade dragging across granite.

"Actually . . ." Her gaze swept over the chair back, but she made no move to retrieve his clothing.

Meeting his eyes, she slowly licked her lips, sending that evil, sexual pulse pounding double-time in his groin.

"I was wondering if it might not be better for you to leave them off a while longer."

She said the words in a great rush, and Walker lowered a brow, wondering what kind of game she was playing.

"Is there some . . . reason you don't want me to put my pants back on?" he ventured.

Two bright flags of color filled her cheeks, but she plodded ahead. "Well, it is my understanding that these things are more easily done when both parties are . . . without clothing, shall we say."

He wasn't sure if his lungs had ceased working or he was swallowing his own tongue, but suddenly he couldn't breathe and a horrible strangling sound worked its way up from his throat.

She rushed forward to pat him on the back, concern etching her expression.

The last thing he needed was her hands on his bare flesh, weakening his resolve, so he stepped away.

"You don't know what you're saying, Hannah. I think it would be better if we both put our clothes back on and headed for the cabin."

"I do know what I'm saying," she emphasized, stepping forward once again to place a small, feminine hand on his well-muscled arm.

"You told me we'd finish things later. This is later"—her fingers stroked upward—"and we're certainly both dressed for it."

Chapter Fourteen

The dark, hair-dappled male skin beneath her fingertips quivered, almost causing her to retreat. Her nerves were dancing on a tightrope of uncertainty, her stomach doing flips only a circus performer could appreciate.

She'd never been so frightened in her life. The words coming out of her mouth were completely foreign to her. For a moment, she even wondered if the purple gown she wore was haunted and a loose-moraled entity had taken over her sensibilities.

But she soon realized the voice she heard was her own. As was the hand resting on David's bare forearm.

She shouldn't be surprised. Hadn't she been working up to this for a while now?

Hadn't she told David that night behind the cabin when he'd kissed her so thoroughly that it wasn't over between them? That they would only have to wait for the right moment to pick up where they'd left off?

She'd meant it then and she was pretty sure she meant it now. David was like a fever in her blood. Heating her skin and pickling her brain. Making her think and feel things she'd never experienced before.

Well, that wasn't quite true. She'd had similar reactions before . . . every time she was within ten feet of David Walker.

Surely that fact alone indicated her feelings were far more than a shallow, passing fancy, but something much deeper and abiding. If it didn't scare her so much, she might even venture to call it love.

Love was such a terrifying word, though. Yes, she loved David; she'd loved him since childhood. But did she love him *that way?* Did she love him madly, passionately, devotedly? Did she love him as a woman loves a man, with all those little minister-inspired dictums tacked on? In sickness and in health, till death do they part.

The answer was . . . *probably*. Probably she did love him in every single one of those ways. What kept her from admitting to anything more definite, however, was her uncertainty about David's feelings.

He'd made it clear on several occasions that

147

he didn't think he had the right to touch her, that his Comanche blood made a difference to him. It didn't make a difference to her.

Perhaps it should. She knew full well what people thought of half-breeds, how they treated them. But she'd never thought of David as part-Indian; she'd only ever thought of him as . . . David.

He was the boy she'd met when she'd first been brought to the Purgatory Home for Unwanted Children after her parents' deaths. The boy who chased the monsters away in the middle of the night. The young man who'd come back to visit even after he'd been adopted and moved away from the Home. And the man she'd dreamed of in a very adult fashion for the past several years, despite the fact that she'd hardly seen him once he'd started spending more time at his mother's village outside of town.

He was just David to her, and any blood other than white that pumped through his veins only aided in making him the man he was today. How could she be sorry about that when there were so many things about him she admired?

It wasn't that she had a problem with his Indian blood, she realized suddenly, but that he did.

She turned her face up to his, took in his strong jaw and soft lips, the dark arches of his brows over deep brown eyes. With two fingers of the hand that wasn't still covering the top of his arm, she traced the outline of his mouth.

Feeling how tense he'd gone beneath her touch, she was surprised he didn't pull away. But he didn't, and she let her thumb trail over his cheek, into the sleek fall of his jet black hair.

"You promised," she whispered softly. "And we're finally together with no one else around."

Her caress alone he might have been strong enough to resist. He was rock hard beneath the inadequate covering of the white sheet and the blood was pounding in his ears, but still he could have walked away. If only she hadn't spoken.

He wasn't sure if it was her words, or the soft, throaty tone she murmured them in, but the second they reached his ears, he was lost.

Without another thought for right or wrong or how much she might regret this in the morning, he grabbed her by the shoulders and hauled her against him, his mouth crashing down on hers. She tasted like springtime and innocence and . . . forever. Too much for Walker to wish for, but enough for him to enjoy, just for a little while.

He kissed her like he'd never let her go. Showing her with his mouth and hands how much she meant to him.

The sheet pooled at his feet, forgotten. His

fingers stroked the supple flesh of her shoulders and upper arms, dancing down to her shoulder blades and back up to caress her collarbone. His hands explored every inch after inch of skin left bare by the skimpy purple gown.

Step by step, he backed Hannah toward the wide four-poster bed. When her legs came in contact with the mattress, they crumpled, and she sat with a heavy thump. He didn't break contact at the abrupt change of position but leaned over her, bracing his body against the soft feather ticking with one arm.

His lips brushed over her own, gently sucking and biting. He teased her mouth open and their tongues swirled together, making him groan.

When her hands, with their slim fingers and sharp, delicate nails began to explore his chest and abdomen, Walker raised his head and stared down at her. This beautiful woman he'd loved since she was a girl gazed at him so trustingly. Her long blond hair mussed. Her blue eyes slightly cloudy and unfocused.

She wanted to make love with him.

The knowledge almost brought him to his knees.

Reaching out, he brushed a few strands of baby-fine hair away from her face, tucking them behind one ear.

"You're a very beautiful woman, *notsa?ka?*. You grew up well."

Her eyes—against her will, he thought, and before she could catch herself—darted below his waist, causing his already burgeoning manhood to pulse even more relentlessly.

As soon as she realized what she was doing, Hannah yanked her gaze away from his privates and back to his face. Bright circles of pink filled her cheeks.

"So did you," she said in a strained voice. "You're so much . . . bigger than I remember."

At that, he laughed. "I sure as hell hope you weren't looking at me *there* way back then. If I'd known, I might have done something that would have seriously decreased my chances of making it to the age I am now."

The rose of her blush turned scarlet. "No," she denied, mortified. "I didn't mean—"

"I know what you meant," he interrupted softly, reassuring her that he was only teasing. He ran the backs of his knuckles over the smoothness of her jaw. "You don't know how happy I am to hear you noticed. That you thought of me at all back then."

"I noticed," she told him, leaning into his touch. "And I thought about you every day, even after you left Purgatory."

Walker's eyes drooped closed, the muscles in his legs quivering so badly, he had trouble remaining on his feet. Her words humbled him. And heated something deep in his gut, something he was afraid to contemplate too closely.

He decided to ignore it and just be grateful they'd arrived at this moment together at all.

Hannah reclined before him, waiting, without a hint of trepidation visible in her expression. It made him not care how many years he'd spent pining for her from afar, or how many years after this he would spend castigating himself for being weak. But it would take a force of nature—a flood of epic proportions or a mammoth tornado—to tear him away from her now. And he didn't ask if she was sure this time because he didn't want to know. It would kill him if she backed away now.

Instead, he pressed a kiss to her brow, buying himself some time to calm his raging emotions, then leaned back on his heels and said, "I want to see you."

He hoped she didn't notice the slight trembling of his hands as he slipped his fingers into the open vee of her bodice to finish unhooking the tiny clasps he'd begun to loosen earlier. One fastening at a time, the stiff material parted until it fell open altogether. Hannah gave her shoulders a little shake to help the straps down her arms, and then the entire contraption was gone, leaving her blessedly naked from the waist up.

Not for the first time, he noticed how light

her skin was, like fresh cream. Flawless, with tiny breasts that would just fill his palms.

He ran the side of his thumb along one plum-colored areola no bigger than a silver dollar and was rewarded with the tight beading of her pearl-size nipple. He gifted her other breast with the same treatment until both were taut and swollen with desire. And then, locking his gaze with hers, he lowered his mouth to swipe his tongue over one distended tip.

Hannah sucked in a shocked breath. She'd expected to feel pleasure and never-before-experienced sensations, but she'd never expected *this*. Just being with David, alone in this room, was enough. It was half of her dream fulfilled. But she'd never imagined he would touch her this way or look so magnificent in the nude.

She'd never seen a man in the altogether before. Not even as a small child in the orphanage; the nuns had been diligent about keeping the boys and girl separated, especially at bath time and while dressing. David's midnight visits were the exception, but he'd been so skilled at slipping in and out of the girls' sleeping quarters without detection that the sisters had never even suspected.

But now here he was, an adult male, standing before her without a stitch of clothing on. Not even the sheet he'd been so careful to cover himself with earlier. Rather than being

153

Heidi Betts

aghast, however, she was mesmerized.

He was amazing. Tall and virile and—dare she think it?—mouthwatering.

His glorious mane of straight black hair, parted naturally in the middle, flowed down his back and over his shoulders. Dark skin the color of an amber sky stretched over thick mounds of muscle and the narrow planes of his abdomen. And lower, where she'd glanced for only a fraction of a second, was the part of him that she'd . . . wondered about. At least upon occasion, very late at night when she was feeling particularly fragile and lonely.

It was nothing like she'd envisioned, and yet awe-inspiring all the same. Surrounded by a dark nest of springy black hair, his member jutted out at what looked to be a painful angle. Almost parallel with his body and straight as an arrow. (She hadn't thought man-parts looked like that at all. She'd assumed they . . . hung down, as on various forms of livestock.) It was also much larger than she'd expected, both in length—or height, as the case seemed to be—and width.

She'd assimilated quite a lot in such a short span of time, she realized. Then again, she'd been waiting for this moment for a long time. She had a right to explore. And memorize. And enjoy.

David's tongue—that wicked, wicked appendage—swept over her other nipple and

154

sent a shiver of pure ecstasy from that spot all the way to her toes. Her breath caught and she curled her fingers into his shoulders like claws in an effort to maintain her balance.

She thought she should feel embarrassed by what he was doing. By being exposed this way, half-naked while a man caressed and touched and licked her skin.

She *should* be embarrassed, but she wasn't. At least not enough to call a halt to what was happening. She'd waited too long. And wanted it too much.

She must have made some sound, some small noise, because David raised his head. Their eyes met and he smiled. Then he wrapped his arms around her. Not just his hands, but the full length of his arms from shoulder to wrist. His chest pressed against hers until not a wisp of air separated them. His elbows hugged her waist, his forearms cradled her back, and his hands kneaded the muscles just below her nape.

Lifting her off the bed, he held her close, kissing her neck and leaving a trail of moisture from where his tongue darted out here and there.

He held her off the ground with his body and she worried that the added weight would tear open his gunshot wound, although it had been healing nicely this past week.

"David," she murmured. Her entire being felt too languid to manage even that much,

155

but she needed to say something. "Your side."

"You're light as a feather, *notsa?ka?*," he whispered back, his lips spending an inordinate amount of time nipping and sucking at the pulse point of her throat. "Don't worry about it."

"But . . ."

Before she could utter more, he swept her up and tossed her high in the center of the bed, near the headboard. She gave a small squeak of surprise, but he quickly followed her down, one knee between her legs, hushing her with the almost smothering sensation of his overwhelming breadth and presence.

"Is that better?" he asked, a teasing glint in his eye.

She grinned. "A little."

One brow quirked upward. "Only a little? What else should I do?"

She shrugged a shoulder, letting her gaze skitter away bashfully. "I'm not sure. You're the one who's supposed to be showing me how this works, remember?"

"What do you want to know?" he asked in a low, husky voice.

Reaching up, she looped her arms about his neck. "Everything."

Chapter Fifteen

Their mouths met in a soft, tender kiss, and when he pulled away, he said, "If you want to know everything, this will have to go."

She followed his gaze to where he held a fistful of purple taffeta. Her bodice had long ago been flung to the floor. She was half-naked and lying underneath a fully naked man. Losing her skirt would be nothing compared to that.

It surprised her to realize she felt not a whit of apprehension over the idea, either. She was completely comfortable with David, trusted him wholeheartedly. With her body, her feelings, and her life.

Arching her hips off the mattress, she reached behind herself to loosen the skirt's

157

ties. With David's help, she shucked out of the voluminous layers. Slipping the garment off her heels, he tossed it aside to join the rest of their discarded clothing.

Hannah waited, watching breathlessly as David's gaze scoured her frame. From head to toe and back again, he studied her, his eyes coming to rest on the apex of her thighs.

Of course, she was still wearing the simple, homemade drawers she'd kept on when he'd first made her change into the gown she'd originally thought of as the purple atrocity. She was now coming to actually appreciate the garish thing, along with the sleek stockings that had been balled up with it. They were a far cry more comfortable than her sturdy linen stockings, which by this time had any number of holes and snags running through them.

One silk stocking was still rolled all the way up her leg, held in place high on her right thigh by a buff-colored garter with a small pink rosette sewn into the outer edge. Her left leg, however, was practically bare, the stocking still flopping around her ankle, the remaining garter holding up nothing but air.

David slipped the tip of an index finger beneath the fabric, running his hand back and forth between the snug, lacy material and the sensitive, never-before-touched-by-man skin.

"Very nice. Is this what you showed the fellow who came here earlier looking for us?"

"You told me to," she countered pointedly.

"I know. I'm just surprised he could bring himself to leave after getting a glimpse of these gorgeous limbs." His finger snapped out from under the pliant band and ran at a snail's pace down the length of her leg. Along the outside of her thigh, into the dip of her knee, over the rise of her calf muscle, to her ankle.

"Mind if I take this off?" he drawled.

His eyes rose to meet hers and all she could do was shake her head. Her mouth had gone dry as the Chihuahuan Desert the minute his perusal had begun.

So slowly Hannah had to bite her tongue to keep from demanding he move faster, David slipped the crumpled-up stocking off her heel. Returning to her thigh, he found the tiny strings of the garter and began unfastening them.

Now one long ruffle, with ties at either end, he laid the strip of lace on her belly and trailed it along her torso. He brought it up and around the curve of her breast, then left it there like the frilly trimming of a fancy décolletage.

He grinned, kissing the underside of that breast before doing the same with the garter from her right leg. Once both articles decorated her otherwise naked chest, he began rolling down the remaining stocking.

He was driving her crazy. His actions were

159

drawn out nearly to her breaking point, making the fine hairs all over her body stand on end in sweet anticipation of what he would do next, where his hands would caress next.

With the second stocking, he agonized her even more by pressing his lips to the small portion of skin he exposed each time he rolled the diaphanous silk farther down. Roll an inch, kiss. Roll an inch, kiss.

She wiggled and moaned, begging him to hurry, threatening to finish the task herself if he didn't. But he merely graced her with a devilish, knowing smile and continued the torture.

When he got to her foot, he peeled the stocking the rest of the way off and kissed the inside of her ankle. Then the top of her foot, then the arch, then each toe in turn. Her toes curled involuntarily under his ministrations, and she tried yanking her leg back, but he tightened his grip on her calf, holding her in place.

Hannah didn't just groan this time, she growled. "Aren't you ever coming back up here?" she bit out in frustration. "You're driving me crazy, taking so long."

He looked at her through long, sable lashes, lips caressing the side of her foot. "Now you know what you do to me," he informed her. "And patience is a virtue, *notsa?ka?*. Don't you like the way I'm touching you?"

160

"I like it too much. I want you to kiss me again."

"I am kissing you." To prove his point, he pressed his lips to a spot near the ridge of her toes.

"Not *there*," she protested. "Here." She gestured toward her mouth like a child beckoning for a peppermint stick.

Leisurely, David crawled his way up her body, moving one hand and then the other along the mattress and pulling his great weight after him. When he reached her stomach, he stopped.

"Where did you want me to kiss you? Here?" And he kissed the gentle slope of her abdomen, his warm breath tickling the tight curls at the apex of her thighs.

"Or here?"

He dipped his tongue into the hollow of her navel, causing her to moan and arch her back up off the bed.

"No, that's not it," he muttered, his voice growing gravelly. Drawing himself up a few inches more, his mouth moved to the side of her right breast. "Here?" He kissed her left breast, a hairbreadth from the beaded peak that ached and strained for his attention. "Maybe here. Or maybe . . ."

He hovered over her, his face directly above her own. "I remember now," he all but whispered a moment before his mouth came down on hers. "Here."

He kissed her until her body grew heavy and her bones felt no more substantial than the wings of a dragonfly. She flung her arms over his shoulders and linked her wrists behind his back, opening her legs wider to cradle his large frame.

He snuggled close, pulling her against him until the perspiration of their two bodies seemed to suction them together as one. His hands, with their long, splayed fingers, played over her waist and hips, and then slipped around to cup her buttocks.

She was heaven, pure and simple. He'd been with women before—even as a half-breed, he wasn't entirely repulsive to the opposite sex. Of course, most of the time he'd had to pay them. No self-respecting white woman would spread her legs for a Comanche, and even the less than respectable ones tended to cross the street if they saw him coming. But women like those Cora employed didn't seem to mind the color of his skin as long as he had the right amount of coin.

Women like Hannah, however, were few and far between. If he hadn't known her since she was the size of a wheat chigger, she probably would have been one of the cross-the-street-when-she-saw-him-coming or even the run-screaming type, too. Even now, he couldn't figure out why she was with him, letting him touch her like this. He only knew he was exceedingly grateful. As soon as he got the chance, he'd get down on his knees and thank the Great Spirit and the Holy Spirit both.

But for now . . . for now, he just wanted to enjoy his good fortune and make love to Hannah the way he'd always dreamed. Long and slow, and then again later, faster and maybe in a new, more creative position.

She was a virgin, though, and he needed to keep that in mind. She might be more beautiful than a thousand Greek goddesses and as passionate as Aphrodite herself, but deep down she was still an innocent. He wanted to make her first time pleasurable, not frighten her away from men—or worse, from him— for the rest of her life.

"Hannah," he murmured against her lips.

"Mmmm."

"I want you to tell me if I hurt you, *notsa?ka?*. All right?"

"You won't hurt me," she told him with confidence.

"I'm told it hurts for a woman the first time."

"You won't hurt me," she said again.

"I want you to tell me if I do. I'll stop; I promise I will."

Her fingers tunneled through his hair, holding tight to his temples as she gazed up at him with azure eyes and smiled her angel's smile. "You won't hurt me, and I won't want you to stop. I trust you, David."

She couldn't know what her words did to him, and because he was afraid she would see his stark vulnerability, he buried his face in the curve between her neck and shoulder and tried to figure out what he'd done to deserve a woman like Hannah.

"*Nu? kamakuru mui,*" he whispered against her throat.

He felt the stroke of her hands over his scalp and through the long sweep of his hair just before she asked, "What does that mean?"

He lifted his head, startled by her question. "What does what mean?"

"Those words. What you just said."

He honestly hadn't realized he'd spoken aloud and his muscles tensed, knowing she'd heard his declaration of love in a moment of weakness.

"It means . . . you're beautiful," he lied, shifting his lower body intimately against her own so she wouldn't notice that he refused to hold her gaze. "The most beautiful woman I've ever seen. And I want desperately to make love to you."

Her soft, rose-pink lips turned up at the corners. "For someone who wants desperately to make love to me, you're certainly taking your sweet time about it."

"I want it to be good for you."

Join the Historical Romance Book Club and GET 4 FREE* BOOKS NOW!

A $23.96 Value!

Yes! I want to subscribe to the Historical Romance Book Club.

Please send me my **4 FREE* BOOKS.** I have enclosed $2.00 for shipping/handling. Each month I'll receive the four newest Historical Romance selections to preview for 10 days. If I decide to keep them, I will pay the Special Members Only discounted price of just $4.24 each, a total of $16.96, plus $2.00 shipping/handling ($23.55 US in Canada). This is a **SAVINGS OF AT LEAST $5.00** off the bookstore price. There is no minimum number of books I must buy, and I may cancel the program at any time. In any case, the **4 FREE* BOOKS** are mine to keep.

*In Canada, add $5.00 shipping/handling per order
for the first shipment. For all future shipments to
Canada, the cost of membership is $23.55 US,
which includes shipping and handling.
(All payments must be made in US dollars.)

NAME: _____
ADDRESS: _____
CITY: _____ **STATE:** _____
COUNTRY: _____ **ZIP:** _____
TELEPHONE: _____
E-MAIL: _____
SIGNATURE: _____

If under 18, Parent or Guardian must sign. Terms, prices, and conditions subject to change. Subscription subject
to acceptance. Dorchester Publishing reserves the right to reject any order or cancel any subscription.

"It's already good for me. I'm just waiting for you to make it even better."

With a groan of defeat, he kissed her again. Sliding a hand over her thigh, he lifted one of her legs to crook over his hip before lightly brushing the short, sun-gold curls that formed an inverted triangle between her legs. He used two fingers to find the moist furrow that led to her center and slowly explored her womanly flesh.

She was wet, arching into him at every touch, nearly panting in need. His gut clutched, knowing he was the reason for her present condition. It made him want to howl at the moon like a coyote on the prowl.

He settled instead for shifting closer, bringing the tip of his shaft to her opening, and entering her the merest fraction of an inch. Hannah stilled beneath him and he sucked in a great gulp of air.

She was tight. Even though he was barely inside her, he could tell, and he gritted his teeth to keep from moving and possibly hurting her. He would cause her pain eventually, he knew, but he didn't want to bring it about any sooner than necessary.

"Are you all right?" he ground out, holding himself up by his forearms and looking down into her bright blue eyes.

She nodded, her chest hardly moving as she held her breath. And then she began to squirm.

Walker's jaw clenched as he fought the urge to simply thrust all the way inside her. He tried to pull back, to keep her from going too far, too fast, but she wouldn't heed his warning. "Hannah, stop. You're going to hurt yourself."

"No. It doesn't hurt, it feels wonderful. And I want it all. Now."

"You don't know what you're saying. You've never—"

She cut him off. "Then show me. Please, David. Don't make me wait any longer."

Holy Jesus. How could he deny such a charming request? Even if he'd wanted to, the needs of his body were fast overriding any thought of patience his brain was trying to impart.

Teeth grinding, nostrils flaring, and heart pounding like horses' hooves through his system, he braced himself above her, shifted her legs higher around his waist, and covered her mouth with his own as he pushed fully into her.

Her lips parted beneath his in a sharp inhalation of breath as he broke through the barrier of her innocence. He took her small cry of pain into himself and prayed the pang would pass quickly.

It hardly hurt at all. She'd been prepared for something much worse and gasped more from anticipation, she thought, than any real sense of discomfort. And then she moaned against David's mouth because it felt so good.

She didn't know what she'd been expecting. No one had ever talked to her about man-woman relations or what she should expect from the marriage bed. Granted, she and David weren't married, but the concept was the same.

Probably thinking he'd hurt her irreparably, David remained perfectly still. Though his mouth was planted firmly on hers, he didn't even move his lips.

Darling man. He was a sweet, caring, generous, darling man, and he didn't realize he was even half of those things.

Looping her arms about his neck, she hugged him tight and started kissing him the way she wished he'd kiss her. Finally, the tension began to leak from his rigid muscles and he kissed her back. His tongue tangled with hers while she stroked the solid planes of his back and lifted her pelvis to bury him even deeper within her silken folds.

It was David's turn to groan when she did so, and his fingers dug into her buttocks. She thought he meant to hold her in place, but Hannah was having none of it. Following the lines of his arms, she pulled them free of her bottom and brought his hands higher, near her breasts.

"Don't stop now," she murmured in his ear. "Things were just getting interesting."

He lifted his head and stared down at her,

the corners of his mouth quirked up in amusement. "Impatient, are you?"

"It's your fault," she chastised. "You promised to make love to me, and if the rest feels as lovely as this, I'm eager to get to it."

He chuckled. "I may be sorry for this later," he said. "You may turn out to be insatiable and I'll never get any rest from pleasuring you."

"Something tells me you won't consider it a trial."

He rotated his hips in a gentle clockwise motion and sent her eyeballs spinning in their sockets.

"No, ma'am. I'd have to say I'm downright looking forward to it."

Chapter Sixteen

Hannah grinned and he grabbed her close, kissing her as he rubbed up and down the sides of her body and slowly started to move inside her. She could feel her muscles expanding to accommodate him and then contracting to hold him in place. The gentle friction sent waves of pleasure up and down her spine and she began to rock her pelvis in contrast to his so that each time he thrust forward, they came together with such force that it caused delightful little stars to shoot to life behind her eyelids.

As her movements increased, so did his. Walker gripped her waist, pounding into her as the temperature of the room shot up and his blood began to boil. Deep in her throat,

Hannah purred. Low, rolling, passionate sounds that all but drove him over the edge.

"Hannah." He said her name, pressing his cheek against her face and nibbling the corner of her mouth. She was the only woman he'd ever truly wanted to be with like this. Probably the only woman he would ever again want to be with this way.

"Hannah, Hannah, Hannah." It became a litany as he moved into her. Heart pounding, muscles surging, he felt her body wrapping around his like a soft, kid-leather glove.

"Come with me, Hannah." He felt the pressure building in his groin, rushing through his veins, and he wanted the same for her. "Come with me."

"Yes." She uttered the word on a sigh, her inner muscles clutching at him and her back arching as she threw herself into the abyss.

Lowering a hand from her rib cage, he very carefully slipped one finger between them and into her moist heat, teasing the tiny bud of desire nestled there.

His touch brought a sharp jolt of pleasure, and she called out his name a moment before her breath hitched and spasms pushed her back into the mattress.

David drove into her a few seconds longer and then his body tensed and a liquid warmth spilled into her, filling her.

His weight covered her, both of them gasping for air. Hannah's limbs were like lead weights; she couldn't have lifted a finger if a troop of soldiers had barged through the door at that very second. She'd never felt so sated, so comfortable. So content.

David made her feel that way. Not only the manner in which he'd touched her, made love to her, but his simply being here with her, holding her this way.

Just as she was thinking that, he raised his head from her chest, shifted to one side, and brought her along so that her body reclined half on, half off his long, solid frame.

She went with him without a qualm, letting her head rest in the crook of his shoulder. His chest rose and fell rhythmically with his breathing and she found herself tracing nonsensical designs over his golden bronze skin with the tip of one finger.

"We're in trouble here; I hope you know that."

The words rumbled in her ear and she raised her head a bit to glance at him. His eyes were still closed, the lines of his face completely relaxed. She thought he looked more handsome than she'd ever seen him. Not that she was biased.

"What kind of trouble?" she asked, fighting a smile. He seemed to always be so worried about her and the situations he got himself into. She found it endearing.

At that, he opened his eyes and turned his head on the pillow toward her. "The kind we

171

may not be able to get out of. Not without casualties."

She shrugged a shoulder negligently, letting her gaze skitter toward the bottom of the bed before he noticed the frown forming between her brows. "I guess that's all right, then, because I don't want to get out of it."

"You will."

He sounded so convinced. And as though his certainty made him distinctly unhappy.

Good. Because it made her unhappy, too. And if she had to suffer through insecurities over this . . . budding relationship, then he should, too.

"What if I don't?" she asked mutinously. "What if I'm deliriously content to continue on with you like this?"

Several long seconds of silence ticked by before he responded. His fingers sifted through her hair, draping it in a ticklish curtain down her back. "You don't know what you're saying, Hannah. You don't understand the way things are, how dangerous this could be. How dangerous it is."

"And you seem to be overly concerned with what other people think of you."

"Is that what you think? That I'm worried for me?" The words were biting and he pulled away from her, deeper into the pillows propped against the headboard.

Sensing that they were about to embark upon a touchy topic of conversation, Hannah pulled the crumpled sheet high enough to cover her breasts and propped herself on one elbow.

"I'm not afraid of anyone, Hannah. White man or otherwise," he continued. "But things aren't the same for me as they are for you. I can take off, leave town and go to ground if I need to. You could be ostracized—or worse—for even being seen with me. Let alone what we just shared. And what would you do? Where would you go?"

"Why don't you let me worry about that?" she challenged. "I'm a grown woman now, David, in case you didn't notice. I've been caring for myself and making my own decisions for quite some time now. If I want to be with you, be *seen* with you, then that's my choice to make."

He was already shaking his head, a sorrowful expression drawing lines around his mouth and at the corners of his. eyes. "You can't know, Hannah. You just . . . don't understand."

"I understand enough," she said softly, leaning closer to him to place a hand on his chest and brush the worry from his brow with her fingertips. "But let's please not talk about this now. We were having such a good time."

Although his eyes remained shadowy and troubled, his lips lifted in the hint of a grin. "We were, weren't we?"

"Mmm-hmm." She climbed a little higher

on his chest. "Is there anything else you'd like to teach me while we're alone? We'll have to go back soon to check on your sister and nephew."

His hands drifted down to her waist, then her hips, then brought one of her legs across his so that she sat above him, straddling his thighs. "We've got a few minutes, though, right?"

"A few."

"Then there *are* a couple of things I want to show you."

"Oh, goody." She raised herself up on her knees, letting go of the sheet and leaving them both completely bare, a thin layer of sweat glistening on their skin. "I was hoping you would."

At first their return to the cabin was awkward. They avoided looking at or touching each other for fear Bright Eyes or Little Bear might notice something amiss. But the more time that passed, the more relaxed they became. They even began sharing warm glances and quick brushes of hands and arms when they thought they weren't being watched. Which wasn't easy in such a small space.

Hannah was back to wearing her red plaid shirt and man's trousers, and putting on the battered Stetson to cover her hair whenever she found it necessary to step outside the tiny shack. And David often made excuses to join her when she did. Then he would back her up against the wall and kiss her so long and hard, it stole her breath.

Whenever he did that sort of thing, she took great delight in teasing him about the possibility of being caught embracing another "man." But he only laughed and said that if anyone else knew what her masculine attire hid, they'd be sneaking out to accost her in a rear alleyway, too.

She was also happy that he continued to hold his tongue on the topic of their previous argument—his heritage and her reputation in the white world. She didn't for a minute believe he'd given up trying to convince her that having anything to do with him was a colossally bad idea. He was simply biding his time and working on an even stronger argument.

But until he decided to throw a thousand more reasons at her for why they should keep their distance, she was content to enjoy his attentions and pretend no problems existed between them.

Perhaps that was naïve of her, but she didn't care. She'd harbored feelings for David Walker more than half her life. This was the first time she'd had a chance to act on those emotions. Their relationship might not last— in fact, she expected it not to. And because of that, she intended to savor every moment she had with him, regardless of the consequences.

Heidi Betts

Early that morning, Hannah had boiled water and used the hunk of soap they'd been bathing with to wash out several pieces of clothing belonging to all four of them. She normally scrubbed dirty laundry on a washboard, but with none available she still managed to get everything fairly clean just by rubbing the fabric vigorously between her two fists.

To dry, she hung the more personal items over the corners of furniture inside the cabin, and the more common ones off different surfaces outside. An empty crate, a shovel she'd found leaning against another shack, a half-empty water barrel.

Now, with the sun well set and a glowing quarter moon hanging high in the sky, Little Bear was helping her fold the dried clothes and put them in piles according to their owner.

They'd eaten dinner a couple of hours before, a bit of chicken and some white potatoes she'd thrown inside the *chiminea* to bake over the open fire.

While she, David, and Little Bear had crowded around the tiny, lopsided table to share the evening meal, Bright Eyes had remained in bed. She'd complained of a backache most of the day that stole her appetite, and Hannah thought she looked more tired than she had since David abducted her from the Bar L.

176

Because Bright Eyes had been recovering from her injuries so well these past few weeks, Hannah wasn't terribly worried. The woman's gaunt cheeks had filled out and regained their color, and she'd put on a good deal of weight. At least what Hannah considered a good deal, given the extent of her pregnancy.

Conversely, David ate what Hannah considered enough to feed three men. And Little Bear did his best to emulate his uncle.

She didn't know where David got the money to pay for everything he'd provided for them during their stay in this outlaw town—or what he bargained with if he worked out trades with the locals—she simply assumed he had planned the rescue of his sister well in advance and come prepared for any number of potential situations.

"*Ara?.*" David, legs stretched out in front of him at the table where they'd eaten dinner, broke the almost stifling silence of the room by catching his nephew's attention. "Come over here when you're finished. I thought I might show you a game of cards the white man is fond of playing."

Little Bear glanced up at Hannah, silently asking her permission, and with only two pieces of clean laundry left to fold, she nodded. "Go ahead."

To David, she said, "You aren't going to teach him poker, are you?"

He grinned. "How did you guess?"

"Poker isn't exactly appropriate for a seven-year-old boy."

"Yeah, but someday he'll be eight, and this way he has a better chance of winning his first real game. Especially if he's playing for money."

She cocked a brow and tried to look stern while at the same time biting the inside of her lip to keep from laughing. "Very funny. Does your sister know you're corrupting her son?"

His glance darted to the cot where Bright Eyes rested and a sudden shadow crossed his face. She followed his gaze and knew he worried about his sister's sudden lethargy and minor discomfort.

"She'll be fine," Hannah said softly. "Pregnancy takes a lot out of a woman, and she's had it rougher than most."

David looked at her and smiled, though the gesture never reached his eyes. "You're right."

He picked up the blue-coated deck of cards from the tabletop and began shuffling. First from one hand to the other, then in a rapid-fire, interlocking bridge between both hands.

He tilted his head toward the piece of linen she was holding, the last that needed to be folded and put away. "Care to join us? You're finished there, and you might get lucky. We're playing for matchsticks."

Moving around the table, she took a seat across from David and only an arm's length from Little Bear. "I *could* use some more matches. My supply is getting a little low."

"I know." David shot her a cocky grin. "I stole them. If you want them back, you'll have to win them."

"If *you* want a hot breakfast, you'd better *let* me win."

He chuckled. "All right, *notsa?ka?*. Do you know how to play poker?"

She rearranged herself on the chair, wishing for a few layers of petticoats between the hard wood and her bottom instead of being stuck in the much thinner, scratchy canvas pants. "Not at all. You'll have to teach me. Pretend I'm seven years old," she added slyly.

"I may have to," he said with a straight face. "After all, it can be hard to teach an old dog new tricks."

Eyes narrowed, she glared at him. "I'm thinking you'll be getting a cold meal in the morning no matter how many matchsticks I win."

He sat back, a hand to his chest as though he'd been shot. "Ouch. I take it back. However the game turns out, how about I give you my share of matches, too? Or better yet, maybe I'll fix breakfast for you. What do you think of that?"

Hannah let her gaze shift to Little Bear, who was squirming in his seat, eager to learn how to play poker from his uncle. "Just deal, Walker," she told him. "We'll negotiate later, depending on how badly you're losing."

David's chest expanded beneath his snug buckskins as he laughed and started dealing the cards, five to each of them. "All right, *notsaʔka?*. Let's see who's the better bluffer."

Hannah didn't know what it meant to bluff, but an hour later she and Little Bear each had a nice-sized pile of matches scattered in front of them. David was down to only three. No doubt he was letting them win, but he was utterly beguiling about it. And while he favored them both, he was careful to let Little Bear win just a little more often. Hannah had to work at it. Or rather, flirt at it.

Soon after he'd explained the rules of the game and what it meant to bluff, Hannah had figured out that the smallest forward gesture on her part tended to win her that hand. She licked her lips and brushed a lock of hair behind her ear, and suddenly her pair of fours beat whatever cards he held. She claimed to be a bit warm and undid the top button of her shirt, and almost immediately he folded.

Because of Little Bear, she didn't do too much of this, but once in a while she enjoyed bringing about the clearing of his throat, the high color that tinged his cheekbones, or the uncomfortable way he shifted in his chair.

Her own skin flushed on several occasions, and she wished they were alone. She could only imagine the game of cards they'd be playing then, but she had a feeling it would end with the rapid removal of all their clothing and a quick dash to the nearest bed. Hannah didn't think she'd mind losing at that kind of poker at all.

"Hurry, hurry!" Little Bear begged, squirming with excitement and pulling Hannah back from her wayward thoughts. "I think I win again."

"All right, *ara?*, what you do you have?"

The boy held his cards close to his leather-clad chest. "Uh-uh. You and Hannah first."

David cast her an amused glance. Laying out his hand, he said, "I've got three of a kind, sixes. How about you, *notsa?ka??*"

Hannah followed suit, spreading out her cards on the table, face-up. "Full house, queens and twos."

"I win! I win!" Little Bear cried, bouncing so hard on his seat, she thought he might take flight. "Four of a kind, I've got four of a kind!"

David studied his nephew's hand. "I'll be damned. You win again, *ara?*. And I am completely out of matches. You've both whipped me good."

Collapsing against the straight, stiff back of his chair, he fixed her with a half-teasing, half-pitiful gaze. "Don't you think that deserves a piping hot meal in the morning?"

Crossing her arms over her chest, she took her time answering and was careful not to commit to anything. "Maybe."

"Eggs, bacon, ham, biscuits . . ." he suggested hopefully.

She laughed. "Even if I did agree to make the *loser* a hot breakfast, I'm afraid our supplies are a little lacking. It would be closer to porridge or simply eggs. Certainly not ham or bacon."

"What if I could get my hands on a nice chunk of pork? Would you consider it, then?"

His eyes glittered. His lips teased. She couldn't help smiling at his adorably amusing antics.

But before she could agree to fry up whatever type of meat he might buy or trade for, a loud moan filled the small cabin. All three of them spun immediately toward the cot where Bright Eyes slept.

Only she was no longer resting. She was sitting up on the thin mattress, clutching her stomach, lines of pain bracketing her mouth.

"*Pia!*" Little Bear called out.

"*Patsi?*, what is it?"

But even though the three of them raced to her side, Hannah reached her first. The woman's gaze met hers, filled with trepidation. Hannah pulled back the covers to see a large, wet stain spreading across the sheets.

"What is it?" David demanded, alarm written clearly on his features. "What's wrong?"

Hannah ran a hand over Bright Eyes's long, ebony hair, then raised her eyes to look at him. "I think we're about to have a baby."

Chapter Seventeen

Hannah had never done anything like this in her life. And the only animals she'd ever seen born were chickens . . . which she didn't think counted since they hatched from eggs that had already been laid.

She was also at a loss as to Comanche birthing customs. From the time they'd realized Bright Eyes was in labor, David had hurried about, collecting materials and constructing what looked like a cooking spit—two thick, forked, branchlike posts with another wedged across the top.

All of this was at his sister's insistence. She wanted to have her baby in the manner of her people rather than the way white women did. None of them had expected this to happen yet, otherwise Hannah suspected he would have already had all of the necessary supplies gathered and at the ready.

As it was, Hannah understood that when the time came, Bright Eyes would loop her arms over the top rung of the apparatus, hanging there until the child was born. Hannah didn't say so, but she found the idea somewhat barbaric. She thought she would much rather be tucked into a nice, soft bed with plenty of sheets to drag at when the pains came.

At the moment, Bright Eyes was standing against one wall, waiting for them to make sure the device was secure and to spread blankets on the ground beneath. Bright Eyes also seemed to believe she would sense when the time was right to kneel and begin the strenuous act of pushing the baby out into the world.

Making one more adjustment to the contraption, David stood. He drew the back of one arm across his damp brow, his face drawn with worry for his sister.

"I guess that's it," he said. "You know what this is for, right? How this works?"

"I think so." He'd explained it to her at least a dozen times. She shifted her gaze to David's sister, giving her a gentle smile. "And if I don't, Bright Eyes certainly will. She's done this before, after all."

David didn't look heartened. "You understand why I can't stay, don't you? In the Comanche village, expectant women go into a birthing lodge with only other women to assist them. Men are never in attendance."

He hesitated. His eyes swept the room as he shifted uncomfortably from foot to foot. "I . . . I can stay if you want me to. If you think you'll need me. But . . ."

Hannah laid a hand on his arm and gave it a small squeeze. "We'll be fine. As long as you don't go far. I can always call out if we need you."

He considered that, studied his sister a few moments longer, then gave a sharp dip of his head. "Come on, *ara?*." He gestured to Little Bear. "Let's wait outside until we find out if you have a brother or sister."

The boy shot concerned glances in his mother's direction but followed his uncle out of the cabin.

Hannah took a deep breath and turned to Bright Eyes. In all honestly, she was scared spitless. She had no idea what she was doing and had never before witnessed a birth of any sort.

But she pushed aside her fears, intent on aiding Bright Eyes in any way she could. Women had children every day. As long as nothing went wrong, things should progress quite naturally.

She would simply have to hope nothing went wrong.

Moving to Bright Eyes's side, she wrapped a hand around the woman's arm and another about the back of her waist. "You'll have to tell me how to do this, what you need. I've never been involved in bringing a child into the world before."

Bright Eyes was breathing heavily, fighting the pain of her contractions, which were coming more quickly and steadily than they had before. She nodded, leaning against Hannah for support. "Little Bear came easily," she said. "This child will, too."

Hannah prayed she was right. Otherwise, they might be in very big trouble.

Hannah helped her across the room and to her knees on the thick padding of blankets David had spread. She was wearing a new dress of tanned doeskin that David had somehow acquired, and while Bright Eyes arranged the top pole of the birthing device beneath her armpits, Hannah lifted up the hem of her tunic around her hips and over the mound of her hard belly.

"This is quite different from the way I've heard these things are supposed to be. Are you sure we shouldn't find a physician to see to you?"

Bright Eyes shook her head, her teeth drawing blood as she bit down on her lower lip through another contraction. "My people do not give credence to your kind of doctors. If the medicine woman of my village were here, she might give me a mixture of herbs to hasten things, but she was not there when Little Bear was born, and I do not need her now. All will be well, Hannah. Do not worry."

It was a little late for that, but Hannah tried to do a better job of tamping down on her anxiety. Or at least of not letting it show.

She stood nearby, dabbing Bright Eyes's brow with a cool cloth, ready to assist in any way she could. When the next wave of pain hit, Bright Eyes started pushing, and from that point on, Hannah's only mission was to stay on her feet.

Outside the cabin, Little Bear was perched, legs swinging, on an overturned barrel that at one time had likely held rum or some other type of ale from the Devil's Den across the street. He either didn't understand the importance of what was taking place with his mother or simply wasn't concerned about the situation. Of course, he was a child and couldn't know the possible dangers involved in a woman giving birth.

Walker, on the other hand, was wearing a hip-deep gully into the dry earth, pacing back and forth along the full length of the outside wall of the shack. He strained his ears to hear the slightest noise, and even the smallest, most muted sound had him stopping in his tracks, craning his neck to try to figure out what it might mean.

Hours passed that seemed like days, and still Walker couldn't stand still. He didn't know who he was more worried for . . . Bright Eyes, who was bearing the actual pain and hazards of childbirth, or Hannah, who had looked more pale and frightened than he'd felt when he'd left her alone in the cabin with his sister. Despite her reassurances, Walker knew she was terrified and had no idea what to expect.

She was willing to stay with Bright Eyes, to help her however she could, but Walker knew darn well she'd never been thrust into a situation like this before. This was all his doing. His fault for ever going to her in the first place when he needed a place to stash Little Bear.

He should have taken the boy to his parents. Clay and Regan would have watched after him as though he were their own son. They would have hidden him if necessary, or fought anyone who came and tried to take him away.

Instead, Walker had thought to save them any trouble and go to someone Ambrose Lynch would have a harder time linking him with, somewhere the bastard would be less likely to look. And, yes, if Walker were forced to be truthful, he'd have to admit he took Little Bear to Hannah just for the chance to see her again up close.

He was a selfish son of a bitch. He should be shot. Or drawn and quartered. Or hanged, just like he'd been telling Hannah he could be.

He'd landed on her doorstep with a boy in need of protection and a bullet in his side. And how had he repaid her for her selfless kindness? By not sending her straight back to Purgatory when he'd discovered her trailing along behind him. By dragging her to this godforsaken town filled with thieves and murderers and criminals of every color, and making her hole up in a one-room shack that wasn't fit for a nest of vermin. And now by leaving her alone to assist his sister in the birth of her second child when he was well aware she knew nothing more about this sort of thing than he did.

How fair was that? What kind of man was he to ask her to do any of this? He was a disgrace to both his white and his Comanche bloodlines.

"That's it," he all but swore, halting in mid-step. His bunched fists went straight to his hips and he turned toward his nephew, fixing him with a stinging glower. The intense look wasn't aimed at Little Bear, however, but at himself.

"Stay right here," he told the boy. "I'm going inside to check on your mother."

Stomping around the corner of the building, he put his hand on the lopsided door panel, ready to yank it open, when a loud, newborn infant squall rent the air.

Walker's heart stuttered in his chest and he burst through the door. Hannah stood in front of a sagging Bright Eyes, a squirming bundle of blankets in her arms.

When she looked up to meet his gaze, she was smiling from ear to ear, and he thought he'd never seen anything as beautiful as this woman holding a brand-new, tiny, pink-faced child. It made him long for things he had no right to even imagine.

"Is everything all right?" he asked in a strangled voice, eyes darting from Hannah to his sister and back again.

"Everything's fine. You've got an adorable new niece, in case you were wondering," Hannah added, beaming at him with that same bright, the-world-is-a-glorious-place grin. "Can you take Bright Eyes to the bed, please? She needs to rest."

Walker hurried forward, eager to do whatever he could, since he'd been of little help so far. He held his sister by the waist and lowered her arms, then lifted her up and carried her the few steps that took them to the narrow cot. He arranged her carefully on the clean sheets Hannah had put down before he'd left the cabin and brought the covers up around her chin. She smiled wearily and let her eyes drift closed.

Hannah came up behind him and he took a moment to study his new niece, no bigger than a minute. Her tiny lips were pursed, her face scrunched and turning red as she readied herself for a good cry.

Before the child could raise the roof, Hannah leaned down and arranged her in the crook of one of her mother's arms. Bright Eyes immediately loosened the laces at the front of her dress and took the child to her breast. The baby settled down to suckle contentedly, and Hannah and Walker slowly backed away to give mother and baby some privacy.

Hannah was just beginning to clean up the area where Bright Eyes had actually given birth when she noticed Little Bear peeking his head around the doorway.

"It's all right," she said sweetly with a wave of her hand. "You can come in now."

Walker took over clearing away the soiled blankets and linens, watching out of the corner of his eye as she took his nephew's hand and led him toward the bed.

"Would you like to meet your sister?"

Little Bear nodded, peering closely over the mound of covers to where only the baby's round face was visible against Bright Eyes's sun-brown chest.

Walker could very clearly picture Hannah teaching a classroom full of Purgatory's children. No matter the age range, he knew she would be patient and understanding with every single student in her care. She'd been nothing but wonderful with Little Bear the entire time they'd been together, and then with Bright Eyes when he'd brought her here, as well.

And with him. She'd been especially nice to him, and not only over at Cora's. She treated him like a man. Not a white man or a red man, just . . . a man.

Face it, Walker, she's the perfect woman. He wouldn't find one better in either his mother's village or Purgatory. Hell, not even if he searched the world over. Hannah Blake was it.

Hannah Blake was *the one.*

His mother, Regan, had always told him that he would find her. Not Hannah, specifically, but the one for him. The woman he would fall in love with and marry. A woman who wouldn't care that his blood was mixed or that he'd spent most of his childhood in an orphanage. She would love him for himself, his mother had said.

Of course, Regan couldn't have known that all the times she'd spoken of him finding his true love, he'd only ever been thinking of Hannah.

He'd never been foolish enough to imagine her as his wife, though. He knew better than to think a white woman would marry up with him, no matter what his mother claimed.

Instead, he'd always believed he would likely end up with a woman from his mother's village. She might not invoke the same gut-deep emotions that plagued him when he remembered Hannah, but he thought he could still be a good husband to a Comanche girl, and a good father to any children they might have together.

Now he knew that was impossible. He could never love another woman the way he loved Hannah. Could never come anywhere close to feeling for someone else the way he felt about her.

Even if he went ahead with that plan, he realized the rest of his life would be a lie. He might be responsible for a wife, but he would never truly love her. That honor belonged to Hannah alone, for she already owned the biggest part of his heart.

This was bad. This was really, really bad.

Walker could almost feel that same organ shriveling in his chest like a pumpkin left too long in the sun. He loved her, all right, but there was no chance of his making a life with her, and he thought he'd rather die outright here and now than spend the next twenty or thirty years pining for her. Seeing her fall in love with someone else, marry another man, have babies with him.

He'd kill himself first. Hell, he thought he might even kill Hannah first. Either that, or he'd steal her away.

If he was already going to live in misery or hang for making love to a white woman, then he had nothing to lose by kidnapping her before she could hitch herself to another man. Some lily-livered white who'd probably do nothing more adventurous with his life than running a general store.

It sounded ridiculous, and if the law ever caught up with him, they'd string him up for sure. But he tucked the notion away in a deep pocket at the back of his mind in case he needed to pull it out someday. Like if he ever caught wind that Hannah was fixing to marry someone other than him.

"I'll take these things outside," he said brusquely, holding up the ball of dirty linens and clearing his throat twice before the words would come out.

Hannah lifted her gaze from where she and Little Bear were oohing and aahing over the new arrival and nodded her head, giving him a smile so angelic, he wanted to hie her away then and there.

He stomped out of the cabin before the urge overtook him. Or before he could do something really stupid . . . like propose.

Chapter Eighteen

When David first left the cabin, Hannah thought nothing of it, though she had noticed he seemed to stomp out in a bit of a huff.

Why, she couldn't imagine. If anything, he should be ecstatic about being an uncle again, and happy that Bright Eyes and the baby seemed to be in perfect health.

But after a little over an hour, when he still hadn't returned, she began to worry. Hell wasn't a large enough town to get lost in, and except for the Devil's Den, there wasn't really anywhere for him to go. At least not where he could lose track of time.

She paused in the middle of fixing supper for Little Bear, who was sitting at the table pretending to be the dealer of a game of poker he was playing with himself. She was also heating a bit of broth for when Bright Eyes awoke from a much needed nap. The baby was still tucked close at her mother's side, and Hannah figured that was the best place for her.

Hannah's mouth turned down in a frown as she considered all the places David might be for this long. If he was at the Devil's Den, he'd better be *downstairs* and drinking rather than *upstairs* doing God knows what.

Well, God knew perfectly well *what*. As did she . . . now. And if David was in one of the upstairs rooms doing *that* with one of Cora's girls, she would personally tan the skin right off his hide.

She set Little Bear's plate on the table in front of him with more force than necessary and immediately smiled an apology so he wouldn't think she was cross with him. He was overly sensitive about that sort of thing, she'd noticed, because of the treatment he'd received from his father.

Little Bear's father was the second thought that popped into her head when she wondered where David could be. Her stomach plummeted at the very idea, but she had to admit that David might have taken one look at his new niece, recalled how Ambrose Lynch had treated his sister and nephew, and gone off to teach him some kind of lesson. David hadn't said anything about exacting revenge, but that didn't mean he wasn't thinking about it.

From everything she'd heard about him so far, Lynch wasn't a man to mess with. David could get hurt confronting him. Even killed.

Her pulse quickened as she pictured all the terrible things that could be happening to David at this very moment.

She needed to find him.

Straightening with determination, she finished serving Little Bear and then prepared him for her absence.

"I'm going across the street to look for your uncle," she told him. If David wasn't there, she might have to pursue his disappearance further, but she would start at the Devil's Den. "Will you be all right here, with your mother and sister? Can you watch over them for me until I get back?"

Little Bear bobbed his head up and down, his teeth busy chomping away on a piece of chicken left over from the day before.

"I heated broth for your mother. If she's hungry when she wakes up and you think you can manage, you're welcome to feed her. Otherwise, give her a bit of bread to hold her over. I won't be long."

He nodded again before swallowing. "Don't worry, Hannah. I can take care of them."

She thought he could, too. He might be only seven years old, but he was quite level-headed and responsible for his age. She would guess he'd been caring for his mother for a number of years now, even if he hadn't been able to protect her from his father's abuse.

"All right." She headed for the door, tucking up her hair into the battered Stetson she was supposed to wear for protection when she left the shack. She hesitated before walking out, casting one last look toward the sleeping Bright Eyes and the baby, and Little Bear, devouring his meal as though he hadn't tasted real food in weeks.

"I won't be long," she said again before pushing open the cabin door and heading out into the night.

Keeping the brim of the hat pulled low over her eyes, she stretched her step and walked more slowly than usual, trying to look as much like just another cowboy as possible. If anyone studied her too closely, she felt sure they would notice she was merely a woman dressed up in men's clothing. Her less than buxom figure did aid in the illusion, however. And hopefully everyone inside the saloon would be too preoccupied to care about the arrival of another stranger.

She made her way across the street, dark but for the dim light shining through the windows of the Devil's Den. Her boot heels echoed hollowly on the boardwalk for a few steps until she came to a halt at the establishment's squeaky, bat-wing doors.

She swept the room with a glance, looking for the straight black hair falling past his shoulders and buckskin clothing that would identify David. Unfortunately, she saw no sign of him. She would have to go in.

Taking a deep breath and steeling her nerves, she pushed through the saloon doors and walked inside. Loud, lively music came from one corner of the room, where a man sat at a scarred upright piano. Men in various forms of dress, from all walks of life, sat gambling at tables covered with faded felt and velvet, curling at the edges.

And Cora's girls—dozens of them, some wearing bright colors, others in little more than a camisole or corset and drawers—hung on them, nearly one working girl to each male customer. They were rubbing suggestively along their bodies and laughing wildly, all in hopes of luring them upstairs for a quick tumble and a bit more profit for the Devil's Den.

Hannah searched the area even more carefully, studying faces and at the same time trying to keep hers half-hidden. Her gaze drifted to the stairs and the ornately carved balustrade bordering the second story. If she found David up there with one of those women, he was in trouble.

She didn't see him. He might not be in the saloon at all. But if he wasn't here, where could he be?

199

Heidi Betts

If he was on his way to the Bar L, she would never find him. Not only was she sure to get lost on the trail if she even tried, but she couldn't leave Bright Eyes and Little Bear for that long.

She started to turn, about to leave, when a tall, hard body sidled up behind her. Whoever it was pressed against her back, tight and warm, and a big hand cupped the side of her waist.

Her muscles tensed, waiting and wondering what in heaven's name she would do if this man accosted her. He must already know she was a woman or he wouldn't be touching her like this. She couldn't imagine any man standing so close to another man and caressing him this way.

"What are you doing here, *notsa?ka??*" a low voice breathed above her ear.

The air rushed from her lungs in a relieved whoosh and the tension melted from her bones. "David!" she chastised through gritted teeth. She started to turn, but his hand on her waist held her in place. "Will you please stop sneaking up on me like that!"

"What are you doing here, *notsa?ka??*" he asked again, no friendlier than the first time.

"I'm looking for you. You left the cabin and never returned. I started to worry."

"Where are Bright Eyes and the children?"

"Back at the cabin, where do you think?" She was getting tired of all his questions and

200

not being allowed to turn around. Every time she tried, his fingers flexed, digging into the tender flesh of her side.

"You shouldn't have left them."

"Why not? You did," she snapped, and then immediately regretted it. "Besides, they're fine. I made sure of that."

"I should have known." His words still held an edge of something she couldn't define, but his tone had eased slightly.

"So if everything's all right back there, you have a few minutes to spare. Care for a drink?" The grip he'd had on her waist lifted and he flicked his wrist toward the bar.

She shook her head. Not only did she not partake of spirits any stronger than chamomile tea, but she was afraid spending too long inside the Devil's Den would lessen her chances of passing as a man.

"Well, I could sure stand to finish mine," he said dryly, taking her hand and starting across the crowded floor.

Hannah tried to wiggle her fingers free as they dodged other customers. "I don't think this is such a good idea," she whispered, throwing nervous glances around the room to see if anyone was looking at her oddly.

"What? Drinking? I think it's a damn fine notion."

He stopped when he reached the far end of the bar where a half-empty glass of amber liquid sat, a half-full bottle beside it. Propping one booted foot on the brass rail near the bottom of the pine wood counter, he hitched his shoulders and slouched over his drink.

"What's wrong with you?" Hannah hissed, moving close to the bar so as not to be overheard by anyone else. "Your sister just had a baby and both she and the infant are healthy, yet you're moping around like . . . like somebody shot your dog."

"I don't have a dog," he replied in a monotone.

Giving in to temptation, she slapped his arm with the back of her hand. "You know what I mean. This is a good day. You should be happy. Why aren't you?"

"Not everyone celebrates the birth of a new child, Hannah," he told her without taking his eyes off the bottle of whiskey before him. "Especially those who don't think they'll ever have children of their own."

Hannah rocked back on her heels, stunned. *That* was why David was acting so strangely? He wanted children and didn't think he'd get the chance to have them?

"What a silly thing to be upset about," she said, trying to lighten his mood. "There's plenty of time for that sort of thing, David, if that's what you want."

It killed her to say it, but David was far from unmarriageable. He had years ahead of him to find a wife. Men weren't considered on the shelf nearly as early as women were, if ever. He could wait well into his later years to marry, if he chose.

He was handsome and virile and so kind, a girl couldn't help but be charmed. Any woman worth her salt would have no problem defying society's small-minded views of his Indian blood and risking the censure of others for a man who treated her as well as David would. Why he couldn't see that bewildered her. Why he couldn't see that she was completely in love with him already was incomprehensible to her.

He shook his head and downed the last of the liquor in his glass. "Not for me."

Walker knew Hannah didn't understand. Couldn't. She didn't know what it was like to want someone, and to know that if he couldn't have her, he'd rather spend the rest of his life alone.

He'd grown up knowing he was different, knowing little girls looked at him differently than they looked at the white boys their own age. Knowing his adoptive parents were more accepting than most of the people in Purgatory, and that even though they'd always told him he could do anything despite others' prejudices, his entire life was going to be an uphill battle. And knowing, too, that he could never have the one girl he really wanted.

Seeing Hannah holding his newborn niece a few hours earlier had driven the point home

203

harder and more painfully than he'd ever imagined.

Clay and Regan were wrong. He couldn't have all the things white men had. He could only walk through life like a ghost, straddling the line between the Comanche world and the white man's, pretending to be satisfied with whatever scraps of happiness came his way.

He'd thought he'd come to terms with that fact years ago. But that was before he'd seen Hannah again. Seen her, talked with her, touched her, made love with her.

Now it rankled. Rubbed his backside like a burr in his trousers.

He cocked his head, fixing Hannah with a sharp glare. "You think I'm such a catch?" he asked her, the words edged with bitterness. "Would you be willing to marry me, *notsa?ka??* Bear my children? Put up with the whispers and straight-out disdain the people of Purgatory would heap on you for hitching yourself to a half-breed?"

One golden brow arched high over a corn-flower blue eye turned stormy with ire. "If I thought you were sincere instead of drunk, I just might. You underestimate yourself, David," she said more softly. "I've never met anyone who worked so hard to belittle himself before anyone else gets the chance. Maybe if you gave yourself the benefit of a doubt once in a while, others would, too."

With that, she whirled around, ready to

head for the door. Only a hard hand on her elbow kept her from taking more than a step in that direction.

"Do you think it's that easy?" he bit out, spinning her back to face him. "Being part Comanche isn't something I can hide, like a birthmark or a bum leg. Folks see it every time they look at me. My hair, my skin . . . they know exactly what I am and cross the street to keep from getting too close."

A muscle in his jaw ticked with each angry word, his fingers wrapping tighter around her arm. But Hannah wasn't intimidated.

"I have never seen anyone cross the street to avoid coming in contact with you. I've never seen anyone look away from you rather than be caught staring at a half-breed. I don't know what it's like in other towns, but the people of Purgatory treat you the same as anyone else. They watched you grow up and think of you as just plain David Walker, son of Clay and Regan Walker."

Her voice gentled as she reached up with her free hand to pry his white-knuckled fingers from her arm. "You're the only one who still thinks of yourself as that little half-breed orphan, David."

Chapter Nineteen

Walker stood, dumbfounded, watching a hat-wearing, trousers-clad Hannah dodge drunken cowboys and saloon girls as she marched out of the Devil's Den. The hinged double doors swung wildly after her exit.

Before she could get too far, he hopped up, threw a handful of coins on the bar, and chased after her. She was nearing the end of the boardwalk that lined the saloon, about to step off into the street. He lengthened his strides, eating up the distance between them in seconds flat.

Reaching out, he slapped a hand over her mouth to keep her from yelling out and looped his other arm about her waist. She weighed little more than a sack of sugar, and he had no problem plucking her off her feet and carting her the short distance around the side of the building.

It was dark here, pitch black. Hell had no street lamps and what little light filtered out of the saloon's windows didn't reach this far around the corner.

Hannah was kicking and struggling against his hold, though he had no doubt she knew exactly who restrained her. She wasn't fighting him out of fear but fury at his heavy-handedness.

When he decided they were far enough away to have a private conversation, he put her down, turned her to face him, and slowly removed his hand from her mouth.

He expected an immediate lambasting for treating her so roughly, but instead she pressed her lips together in a grim line, crossed her arms beneath her breasts, and glared at him from under the rim of her Stetson.

His mind raced with the multitude of things he could say to her. They all scrambled together in his head, pounding painfully against the insides of his skull, but none of them found their way to his vocal chords.

Instead, he felt an overwhelming urge to kiss her. No one had ever thought as highly of him as Hannah seemed to. No one had ever defended him before. And certainly no one had ever been brave enough to tell him he was acting like an idiot.

He wasn't sure he believed her every word. He'd spent too long being ostracized to suddenly think the town of Purgatory paid no attention to the color of his skin.

But she'd given him something to consider. Memories to reassess. He thought he should maybe even talk with his mother and father to find out how they felt he'd been treated, both before and after his adoption.

"I really upset you in there, huh?" he asked. His gaze stayed latched on the light pink rosebud of her mouth, so he saw the minute her lips pursed even tighter.

"I have that effect on people now and then," he went on, thinking of how many times he'd sent his mother into conniptions while growing up. His father used to say Walker was the only kid on earth who could turn Regan's corkscrew curls straight as a board.

"I'm sorry," he said, still focusing on the fine features of her delicate face. "As soon as my sister is able to travel, I think we should head for Purgatory. You need to get back before the town starts to think you've been abducted, and hopefully I can find a place there to hide Bright Eyes and the children. My father is there, too, and it can't hurt to have a sheriff on our side in case Lynch does come calling."

Her expression remained impassive, her

crossed arms making her look prickly as a porcupine. He blew out a frustrated breath, not knowing where the hell to start or how to go about getting her to forgive him.

"I'm trying to apologize here, Hannah. Not doing a very respectable job of it, I'm afraid, but what I'm saying is that when we get back to Purgatory, I'm going to give some serious consideration to what you said inside. Maybe I'll take a stroll down the middle of town and see how folks react. Maybe you can go with me and we'll see how they react to the two of us together."

Even in the darkness of the alley, he saw her eyes widen at that. He liked to think the stiff set of her shoulders loosened a bit, too.

"That's terribly . . . agreeable of you," she said, finally unpursing the thread-thin line of her lips.

"I know. Don't get used to it, though. I'm bound to switch back to my usual disagreeable self at any minute."

She smiled. The first real sign of happiness he'd witnessed since he'd seen her cradling his newly born niece.

He leaned forward, resting his forehead against her own. "So do you forgive me?"

"For what? Being disagreeable?"

He chuckled. "Among other things, but mostly that, yeah."

Dropping her arms from their earlier hostile position beneath her breasts, she brought them to his sides, her fingers curling into the soft leather of his dun-colored shirt.

With an exaggerated sigh, she said, "Well, I've forgiven you for less, so . . . I suppose."

He couldn't remember ever doing anything that required her forgiveness before but thought it better not to press his luck by questioning her generosity.

Glad to be in her good graces again, he laid his lips just below her left ear and pressed both palms flat on the vertical planks of wood that sided the building at her back. "Has anyone ever told you you've got a smart mouth? I hope you don't talk to your students like that."

"I speak to my students however I like," she replied primly. "I am the teacher, after all. And besides, my mouth isn't the only part of my body that's intelligent."

"Is that right?" He grinned, letting his hands slide down the wall, over her back, to the curve of her rear end. "Is this one of those other places?" he asked, giving the rounded globes a licentious squeeze.

She gave a short yelp and pressed herself more tightly to his front, trying halfheartedly to shift away from his roving hands.

"It's one of them," she said breathlessly, "but there's another part of me that's wishing you'd use a little bit of your own smart mouth to hush up and kiss me."

He pushed the hat back on her head and

looked deep into her eyes. Loose plaits of blond hair fell free, glowing silver in the pale moonlight as it dusted her shoulders.

"That, I can do," he said, his warm breath dancing on her face. And then he gently took her bottom lip between his teeth. Toying, teasing.

His hands tightened on her bottom, drawing her against him until his jutting arousal settled in the vee of her legs. They were separated only by their clothing, which did nothing to keep even the smallest sensation from rushing to his nerve endings.

He kissed her wildly, absorbing every nuance of her mouth, every scent and taste and impression. He wanted to soak her into his system so he could carry her with him everywhere he went and never again be without her. She was a dizziness in his blood, like the strongest opiate or hundred-proof liquor.

Leaning his full weight into her, he pressed her back against the building. His knee found its way between her legs and she eagerly opened to him, straddling his thigh and rubbing there like a cat in heat.

Walker wasn't far behind, feeling like the tip of a lucifer held too close to the campfire, ready to explode.

"Now," she whispered raggedly, tearing her mouth away from his own. "Now, David, now."

No woman had ever begged him so sweetly,

so desperately. And he'd never wanted one as badly as he wanted Hannah. She was right; it had to be now.

His fingers fumbled at the front of her pants, struggling to get them undone. She reached out to do the same for him and their arms tangled together like an ivy vine gone loco. But soon her trousers fell loose about her waist and he shoved them roughly down her legs, until she was bare from hip to calf.

With his other hand, he unbuttoned the flap of his own breeches. His throbbing member sprang free and he lifted Hannah off her feet, bringing her down again so fast, they both gasped at the sudden force of their bodies coming together.

But she didn't give him time to catch his breath. With her hands on his shoulders, her feet flat against the wall at her back, and her knees braced on his hips, she rocked her body up and down, riding him like a quarter-miler on the last leg of a cash prize race. He could only keep his hands on her waist for leverage and pray he lasted. At the pace she was setting, he wasn't sure he would.

"God, Hannah," he groaned, biting her neck, flexing his fingers in her supple flesh, grinding his chest against the budded nipples poking through the thin material of her shirt.

"Yes," she answered him, with both her mouth and her body. "Yes, yes, yes."

"*Haa, haa, haa,*" he repeated her litany in

Comanche, driving into her even as she came down on him.

Their hard, thrusting movements struck like lightning, sending a flash of hot, almost indescribable pleasure from the place where their bodies met, through every bone, muscle, and vital organ. The top of his head all but shot off, and he felt nothing but her damp warmth surrounding him, drawing him in, driving him insane.

Suddenly, her nails curled into his arms like talons and she stiffened above him, crying out as her climax hit. He covered her mouth with his own, muffling the noises of her completion, not knowing who might be passing the corner of the building at just that moment.

And then he was kissing her for real as his hips lurched forward and an orgasm more powerful than any he'd experienced before washed over him like a strong ocean wave. It shook him to the soles of his boots and left him weak as an orphaned calf, barely able to keep himself on his feet.

Hannah's lifeless weight bore down on him, too, and it was all he could do to let her slide slowly down his tall frame and get her feet beneath her before collapsing on top of her, pinning them both to the wall.

"Shit," he muttered, and was glad to get out that much.

He didn't know where she found the energy, but she chuckled, her head resting against his shoulder as they both struggled for air. Their trousers were still down around their knees, their backsides visible to anyone who cared to see, and Walker couldn't say he gave a stallion's left nut. He wouldn't have the coordination to pull up his pants if he tried.

"I hope that's a complimentary expletive," Hannah rasped just below his ear, "and not a complaint."

"Definitely. It's times like these I'm glad I can cuss in two languages." He took a moment to catch his breath. "Is your behind getting cold?"

She laughed again. "Not cold, exactly, but there is a slight breeze blowing through. And I've got a bit more than my . . . bottom hanging out, in case you hadn't noticed."

He'd noticed. He just hadn't wanted to cover her up anytime soon. But what kind of gentleman would he be if he ravished her standing up against the outside of a whorehouse and didn't even pull her trousers back up afterwards?

Walker grimaced, realizing there wasn't a single part of that sentence he ever wanted his mother to overhear. She'd drag him out back by his ear faster than he could say, "It was all Hannah's idea!" And when it came to wielding a birch stick over something she considered unsuitable, Regan didn't much care how old he was. She'd just get herself a bigger switch.

Forcing himself to move, he stretched down, careful not to dislodge Hannah from where she rested on his chest. With one hand, he dragged the canvas breeches up the length of her legs, holding them in place with his hips until he could get the tail of her shirt tucked in and the front buttons fastened.

"Better?" he asked, breathing hard again from the effort of doing all that practically one-handed.

She nodded, then reached around the width of his body to tug at his own trousers. Her motions brought her in direct contact with every inch of nether flesh still exposed to the night wind.

Wrapping his hand around her wrist, he stopped her. "Maybe I should do that."

"Why?" she asked, glancing up at him with complete innocence in her shadowed eyes. "Did I do something wrong?"

He gave a harsh laugh. "No, *notsa?ka?*, you do everything absolutely right. Believe me. I'm just afraid that if you keep rubbing against me like that, pulling our pants up at all will end up being a big waste of time."

And sure enough, it took some doing to get himself properly adjusted and shut behind the placket of his trousers.

By the time he finished, Hannah was leaning against the building, hands clasped behind her back. She looked relaxed, almost boneless, and was watching him with a cross between unbridled lust and complete dazedness.

The dusty black hat sat at a cockeyed angle on her head, and tendrils of hair fell haphazardly about her heart-shaped face. It made him want to grab her up and kiss her, then strip her of her clothes and ravage her all over again.

"We'd better get back to the cabin. Check on Bright Eyes and the kids," he said.

Lifting her hat, he swept up the loose strands of hair and tucked them beneath the brim, thinking that if they didn't move out of this alleyway soon, they might never leave. And eventually the sun would come up. People would find them, naked and slaked and wrapped around each other like a couple of cuddlebugs.

She inclined her head in agreement, seeming to use every spare bit of energy she possessed to push herself away from the wall. He lifted a hand to her and she took it without a second's hesitation.

"What does that word mean? The one you keep calling me—*notsa?ka?*"

He didn't answer her right away, his mind racing to think of a proper explanation. The truth was too frightening a prospect—at least to him—and not something he wanted her to know.

He'd told her once it was the Comanche word for her name. Maybe that reasoning would work again. "I told you—"

"You told me it was my name in Comanche, but I don't think that's right. Not the way you've been using it."

Uh-oh. Had he been caught?

She tipped her head to the side, gazing at him from under the wide brim of her hat. The sliver of moonlight in the night sky gilded her face and reflected in her eyes like a full moon on the surface of a lake.

"I can ask Little Bear, I suppose. He's been trying to teach me a bit of the language. Although, from the faces he makes when I repeat the words back to him, I don't think he believes I'm doing that great a job. Still, he would probably know what *notsa?ka?* means. Is that how you pronounce it, *notsa?ka??*"

Her arm was tucked through his elbow now and she leaned into him with every step toward the cabin where his sister, nephew, and niece waited. Whether she intended to or not, she was weakening his resolve.

And offering to ask Little Bear what Comanche words meant was a serious threat. The boy would be more than willing to help Hannah learn his people's native tongue, never realizing why she was asking or what affect it might have on his uncle's life. His life, his relationship with Hannah . . . and his well-being if she found out from a seven-year-old what he'd been calling her these past couple of weeks.

He took a deep breath. Better to do it himself and get it over with, he supposed.

"It's just an . . . endearment. A term of affection we use in the village."

"But what does it *mean?*" she prodded, pressing against him in such a way that the side of her breast brushed his chest.

It was hard for him to think straight when she did that. And then he made the mistake of glancing down . . . and meeting her fathomless, well-deep eyes.

"Sweetheart," he blurted out before he lost his courage. "It means sweetheart."

"It does?"

She beamed up at him, and Walker couldn't decide where he felt it more—the lightness in his brain, the punch to his gut, or the steel-gloved clench to his groin. He only knew that she was staring at him like he'd hung the stars in the sky just to make her smile. And if she continued looking at him that way, he'd do everything in his power to ensure that she never discovered the truth.

But the awed expression on her face worried him, too. Because he knew what kind of man he was; he knew what he'd done to deserve a look like that—and what he hadn't. It would be better for her to be a little disappointed now rather than a lot disappointed later.

"Don't get excited," he told her, forcing his voice to sound gruff and making sure his arm didn't purposely pull her too close to his side. "It's just a word we use in the village."

"Oh, yes. I believe you."

Chapter Twenty

She didn't believe him for a minute.

Two days after their encounter outside the Devil's Den, they packed their things and headed for Purgatory. Bright Eyes and the baby—who still didn't have a name—rode David's stallion, Thunder. The child was safely ensconced in a cradleboard David had crafted when he realized they'd be traveling with the infant. Now, David led the mount while Hannah and Little Bear walked alongside.

She was once again wearing her pink dress. It had been clean when she'd donned it early that morning but was already covered with trail dust up to the elbows, and several pieces of lace trim dangled loose from such harsh treatment. She would have to sew them back on as soon as she arrived home.

But none of that mattered. Not the blistering sun beating down on them, her bedraggled state, the miles they'd already covered, or the miles they had yet to traverse.

All that mattered was David and the word he used when he spoke to her: *sweetheart*.

She'd been grinning from ear to ear ever since the night he told her that was what he'd been saying each time he'd called her *notsa?ka?*. He claimed it meant nothing, of course; simply a general form of address commonplace among the Comanche. But she didn't believe him, and to be sure, she'd gotten Little Bear alone to ask him about it.

The child had seemed confused by her question at first, then told her he had only ever heard his uncle use it with her. His mother, it seemed, wasn't fond of the term, nor had Little Bear ever heard of it being uttered regularly among the Comanche.

He also wanted to know why she pronounced it so well when all the words he'd tried to teach her rolled off her tongue like gravel instead of honey. But Hannah didn't dare tell the boy she'd learned it while in the throes of deepest passion with his uncle. That wouldn't do at all, so she merely brushed off the question and let him try again to teach her a few simpler words.

After that conversation, she was certain of

David's motives and took great pleasure in knowing he considered her, if not *his* sweetheart, at least *a* sweetheart.

She rather hoped it was the former, though. She was coming to realize that she loved the man desperately, and with each day that love only grew. If he felt even a fraction of the same type of affection for her, she would count herself lucky. And his calling her sweetheart was certainly a start. It heartened her and put a spring in her step, even though she should have felt exhausted and collapsed hours ago.

"You seem awfully happy," David commented, gifting her with a rare glimpse over his shoulder as he trudged ahead, one foot in front of the other, leading the horse his sister was riding.

"Mmm-hmmm." She couldn't help smiling at the sight of his broad back and muscular legs as he walked, his ebony hair glistening in the midday sun.

"Eager to get home, huh?" he asked.

Actually, she hadn't given much thought to returning to her little cabin in the woods, or her position as schoolmarm of the Purgatory school. She supposed she should be excited about getting back to her life there, but the truth of the matter was that she almost missed the rickety shack in Hell simply because the outlaw town was where David had first touched her so intimately and finally made love to her. Twice. Or at least on two separate occasions. And the second time, in a way she hadn't imagined possible, yet was more than willing to repeat, if only she could once more get him alone.

She glanced up at Bright Eyes, cradling her baby daughter, and then at Little Bear trailing beside her, and knew it might be some time before she and David got that kind of chance again. She almost sighed aloud with disappointment.

"It will be nice to be back," she said in response to his question, taking the opportunity to skip ahead a few steps and keep pace with his long strides. "People must certainly be wondering over my whereabouts by now. Several of my older students are kept home at this time of year to help their parents' with summer crops, but the younger ones still would have shown up for classes the first day or so after my absence. Hopefully someone went to my cabin and saw the note I left on the door."

He gazed at her through narrowed eyes. "You left a note?"

She nodded.

"What did it say?"

"Simply that I'd been called away suddenly. They'll understand, especially if I concoct a decent story about a friend falling ill in another town. They certainly wouldn't believe I'd gone to a relative's."

She grinned and shot him a look that only another who'd grown up in an orphanage could understand. "Visiting Heaven for a couple of days would certainly be an acceptable excuse," she continued. "Either way, I don't expect it to be much of a problem."

"It will be if they find out you ran off with a half-breed," he muttered.

This time, he didn't bother meeting her gaze. Probably because he knew she'd be scowling at him.

"That again?" Not bothering to hide her annoyance, she raised her chin and gave a little tug to the brim of her wide straw bonnet. She tried to ignore the strip of artificial flowers that had come loose and now dangled in front of her nose in the most annoying manner. "I thought we'd settled that nonsense back in Hell."

"I agreed to take a closer look at things when we get back to Purgatory, but nothing's settled, Hannah," he said wearily. "I doubt it ever will be."

"Well, it certainly won't with an attitude like that. Don't you ever get tired of thinking the worst of people?"

"It comes from a lot of years of experience, *notsa?ka?*. You've just got too kind a disposition to see it."

He wouldn't think her so kind after she walloped him in the head with her disintegrating hat, she thought sourly, flipping the flowers out of her eyes once more. He was the most stubborn man she'd ever met and it was beginning to grate on her nerves.

Then again, he had called her sweetheart when it wasn't a typical endearment, according to his nephew. The knowledge warmed her heart and brought her forgiving nature to the fore.

Plus, he had agreed to walk down the main street of town and see for himself—a little more clearly this time, she hoped—how the people of Purgatory truly treated him. That was something, at least.

"Why don't we change the subject before we both get angry again?" she suggested brightly. "I, for one, am getting rather hungry, and we're not far from my cabin. What would you like for lunch?"

Before David had a chance to answer, Little Bear piped up from several paces behind Thunder. "Anything, as long as it's not chicken or soup," he almost groaned. "Or eggs. No chicken soup or chicken broth or cold chicken sandwiches, or fried eggs or fried egg sandwiches."

Hannah and David exchanged amused grins as the boy listed the meager food choices he'd been forced to choke down the past several days. There had been quite a bit of chicken and eggs served, in all their many forms.

225

"I guess that answers that," David replied dryly.

"I guess it does. The only problem is that a chicken and some eggs may be all I have at home."

A loud, seven-year-old groan drifted across the dusty trail, followed by heavy, petulant footfalls emphasizing Little Bear's displeasure.

David cocked his head in her direction, one side of his mouth twisting into a grin. Hannah smiled back and they lapsed into silence the rest of the way back to Purgatory.

An hour or so later, they reached Hannah's cabin, every one of them exhausted right down to their toes. David immediately lifted his sister and niece from Thunder's back and carried them toward the tiny house while Hannah rushed ahead to hold the door open.

Just as she'd suspected, the note she'd left nailed to the weathered wooden planking was missing. Someone had come by and the entire town must know by now that classes were postponed due to their teacher being temporarily gone.

David laid Bright Eyes on Hannah's small bed in the corner and took the baby from its cradleboard, settling her against her mother's breast. "Rest, *patsi?*," he said, pressing a soft kiss to her brow. "It was a long trip."

"*Ura, samohpu,*" she replied and closed her

eyes, tightening her arms around the tiny bundle at her side.

The child had been very well behaved for being only a few days old. She slept most of the time, only fussing when she was awake until Bright Eyes nursed her or changed her soiled diaper.

Hannah wondered why Bright Eyes hadn't named her daughter yet, but David had explained that the Comanche sometimes waited a few days before deciding what to call newborns. And names were chosen either from nature or in association with the child's clan.

Hannah wasn't sure she understood it, exactly, but she was eager to know what Bright Eyes would call the little girl. For now, they referred to her simply as "the baby."

David took Thunder around back to feed and unsaddle him while Hannah busied herself in the kitchen, looking for something for Little Bear to eat—something other than chicken or eggs or soup of any kind.

Hannah found it comforting to be back in her own kitchen, with many more amenities than the shack in Hell offered, even if Little Bear, sitting at the oaken table in the center of the cabin, was kicking his feet impatiently and complaining about how hungry he was.

It almost cheered her, remembering how quiet and sullen he'd been the last time they'd been alone together in this room. The boy was blossoming, she thought. Or at the very least opening up to her and becoming more comfortable in her presence.

David came in through the rear entrance just as she was setting a plate of cheese and dried bread on the table before Little Bear. And the child who had bragged to her when they first met that his uncle had taught him to track prey and live off the land by eating bugs and dirt if need be, whined about the bread being stale and crunchy. He finally stopped complaining and settled for plopping chunks of cheese in his mouth when Hannah promised to make him a cup of cocoa so he could dip the bread.

Walker watched the exchange with amusement from across the room. Turning his back to Hannah and Little Bear to hide his smile, he pumped water into the metal kitchen basin and scrubbed his hands.

On her way to make hot chocolate for the boy, Hannah brushed much too close for his comfort. The moment the sleeve of her cotton dress made contact with the leather of his shirt, a rush of pure desire shot through his veins. That was all it took, a single innocent brush of limbs with two layers of fabric between, for him to be hard as a rod and randy as a rabbit.

If that wasn't bad enough, being in her house, watching her interact with his nephew, brought to mind future scenarios he had no business imagining. Living here with her, watching her prepare meals for him and *their* children. Spending evenings with her in the narrow bed his sister now occupied.

No matter what vision appeared in his mind's eye, it always led back to the fact that he wanted to spend the rest of his life with her. And since that was impossible, he had no business dreaming such stupidity.

Deciding it was a good thing his buckskin shirt reached to mid-thigh so it covered his rather blatant condition, he cleared his throat and turned, leaning back against the edge of the cast-iron sink.

"After Bright Eyes wakes up and gets a bite to eat, I thought I'd take her and the children over to my parents' house. Regan and Clay should know of a safe place for the three of them to stay until we can get this trouble sorted out, and I can describe Ambrose Lynch to my father so he and his deputies can be on the lookout."

"You . . . you'll be back, though, won't you?"

He didn't miss the catch in her voice or the way she wound her fingers together at her waist.

Avoiding her gaze so he didn't have to see the hurt in her sky blue eyes, he said, "I don't think that's such a good idea, Hannah. I've caused you enough trouble. It might be better if I just take my sister and her children to Clay

229

and Regan's and stay away from you for a while."

"What if Lynch finds you, though? What if he asks around town and they tell him where your parents live and he tracks you there?"

"I hope Bright Eyes and the children will be hidden somewhere else by then, and I won't stay at my parents. I'll probably go back to the Comanche village."

Hannah's fidgeting stopped as abruptly as it had begun. She crossed her arms over her chest beneath the gentle swell of her breasts and stared daggers at him. "What you're saying, then, is that you're leaving and I'll probably never see you again."

He'd been trying very hard not to say those exact words, but they both knew it was what he meant. Seeing her was hard enough. Being with her without touching her was damn near impossible. And making love to her without knowing he would wake up beside her for the next thirty years was enough to rip the heart right out of his chest and stomp it into the ground.

Better to leave and never return. Ride away and never look back. Find refuge in his parents' support and forget he'd ever experienced even a hint of heaven in this woman's arms.

It would be better that way.

Even if it burned like hell and felt like his guts were being torn out and stretched across the land like barbed wire.

"It's better this way, Hannah. Trust me."

"I do trust you," she said simply, her lips pursed in disapproval. "But I also disagree with your reasoning completely. Take your sister to your parents, if you must. Tell them what's going on and let them help you. Bring Bright Eyes and the children back here if you need to, or leave them there if you think it's best. But whatever happens, I want *you* to come back, do you understand?"

"Hannah—"

"No. I don't want to hear it. I want you to come back—alone or with your family, I don't care. And when you do, we're going to sit down and talk. We're going to walk through town and see how Purgatory's citizens react to us being together. And we're going to talk," she repeated.

Having said her piece, she uncrossed her arms and moved to the stove, where the milk for the cocoa was beginning to boil.

"I waited ten years for you to come back, David Walker. I'm not going to let you get away again."

Chapter Twenty-one

By the time David collected his sister, niece, and nephew and set off for his parents' house, Hannah was still shaking. With fury, with anxiety, with disbelief, with dread.

How could he even think of just walking away? He'd come to her when he was injured and in need of someone to look after his nephew, dragged her to that outlaw town and made her live in little more than a hovel for nearly two weeks, and now he thought he could return her to her cabin and abandon her without a backward glance. After he'd made love to her, too. Twice!

If the man thought she was going to tolerate that kind of behavior, he had another thing coming. She knew where the Walkers lived and would follow him there, if need be. She would even ask someone to point her in the direction of his Comanche village and track him there if she had to.

Honestly! She didn't tolerate this sort of pigheadedness from her students, and she wasn't going to put up with it from David, either.

Slamming back into the house, she began clearing the table and ended up cleaning the entire cabin. From top to bottom, she dusted and scrubbed, changed bedclothes and washed curtains. Her body had an excessive amount of energy to burn off, it seemed, fueled mostly by anger and frustration.

And all the while, her mind raced. It catapulted from wanting to shake David until his teeth rattled to being heartsick over his feelings of not fitting in.

She had a bit of experience with not fitting in herself. She'd been somewhat of an outcast as a child, having grown up in the Purgatory Home for Adoptive Children. She knew what it was like to be teased at school for not having any parents. And later, as a schoolteacher, she'd had to deal with a handful of children picking on others because they were taller, skinnier, shorter, fatter, poorer, walked with a limp, spoke with a lisp, or had hair just a shade lighter or darker than was fashionable.

Struggling with that sort of teasing as a

child was bad enough; she couldn't imagine what it must be like to deal with it on a daily basis even into adulthood, as David did. To feel that no matter where you went, someone was staring at you, judging you, thinking less of you without bothering to say so much as hello. And for no better reason than because his hair was a bit straighter and longer than others' or because his skin was more sun-kissed. It was ridiculous, and yet she knew it to be a prejudice that permeated more than David's small world; it seeped through the entire continent and possibly beyond.

But when Hannah had left Purgatory to attend school, she'd learned that if she acted like an outsider, people treated her as one. In direct contrast, if she acted as though she fit in, then she soon did.

She couldn't help but think the same rationale could work for David. If he looked at everyone as though they were censuring him, then chances were they would. But if he put aside his own apprehensions about his heritage, perhaps others would, too. There was no guarantee, of course, but she planned to put her theory to the test as soon as David returned to the cabin.

She wiped the back of one arm over her sweating brow, taking a much-needed break from scouring the floor to catch her breath.

And he'd best return soon—of his own volition—or she would march off after him and drag him back by his ear.

Walker made his way back to Hannah's cabin early the following morning and felt for all the world like a flea-bitten mongrel returning home with its tail tucked tightly between its legs—as though he knew he deserved a scolding for running away. Which didn't explain one whit the rapidly increased beat of his heart at the prospect of seeing her again.

He was torn between knowing he should keep his distance and not ever show his face near her house again . . . and wanting to curl up under the covers of her bed, wrap his arms about her waist, and never move so much as a muscle from that position.

When he'd arrived home last evening, with Bright Eyes, Little Bear, and the newest addition in tow, his mother had practically squeezed the life out of him, she was so happy to have him home. She'd been more than willing to welcome his Comanche sister and her children as well, and had insisted he spend the night in his old room before racing off again for—as she put it—God knows how long.

He'd been surprised by how nice it felt to be home again and hadn't argued. There wasn't much he argued about with Regan, anyway. He rarely won such battles.

And he could hardly tell his parents that the

only reason he very much wanted to sleep elsewhere was because he had an invitation to return to Hannah's place. She hadn't invited him into her bed, exactly, but he was optimistic enough to believe that if he returned as she'd commanded, before long he'd be able to woo her in that direction.

Now, he wasn't so sure. For one thing, it was daylight. Not that anything so immaterial would deter him from making love to Hannah if he got half the chance. He was more concerned, though, with how she would respond to his arrival after staying away through the night, and what she planned to say when they sat down for the conversation she'd promised.

The idea of having a *talk* with Hannah disconcerted him more even than the idea of walking down the main street of Purgatory with her on his arm. Maybe because any time his mother or father had sat him down for a talk as a boy, he ultimately ended up going to bed without supper or doubling up on his chores because of some childish prank he'd gotten caught at.

Only this was much worse. This was a grown-up discussion about issues much more dire than putting a grass snake down his little sister's bloomers.

Dragging his feet the last several yards, he finally reached the front of Hannah's cabin and knocked lightly on the door. It opened almost immediately, and a smiling Hannah greeted him.

She wore a long, smoky blue skirt and a simple white shirtwaist today, with a lighter blue cameo broach pinned at her throat. Her glorious honey tresses were pulled up in a loose twist atop her head, held in place by two large silver combs. Loose strands fell about her face, softening the arrangement and making Walker want to reach out and run his fingers through what was surely straw spun into gold.

He swallowed hard, curling his fingers into his palms and forcing himself to remain perfectly still for fear he'd do something crazy like sweep her into his arms and declare his undying love.

"Good morning," she said brightly. "Would you like to come in?"

For the life of him, he couldn't get a single word to pass his lips. He felt no better than the town idiot, standing there with a blank look on his face, shuffling his feet in the dirt.

"All right, then, why don't we go." Leaning to the side of the open doorway, she picked up a straw-woven bonnet with a wide blue ribbon in much better shape than the one she'd worn on the trip from Hell yesterday. She placed it on her head, pinned it in place, then stepped outside, closing the door behind her.

The sides of her mouth turned up cheerfully and she linked her arm with his. "I'm glad you came by so early. This will be fun."

Finally getting his tongue to function, his voice only cracked once as he asked, "What will?"

"Our trip into town. I know you don't really want to go," she added, gazing up at him with an expectant, almost imploring look in her eyes, "but I think you need to, and I appreciate you indulging me just this once."

If she only knew, Walker thought. If she only knew that deciding to grant her requests wasn't even an option anymore. He could no more deny her than he could change the color of his skin or stop his lungs from needing air. If she asked him to climb the highest mountain, swim the deepest sea, turn the sky green and the grass blue . . . whatever she asked of him, he would do his utmost to fulfill her slightest desire.

He knew now how his father felt about his mother. As a child, he'd often thought Clay's affection for Regan too lavish. Later, he'd understood it better but still hadn't comprehended how a man could turn soft at no more than a woman's smile, why a man would set aside his masculine pride and his own inclinations to please a woman. Now, he more than understood; he found himself suffering under the exact same spell.

It was embarrassing. It was frightening. It was frustrating as hell.

"And what is it you hope to accomplish by parading me down the middle of Purgatory?" His words were edged with a touch of disdain. Not for her, but for himself. To give him courage and remind him not to let this blond-haired, blue-eyed sprite of a woman wrap him entirely around her little finger.

"I want to see how the townspeople react to you. If you're right and they treat you badly simply because you're part Indian, then I'll apologize profusely for ever doubting you."

She raised her face to his, seemingly waiting for some form of acquiescence or agreement. When he refused to respond, she continued.

"But if they treat you well, like just another friendly face or the son of the local sheriff, then I want you to stop acting like a pariah, expecting people to turn you away before they make a move to actually do so. Does that sound acceptable?"

Her skirts brushed rhythmically against his pants leg as they walked, and he fought valiantly to ignore the soft, lulling sensation they created.

"I think you're going to be sorely disappointed, Hannah," he answered finally. Carefully, because he knew for a fact now that this demure, diminutive woman had a streak of temper running through her that could ignite at the drop of a hat.

But he'd purposely dressed in a fresh set of

clothes this morning that looked much like the ones he'd worn the entire time they'd been in Hell—buckskin trousers and a long, fringed leather shirt. He couldn't look more Indian if he'd donned a loincloth and moccasins and tied feathers in his hair.

By doing so, he honestly didn't know if he was daring the townspeople to shun him, or simply making the statement that he was a half-breed and had no intention of hiding that fact, regardless of their opinion.

"You're being negative again, David. Stop that. You have as much right to be here—and I mean *here* on this earth, in this state, in this town—as anyone else. Maybe even more. You were born not far from Purgatory. Your real father lived here until the time of his death. Your Comanche mother's family has lived on this land, not far outside of town, for more years than probably either of us can count. You grew up here, even if it was in the orphanage, and were adopted by two of Purgatory's most prominent citizens. The Walkers have always treated you like their very own, and your father is the town sheriff. He wouldn't put up with people treating you badly, no matter who they were."

He looked down at her with wide eyes, surprised by her vehemence. "You've really thought this through, haven't you?" he said slowly.

240

"Yes, I have," she answered with a proud tilt of her chin.

The early morning sun danced on her shoulders and over the lower portion of her face as she glanced up at him. Once again, he was struck by how beautiful she was, with her pert nose and gentle features, her bright blue eyes and full, generous lips.

Lips made for kissing—something he knew to be absolutely, 100 percent factual. He wanted to kiss her now, except he was afraid it would lead to more than that . . . and they would end up rolling around on the ground, dirtying her pretty blue skirt and mussing up her carefully coifed hair.

Still, it was a notion well worth considering. And it took him a good two minutes to firmly decide against it.

By that time—thank *Ta?ahpu*—they'd reached town. They came in at the far end, rounding the backs of a few stray buildings. The livery, for one, and a new office where a highfalutin' dentist from St. Louis, Missouri, had set up his practice.

Walker took a deep breath, his grip tightening reflexively on Hannah's arm where it looped through his own. "All right," he said, steeling himself for what was to come, "where do you want to start?"

"How about the mercantile?"

241

He quirked a brow. "You don't believe in starting small, do you?"

Grinning up at him, her lips curled and she responded with a word she would probably never let her students use. "Nope."

Chapter Twenty-two

They stepped up on the boardwalk where the wooden promenade began in front of the half-constructed dentist's office and made their way toward the general store. As they passed the post office, a woman stepped out. She hardly glanced at them before turning the other way, but then she stopped, turned back, and gave them a wide-eyed once-over.

"Well, I'll be. Folks have been wondering where you got yourself off to."

Hannah smiled politely. "I was sorry to leave so suddenly without letting anyone know where I was going, but an acquaintance of mine in Heaven took ill, and I wanted to see that she was properly cared for. I hope my absence didn't cause too much trouble for the students."

"No, no, not at all," the buxom woman assured her, the long slope of her mud brown bonnet bobbing up and down as she spoke. "We understand. And the children were certainly happy to play in the sun for a couple of weeks instead of being trapped inside that schoolhouse all day."

"Well, classes will start again on Monday. I hope you'll pass the word along to everyone you see."

"I sure will," she promised.

And then the woman's hawklike gaze settled on Walker. "David Walker, if you aren't a sight for sore eyes. Every time I see your father, I ask after you. He always says you're fine as far as he knows but spend too much time gallivanting about and not stopping back home often enough to keep your mother from fretting. You should think about sticking around for a while. Your mama would appreciate that."

Feeling like he'd just been poleaxed, Walker inclined his head. Hannah nudged him in the ribs with her elbow and he mumbled a quick, "I'll try, ma'am."

"There's one more thing," the woman put in after a moment of consideration. She spared a quick glance at Hannah before focusing once again on him. "My youngest, Melissa, is supposed to write a paper about how the Indian tribes of Texas hunt and gather food, and how they build their little tents."

"Tipis," Hannah corrected her.

"Yes, yes, tipis. The paper is for one of Miss Blake's lessons," she added, casting a brief glance in Hannah's direction, "and as you can see, I know very little about that sort of thing. Neither does her pa. I thought maybe you'd be willing to talk with Melissa and answer some of her questions. We'd be mighty grateful, and I'd be more than happy to bring her by your parents' house whenever it's convenient for you."

Walker turned to Hannah, his mouth hanging open slightly as he gaped. He wanted to ask if she'd set this up. If she'd cornered Melissa's mother—he couldn't remember the woman's name, though he'd seen her in town before on several occasions—and asked her to be extra nice to him just to prove her point.

But if she hadn't—and he didn't know when she could have managed it, unless she'd gone out after he'd left her cabin yesterday—he didn't want to embarrass her in public or make a fool of himself by overreacting to such a simple request.

"That, um . . . that would be fine," he choked out. And then, unable to withstand any more shocks, he tipped his head to the woman, stepping around her with Hannah in tow. "It was nice to see you again. Bring your daughter by whenever you like; I'd be happy to help her with that essay."

"Bye-bye!" she called after them, waving frantically.

Walker quickly averted his gaze and stalked down the sidewalk. "What the hell was that all about?" he growled in Hannah's ear. "Did you concoct that little meeting on purpose, just to show me how wrong I've been about the people of Purgatory?"

He kept stomping, belatedly realizing Hannah was no longer at his side. When he turned to see what held her up, he found her glaring at him through eyes the color of an icy blue glacier.

"Is that what you think?" she demanded, crossing her arms over her chest as he retraced his steps. "Do you really think I would stage something like that just to win an argument?"

All the irritation seeped out of him on a worn-out sigh. No, he didn't. Hannah didn't have a devious bone in her body, and he knew it. She also wanted desperately for her convictions to be proven correct. Not simply to be right, but to show him that the people of Purgatory didn't look down on him for being a half-breed. She wanted him to realize that they accepted him as part of their community.

"I'm sorry. I overreacted. That woman—"

"Mrs. Forrester."

Walker snapped his fingers. "That's it! Mrs. Forrester. For the life of me, I couldn't remember her name."

His declaration brought a hint of a smile to Hannah's lips.

"Anyway, I haven't seen Mrs. Forrester for months, and all of that . . ." He waved a hand, not knowing quite how to describe the conversation that had taken place. "Came as a bit of a surprise."

"Good," she said, tucking her hand back into the crook of his arm. "I hope a lot of things surprise you today."

They started back down the street, nodding to folks as they passed. Walker paid particular attention to how people looked at him, the expression in their eyes when they saw him, how they greeted him, and how they reacted when they saw Hannah on his arm. To his astonishment, no one seemed to be frowning over the company Hannah kept. No one sneered at him or mumbled insults beneath their breath about his heritage or upbringing.

Could Hannah have been right? Could a few negative childhood experiences and his own defensiveness about his Comanche blood have so prejudiced his current point of view?

Worse, if he treated people badly because he expected them to do the same to him . . . and if they *weren't* treating him badly . . .

didn't that make him the same sort of person he'd always claimed to despise?

That thought didn't set well at all.

"So whose idea was it to assign a paper on Indian hunting methods?" he asked as they stopped to check for passing wagons before crossing the street.

An attractive blush rose to her cheeks as she turned away self-consciously. "Mine, of course. I've been making the students do short essays on that sort of thing for years now. There's a Comanche village not far from town. They should know how their neighbors live, even if they've never met them."

A wide grin spread across his face, because he knew that wasn't even half the story. She was forever defending him, defending his people, even if she didn't know a single one of them.

"Don't look so cocky," she castigated him haughtily, finally meeting his eyes. "I've also assigned reports on the Pilgrims, the Civil War, and the Texas Rangers. Your father inspired that last one, since he used to be a Ranger himself."

"Uh-huh." He was still smiling as he opened the door to the general store, ushering her in ahead of him. The overhead bell tinkled, announcing their arrival to the store's proprietor.

"Be right there," a muffled voice called out, and a few seconds later old Fergus McGee waddled out from a back room and up to the counter.

"Can I help ya?" he asked, squinting from behind his round spectacles and licking his lips around the pink flesh of his toothless gums.

"Morning, Mr. McGee. It's Hannah Blake." She had to shout to be heard, but the moment she announced herself, the hunched-over old man beamed.

"Hannah! Good to see you, gal."

Judging by the thickness of the lenses perched on the fellow's nose, Walker seriously doubted that.

"What can I do you for today?" he wanted to know.

"I've come to buy a few peppermint sticks for my students," she answered. "And I've brought a friend with me. You know David Walker, don't you?"

Walker tensed, not knowing what to expect and not yet used to this new demeanor the people of Purgatory seemed to have toward him. Even if it wasn't really a new attitude at all. Besides, Mrs. Forrester was only one person; what if others didn't agree with her seemingly high opinion of him?

But Fergus McGee merely rolled his head back on his shoulders, looked through the glinting glass of his spectacles, and nodded. "Sure, sure. The sheriff's son. Good to see you again. Whatcha been up to?"

"I've been away," Walker replied, following Hannah's example and raising his voice to a near bellow that echoed off the walls of the high-ceilinged mercantile. "Visiting family in my mother's village."

He wasn't sure why he felt the need to make that announcement. Possibly to test this man, this community. To see if they were willing to accept him even when he flaunted his heritage under their noses.

But instead of condemning him, the man nodded his bald head with its ring of thin gray hair just above the ears. "Good boy. Family's important." And then he turned to Hannah, the topic all but forgotten. "Did you say you wanted cinnamon or peppermint sticks for the kiddies over at the schoolhouse?"

"Peppermint," she answered, flashing David an I-told-you-so grin before flouncing off to make sure Mr. McGee got her order right.

Over the next half hour, David chatted with at least a dozen other people. All of them tipped their hats or smiled politely. None shot him foul glances or spat at his feet.

"What do you think?" Hannah asked as they made their way along the boardwalk, the small brown bag of candy for her students clutched in her hand.

"I'm not sure," he answered honestly. "Everyone was downright nice to me, but I can't believe they've always been like that. They

weren't like this the last time I came to town
. . . were they?"

Hannah studied his strong, sculpted jaw
carefully. Poor David; he was truly perplexed.
He'd genuinely expected people to curse him
or throw stones, and had no idea how to handle the fact that they'd done nothing of the
sort.

"You've been away for a while, David," she
told him softly. "Even when you did come
back to Purgatory, you spent most of your
time at your parents' house, avoiding town.
You didn't give anyone outside your own
family a chance to show you how welcome
you are here." She cast him a sidelong glance.
"I'm not sure you even wanted to know."

"In other words, I've been walking around
for the past ten years with a giant chip on my
shoulder. Is that what you're saying?"

Instead of being angry, he sounded almost
amused. Self-castigating, but amused all the
same.

"I'm glad you finally figured that out," she
said, giving him a pert half-grin.

"So it seems the people of Purgatory don't
hate me as much as I first thought."

"They never hated you," she put in ada-
mantly. "They just didn't know you at first.
And they didn't understand that you're the
same as anyone else, regardless of the color
of your skin or your part-Comanche blood. It
took your parents to show them that."

She turned to him, clutching at his sleeve, her heart pounding with excitement. "Think what it would mean if only one person became more accepting of another and then convinced others to be more accepting, too. Imagine how wonderful that would be."

He smiled down at her indulgently. "You're a good woman, Hannah, with a big heart."

"It could happen, David," she insisted. "You're proof of that."

"I hope you're right. I only have one question."

When she lifted her face, she noticed the wicked glitter in his dark, coffee brown eyes. She grew immediately wary. "What's that?" she asked.

"How tolerant do you think these folks would be of me if I wrapped my arms around you right here and now and kissed the breath out of you?"

The air froze in her lungs at his low, sensual proposition. She knew it was disgraceful, but at that moment, she wanted nothing more than for him to do just that. It would be like branding her as his. Publicly declaring that she was his woman.

A shudder rippled through her and she squeezed her legs together in an attempt to calm the sudden erotic pulse pounding there.

"I think they would understand," she said carefully, her voice squeaking like a rusty gate. "But they would probably expect a wedding invitation to follow within the next couple of days."

His eyes narrowed as he considered her response. Then he rubbed his jaw and gave a cursory nod. "I'll keep that in mind."

Hannah inhaled deeply, disappointment seizing her belly. It seemed he wouldn't be kissing her on the main street of Purgatory after all. What a shame.

As they continued on their way, a lovely young woman crossed their path. Her violet eyes sparkled and the peach of her expensive gabardine gown made her skin glow like clotted cream. She smiled coyly at David, and the image of a hungry wolf, with long, sharp claws, flashed through Hannah's mind.

"Why, David Walker," she all but purred, "when did you get back to town?"

The girl ran a hand down the length of his arm, and Hannah suffered an unexpected wave of jealousy, wanting to reach out and snatch the shiny brunette tresses straight out of the strumpet's scalp.

Lord, what a harridan she was becoming. She'd never known she possessed so much as an ounce of envy before.

Of course, she'd never been in love with a sinfully handsome man before, either.

She would have to get used to the stares and coquettish glances of other women toward David, she supposed. It was, after all, impossible for them not to be attracted to him. But if he so much as *thought* about returning one of their moon-eyed stares, she would do more than pluck him bald. She would aim much, much lower, and likely use a very sharp instrument to aid her act of revenge.

The girl didn't even give David a chance to answer her question before she was snuggling up against him, thrusting her udder-sized breast as close to his face as standing on tippy-toe could get her.

"It's been ages since we've seen you. Mama and Papa would just love it if you'd come to supper one day this week. I'll make my famous fried pork chops," she added, batting her lashes.

"I appreciate that, Miss, um . . ."

Hannah watched the girl's lips level off with displeasure. "Louisa. Louisa Prescott."

"That's right, Miss Prescott. I appreciate the offer, Miss Prescott, but I'm afraid my mother expects me at her table every evening for dinner. I haven't been home in so long, she wouldn't hear of letting me miss one of her meals."

"In that case," the girl tried again, "perhaps . . ."

Hannah cleared her throat, having swallowed about as much of Miss Louisa Prescott's overexposed bosom as she could take. "Shouldn't we be going, David?" she interrupted, purposely using his first name to demonstrate their familiarity. If David wasn't going to lay claim to her by kissing her breathless in the middle of the street, then she could at least mark him as her own in front of this top-heavy little twit.

"Yeah. It was nice seeing you again, Miss Prescott," he said, inclining his head. And then he stepped past her without a second glance, tucking Hannah's hand around his elbow.

Her heart swelled at his touch, at the natural way he took her arm. But as much as that gesture warmed her, Louisa Prescott's antics still roiled in her gut.

"That trollop. Did you see the way she was rubbing her bodice up against you? I'm surprised she didn't pop out over the top of her dress; it had to be two sizes too small."

"What are you talking about?" he asked, his brows drawing together.

Her mouth fell open. "You can't be serious. Didn't you notice she was all but throwing herself at you? The hussy."

"Who, Louisa Prescott?"

"Of course, Louisa Prescott!" she snapped. "She was fluttering her eyes like a butterfly in a sandstorm. I'm surprised she didn't take flight," she added on a growl.

"Are you saying she was flirting with me?"

"I wouldn't call it flirting," Hannah muttered. "More like inviting you into her bed."

"I thought she invited me to dinner. Pork chops."

"Hmph." Her nails curled into his forearm, and she could feel her brows coming together, almost reaching her nose, she was scowling so hard.

"So she was flirting with me, hmm? I don't think that's ever happened before."

Her frown slowly disappeared, replaced by a look of utter astonishment. When she turned wide eyes on David, he was grinning, his chest thrust forward like a strutting peacock. Did he honestly not realize the blatant sexuality he exuded? Or how many women came close to swooning over his rugged, swarthy good looks?

She swallowed around the lump in her throat. "Maybe we should go home now."

"Why?" A look of concern washed over his face and his body tensed. "Do you feel all right?"

Before he could reach out to check her for a fever, she said, "I feel fine. I just think we should get back before . . . before . . ."

"Before what?"

"Before you get a craving for fried pork chops," she blurted.

Chapter Twenty-three

Walker couldn't get Hannah back to her cabin fast enough. From the moment she'd invited him home—and into her bed, he presumed—his body had been humming with unleashed desire. His muscles were taut, his brain racing, his loins throbbing in anticipation.

It was a good mile and a half from town to her cabin. If one kept to a brisk pace, the walk probably took about a half hour. Walker rushed Hannah so much, they made it in just over twenty minutes, which included stopping upon occasion to devour her mouth and stroke the soft contours of her face, and then picking her up and carrying her a short distance to make up for lost time.

For once in his life, he couldn't care less who might see them. The citizens of Purgatory didn't seem to hate him as much as he'd once thought, but even if they had, he wouldn't have been able to resist kissing her out in the open. Let them condemn him, hang him. It would be well worth any punishment they could devise.

When they finally reached her doorway, he whirled her around, pressed her flat against the solid wooden panel, and plundered her mouth until their teeth scraped together. He rubbed his chest up and down hers, feeling the abrasion of her peaked nipples through the layers of their clothing. His hands clutched at her back, her waist, her buttocks. He settled his hard length into the crux of her legs and slowly rotated his pelvis until she moaned.

She clawed at his shoulders and he groped behind her for the door latch. His fingers fumbled for a minute before the door swung open, spilling them into the room.

Walker stumbled and nearly fell. Hannah would have if he hadn't caught her around the waist and kept her from landing on her rear end. She looked up at him—hanging backward over his arm, her hat lost somewhere on the floor and her hair spilling out of its artfully arranged bun—and laughed.

He joined her, kicking the door closed behind them, then lifting her fully into his arms and carrying her toward the narrow bed in the corner. His lips remained on hers the whole way and her hands feathered through his hair as he tried not to trip over a spare piece of furniture and kill them both.

At last, he reached the bed and laid her down. The mattress creaked as he lowered himself over her. His elbow cracked into the wall as he straddled her thighs and he gave a short grunt of pain.

"You've got to get a bigger bed, *notsa?ka?*. This one is barely wide enough for the both of us." His voice grew hushed as he propped himself on the heels of his hands and trailed his bottom lip across the corner of her mouth. "And definitely not large enough for everything I want to do to you."

"If you plan to stick around," she informed him bluntly, "I'll consider it."

Walker decided to ignore that particular lure in favor of licking the long column of her neck which exuded a natural, lemony scent. Whether or not he'd stay in Purgatory and in contact with Hannah remained to be seen. And if he did, there was a chance she would be discharged from her position as schoolmarm simply for consorting with him. Halfbreed or not, parents would be none too happy to find out the woman teaching their little darlings to read and write had spent the better part of two weeks alone with a man in a tiny shack in the infamous outlaw town of

Hell. Once she was kicked out of the cabin and possibly run out of town altogether for consorting with a gentleman, the size of her berth would be a rather moot point.

"You know what I'd like?" he murmured, nibbling at the erratic throb of her pulse. "I'd like to take you to the Comanche village and introduce you to my family and friends there. Spend the night with you in one of the lodges. Make love to you on a thick layer of soft animal pelts, with a fire blazing only feet away."

"Mmmm." She moaned deep in her throat and threw back her head, arching her small breasts into his chest.

"Would you like that? Would you let me make love to you on a bed of furs?"

"Anywhere," she said, her breathing growing labored.

Her eyes were closed as she absorbed every sensation he created with his ever-moving hands and lips. She didn't even seem to notice when he released the catch of her brooch and set it aside.

He pictured her there, in his people's village, on that bed of furs, and experienced an almost crippling wave of deep-rooted contentment. He'd never wanted her to be his wife as much as he did at that moment.

There had been times in his life when he'd imagined marrying her, but never had his longing run so deep. He wanted her forever, in both the white man's and the red man's worlds. He never wanted to let her go, no matter what anyone else thought or said.

That terrified him most of all. It was one thing for him to be willing to tolerate the bad things that might come of taking up with a white woman. But they would be nothing compared to what Hannah would be put through. She'd shown him today that not everyone hated him because of his Indian blood, but that didn't mean everyone accepted him, either. And there was no guarantee they would continue to be accepting of Hannah if she married him.

He didn't want to think about any of that now, though. He was too happy, too at ease, and too eager to make Hannah's eyes roll back in her head.

While his mouth was busy sipping at the tiny dip of satiny skin above her collarbone, his fingers worked to loosen the buttons at the front of her blouse. One by one, they slipped through their holes, the white cotton fabric falling open to reveal the porcelain perfection of her chest and breasts.

He pulled the tail ends of the shirtwaist free, then reached around to unfasten the waistband of her skirt. It took all of three seconds to relieve her of her outer clothing, leaving her in a sleeveless camisole with pink edging, matching drawers, and thin linen stockings held in place by garters the same pale pink as the ribbon on the camisole bodice and around the legs of her drawers.

"Very nice," he whispered, the air catching in his lungs as he admired the vision of delightful femininity she made, lying before him with her eyes closed and her lips slightly parted.

Crossing his arms over his abdomen, he shucked his shirt in one quick upward motion, pulling the buckskin garment over his head and tossing it somewhere on the cabin floor.

His fingers explored the silky smoothness of her leg, running around her slim ankle, up the back of her muscled calf to the bend of her knee. Lifting her booted foot to his chest, he began to undo the laces and tossed the scuffed piece of footwear over his shoulder. It hit the wall with a thump and plopped to the floor, soon followed by its mate.

With her shoes removed, he hooked her stockinged legs over his shoulders and slid down until the bulk of his body rested in the cradle of her thighs. She opened her eyes and flexed her feet until her toes pointed straight at the ceiling, and smiled.

When his face came within reach, Hannah grabbed him playfully by the ears and pulled him down for a kiss. While their lips melded and their tongues dueled, Walker slipped his hands under the hem of her camisole and slowly worked it up her midriff. Beneath the confining material, he stroked her breasts, teasing the sensitive centers into tightened peaks.

Stretching her arms high above her head, he slid off the flimsy top and let it fall to the floor. He took a moment to admire the modest upthrust of her breasts before curling his fingers into the waist of her drawers, sliding them over the curve of her bottom and down the length of her legs.

While he was busy and half turned, divesting her of that piece of frippery, she wiggled onto her knees so that her face was level with his. She kissed his forehead and brows, the bridge of his nose, his eyelids, his high cheekbones, the tiny indentations on either side of his mouth . . . Feather-light touches to show him how much she loved him.

She ran her hands over his broad shoulders, the firm sinews of his upper arms and chest. Her thumbs dusted the darker, coin-size circles of his nipples with their sharp centers before running down the wash-board ripples of his ribs and abdomen. From there, her fingers found the bulge at the front of his trousers and gently cupped his throbbing erection.

Letting his head fall back, David's eyes closed. A clutch of excitement quavered through her belly at his low groan of pleasure, spurring her to increase the pressure of her hold and begin a slow, back and forth caress.

"Stop. You're killing me," he hissed, his

hand closing in a viselike grip about her wrist.

"What's the matter?" she purred in return. "Don't you like it when I touch you this way?" Despite his attempt to halt her movements, she was able to stroke the hard ridge of trapped flesh.

"I do like it. Too much. But if you expect this to continue more than another three seconds, you need to stop driving me mad."

"I want to drive you mad," she retorted, sounding almost petulant, even to her own ears. "You've driven me crazy enough in the past. Now it's my turn."

He studied her closely as several silent heartbeats passed, his deep brown eyes drilling into her like twin flames. "I'm not promising anything," he said finally, releasing her hand. "But I'll let you play your games and we'll see how long I last."

She grinned, her mind spinning with all the wicked, forbidden, erotic games she could play with him. No doubt both of them would crumble and give in out of sheer desperation before any of them reached their ultimate conclusions. But they had time, and hopefully many opportunities to try again and again. A shiver of anticipation raced down her spine.

With his blessing, she unlaced the strings at the front of his buckskin trousers. Following the line of thin, dark hair that trailed down his abdomen, the backs of her fingers rested against his coal-hot flesh. Delving even farther, she loosened the ties more and dipped her hand all the way into his pants, fondling his throbbing member.

David growled again and his nostrils flared. The top row of his straight white teeth appeared to bite down on his bottom lip. She watched blood rise to the surface of that delicate skin. Not wanting him to leave marks, she stretched up on her knees and kissed him.

Keeping him distracted this way, she managed to skim the rough material of his trousers down his thighs, baring him to the meager sunlight filtering from the small window near the door. Still, she had no trouble seeing everything that mattered.

"Lie back," she whispered against his lips.

He did so without question and only gave a slight grunt and grimace when his head cracked into the too-short wooden bed frame. Hannah giggled, amazed at how much mistreatment he was willing to overlook while she had her hand down his pants.

He gave her a long-suffering look and then returned her grin. "You're a bad girl, Hannah Blake," he told her. "Father Ignacio and the sisters over at the Home would be horrified if they knew what you were up to."

She tugged at his boots and removed his trousers the rest of the way. "I've always wanted to create a scandal," she tossed back impishly.

He gave a hearty chuckle, his hands spanning her narrow waist, stroking the baby-soft skin below her rib cage. "Well then, you've hooked up with the right man for sure, *notsa?ka?*. And if a scandal's what you want, I'll be more than happy to oblige."

"We'll see about that," she said, thinking of how high he was likely to jump if someone came knocking at the door in the next few minutes. He'd be hopping into his pants, racing out the back before she had a chance to ask who was there.

Then again, if anyone discovered she was in bed with a man without the benefit of marriage, she'd find herself out of a job faster than a flea could jump off a wet dog. If someone came to the door just then, she'd probably be right behind David, dashing for cover with a sheet wrapped under her arms.

Crouching over him, she ran her hands through his hair, letting the long, silky strands fall through her fingers. She pressed her lips to the hollow behind his ear and then took the lobe into her mouth, suckling gently. His hands on her waist tightened, but he didn't try to stop her.

Good boy, she thought with a devilish smile—one she hid behind the veil of her own hair, of course.

From his ear, she followed the line of his

jaw, the pulse at his throat, the fluted prominence of his collarbone. She kissed and licked every spare inch of his body, ignoring the clutch of his fingers at her hips. She thought the piercing dig of his nails might leave bruises, but she knew from previous experience with this man that any injuries she incurred during their lovemaking would be well worth the pleasure he could provide.

Her tongue dipped and whirled around his tiny male nipples. Her teeth nipped at the ladderlike ridges of his ribs, sticking out in sharp relief against his golden skin as he drew in an agonized breath. She explored the indentation of his navel and smoothed her palms over the twin rises of his jutting pelvic bones.

He gave an audible hiss as her fingers dusted the short, crisp hairs that formed a triangle around his hardened length. Her heart was pounding at the idea of what she might do next, but she loved David and knew she was safe with him. No matter what she might say, or do, or think, or ask. He would never demean her or make fun of her for her actions or beliefs. She was also pretty sure he would enjoy what she had in mind, which only increased her level of courage and peace of mind.

Lifting her gaze, she cast him a timid smile before lowering her head once again. She'd never done anything like this before, wasn't sure she knew quite how to go about it. But she often told her students to take chances, to try new things, and it seemed now was the time to put her words into deed.

With her hand at the base of his manhood, she lightly kissed the tip. She stiffened, startled, when he gasped and his hips arched off the mattress.

"Are you all right?" she asked, concern etched between her brows.

"Not even close." His tone was harsh and halting.

Unsure, her hold on his member loosened. "Do you want me to stop?"

"Never."

She took a moment to absorb that. "Hold still, then," she told him, readjusting her grasp and inclining her head.

This time, she took more than just the tip into her mouth. Making a moue of her lips, she slipped them over the plum-shaped head of his manhood, letting her tongue taste and caress.

She felt David struggling for air, his body heaving as his fists curled savagely into the bedclothes. A blossom of power bloomed in her chest and spread out in all directions as she realized the powerful influence she had on him. Continuing her delicate ministrations, she licked the full length of his arousal. Up. Down. Around. Up again.

Her fingers fell away from the root of his

shaft and drifted south until they gently tickled his velvety pouch.

"That's it!" Bolting upright, he clamped his hands around her upper arms and forcibly pulled her away from his groin. "I can't take anymore."

Instead of pushing her to her back and hovering above her as she'd expected him to do, he dragged her toward him, until she reclined across his chest, her breasts pressed flat between them.

"I want you to try something new," he said. "This time, I want you on top."

Chapter Twenty-four

A spiral of desire unfurled low in her belly at the image his words invoked. He was the only man she'd ever been with, so all of this was new to her. But she was willing to try anything once—with him. She wanted to memorize every line and groove of his well-built frame, find out what made him sigh and moan and go tense beneath her touch.

His hands stroked over the rounded mounds of her backside and between her thighs to spread her legs and move them to straddle his hips. She'd always been a fast learner and didn't need to be told to slide up just a bit farther, center the cleft of her feminine opening over the head of his shaft, and slowly sink herself down on him.

Hannah's Half-Breed

Hannah bit her lip, fighting a sigh of complete and utter bliss. Her blood flowed hotter than the Texas sun. Her body was connected with David's in the most intimate fashion, in a position that made her feel dominant and in control. It was a heady sensation.

Placing her hands flat on his smooth, broad chest, she began to move. Slowly at first, forward and back, just enough to create a tempered friction.

David's fingers flexed and relaxed, flexed and relaxed in the cushiony swells of her hips. "I like this," he said, sounding slightly breathless. "You look good from down here."

She grinned, landing particularly hard on the downslide. "You look good from up here."

"Maybe we should make a pact to never"—*grunt*—"leave this bed. We could"—*deep breath*—"stay this way forever."

The heavy rise and fall of her chest matched his as the speed of their movements increased. "People would start to wonder"—*inhale*—"where we'd run off to. And"—*up*—"we'd likely starve"—*exhale*—"to death"—*down*—"if we never left the bed."

"We'll live on love"—*sigh*—"and whatever unlucky little birdies"—*moan*—"happen to fly through the window."

Grinning at his idyllic meanderings even as shocks of indescribable delectation rippled through to the tips of her fingers and toes, Hannah didn't know if she'd ever felt such

271

pleasure. His hands on her hips tightened, governing more of her motions.

"Whatever you want," she agreed, her body alive with molten delight.

When he answered, it was with a deep, rolling rumble of three simple words. "I want *you.*"

With that, he grabbed her by the shoulders and flipped her beneath him, thrusting faster and harder until neither of them could speak even if they'd wanted to. Hannah closed her eyes, arching her neck and back and locking her legs high about his waist.

Walker kept his eyes open even as the lightly veined, almost transparent lids over her own cornflower blue irises fluttered closed. Her long, sand-blond lashes curled delicately against her cheeks.

"*Nu? kamakuru mui,*" he whispered, knowing she wouldn't understand the meaning. "*Nu? kamakuru mui, nu? kamakuru mui, nu? kamakuru mui,*" he whispered over and over again.

Slipping his hand between their bodies, he found the tiny bud of her greatest pleasure and teased it with the tip of his finger, drawing a gasp of surprise from her lovely, dew-kissed lips as her body began to convulse in climax. A moment later, he bowed his head to join their mouths and followed her over the edge into ecstasy.

*   *   *

"Where are your sister and nephew, by the way?" she asked a good while later. She lay stretched across his long, hard body, drawing nonsensical designs along his chest and around the dark medallions of his nipples. He'd warned her a couple of times not to taunt the beast, but she ignored him and continued her cruel game.

"They're with my parents," he answered drowsily. "I don't want to leave them alone for long in case Lynch finds his way over there, but I thought they'd be all right for a few hours."

"You should bring them back here. If Lynch asks about you in town, people will point him directly to your family's home. But no one knows you've been staying here; they'd never suggest he look for Bright Eyes and the children anywhere near me."

Lifting her head, she propped her chin in the center of one well-defined pectoral muscle. He gave a small grunt of pain as the point of her jawbone dug in but didn't make her move.

His eyes drifted open, slowly revealing dark chocolate pools of cunning intelligence. He was entirely too handsome and too charming for his own good. And her virtue.

"That was before. Now that you've paraded me through Purgatory in the full light of day, tongues will be wagging about how well we've been getting along since our days at the Purgatory Home for Unwanted Children, and just what we've been up to more recently. Your name is bound to be mentioned somewhere along the line, and Lynch will surely hear it."

"So where are you going to hide them until he gives up looking?"

Lines of worry bracketed his soft mouth. "I have no idea."

Closing her eyes, she turned her head and rested her cheek on his chest. And then they popped open again as an idea came to her.

"Isn't your father friends with Wade Mason?"

"Who?"

"Wade Mason. He was sent to prison for murder and then later proved his innocence. I think your father helped him. He's married to Callie Quinn now and runs a very successful ranch."

David nodded in remembrance, but his brow was still pinched in confusion. "I know who he is, but I'm not following you. Why bring up his name?"

"Well . . ."

Drawing out her response, she sat up, stealing the crumpled sheet from where it covered his lower anatomy and tucking it about her breasts. David never even blinked, not the least bit abashed by his naked—and semi-aroused, she noted as warmth stained her cheeks—state.

"As I understand it, he has line shacks on his property so he or his ranch hands have a place to stay if they're out overnight repairing the fencing or looking for lost steers. Wouldn't a tiny shack that belongs to someone you barely know and have never had any real connection to be a good place to secure your sister and her children until the danger of Lynch finding them has passed? And if that doesn't work, I believe Mr. Mason owns a mine of some sort, too. Surely no one would think to look for a woman and two small children in a place like that."

A slow smile began to spread over David's face. He said nothing as the corners of his lips curled upward and his eyes took on a devilish glow.

"What?" she asked warily, leaning back even farther on the narrow mattress.

Propping himself up on his elbows, he asked, "Has anyone ever told you you're the brightest, most beautiful woman in all creation?"

She flushed self-consciously. "Not that I recall."

"Well, you are. The entire town of Purgatory is going to be university-bound with you as their teacher."

She averted her gaze, more flattered by his praise than she cared to admit.

"Don't turn shy on me now, *notsa?ka?*." He levered himself closer to where she sat cross-

275

legged at his side and ran the tip of one finger over her cheek, down the column of her neck, along one pale swell of breast sticking out above the edge of the sheet that covered her.

"Since you've got such a smart head on your shoulders, I'll let you tell me what you think we should do next: Go over to my mother's to collect Bright Eyes and the kids, then take them to Mason's ranch and see if he'll hide them for a while . . . or stay here a bit longer and make love again."

"You're asking me what I think we should do?" she charged, not at all happy with the decision she was apparently supposed to make. Already her heart was beating faster, and a slow, needy warmth was beginning to simmer in her belly.

He nodded, his wicked, dangerous fingertip sliding into the valley between her breasts and then back up over the opposite rise.

"My brain says we should probably leave for your parents' house now, before we get . . . distracted."

"And your body . . . ?" he prompted, pressing harder and letting his finger delve just beneath the doubled-up ridge of the bed linen.

She didn't even think about trying to lie to him or denying her own reactions. "Wants to stay right here, in this bed. Possibly for the next several days."

David chuckled, moving his face so close to hers, their noses brushed. His breath fanned her lips as he looked deep into her eyes. "We may not have days," he told her quietly, "but I think we can spare a couple more hours."

"I'm not sure that will be long enough, David," she said in a hushed voice, looping her arms about his neck.

The air caught in his lungs for a moment at her use of his Christian name. He opened his mouth to speak and ended up clearing his throat twice before the words came out.

"Why do you call me that?"

Her eyes rose to meet his. "Call you what?"

"David."

She laughed, a short huff of breath. "It's your name, isn't it? Why shouldn't I address you by your given name?"

"I told you to call me Walker." He wasn't angry with her, simply making a point. He didn't feel like David anymore; that frightened, outcast child with questionable bloodlines. He was Walker now, and no one in a long time—save his mother—had disputed his decision. That Hannah would caught him off guard and made him uneasy.

She sat up straighter, her shoulders tensing and her lips going flat. "Just because you tell me something, David Walker," she told him primly, "doesn't mean I'm going to do it."

He shook his head. "That's not what I meant. It's only . . . when I ask anyone else to call me Walker, they do, even if they're aware that I used to be known as David." Meeting her eyes, he asked quietly, "Why don't you, Hannah?"

Reaching out, she brushed her knuckles softly across his temple. "Because you're not Spirit Walker or Walker to me. You're just David, David. The boy I grew up with. The adolescent I dreamed about and followed around like a lovesick puppy dog. The man I fell in love with. You'll always be simply David to me."

His chest hurt. Drawing a breath was impossible and his head began to spin. His hand darted up, grabbing her wrist as she caressed his scalp. But he wasn't upset, he was . . . moved. Profoundly humbled and unsure of how to respond.

Bringing her hand to his mouth, he kissed the palm and then the pulse point half hidden by his grip. He loved her, too. And though the words were clawing their way up his throat, he couldn't seem to say them. Not in a language she would understand. He was still too scared and floundering from everything he'd learned today. The trip to town, Hannah's revelation. It all coiled together, putting him off balance and muddling his thoughts like the aftermath of a hailstorm.

But he could tell her in Comanche, as he had before. And he could show her with actions what he couldn't seem to say in plain English.

He pressed his lips to hers and whispered, *"Nʉ? kamakʉrʉ mʉi,* Hannah."

She pulled away slightly, looking at him askance. "You've said that before. What does it mean?"

With a shake of his head, he repeated, *"Nʉ? kamakʉrʉ mʉi,"* and pressed her back into the mattress.

He covered her mouth with his own before she could question him further and used his hands and body to convey the emotions he was still too weak a man to confess.

Chapter Twenty-five

It was just past lunchtime when Hannah and Walker finally began to make their way to his parents' house. She'd insisted on washing up and changing clothes after they'd made love a second and then a third time. He'd been happy to remain reclining across the lumpy, narrow mattress, the covers even more rumpled than before and twisted over the more prominent parts of his form.

He enjoyed watching her, studying her lithe, graceful movements, and even offered to brush her hair before she plaited the long, silken tresses into a loose braid and fastened a bright yellow ribbon on the end.

When she was dressed and ready to go, he rolled out of bed and tugged his shirt and trousers back on. With his old, dusty boots on his feet and his own shoulder-length hair tied back with a thin strip of rawhide, he held out his arm to her and they set off.

Along the way, they chatted and laughed and exchanged kisses that were positively chaste compared to the kind they were used to sharing. But Walker knew better than to let things get carried away. If he did, they might never make it to his mother's.

High-pitched, excited children's voices reached their ears long before the sprawling, two-story house came into view. As they neared the yard, Little Bear charged around the corner of the barn, closely followed by Walker's much younger sisters, Olivia and Emily. Both wore plain, unadorned dresses that fell just below their knees, splotched with dirt and grass stains. Both wore their curly, dark red hair in double braids halfway down their backs.

Poor Little Bear looked like he was being chased by a band of armed warriors. And Walker knew from past experience with his sisters that if they caught the boy, he'd likely be wishing for torture at the hands of brutal, spear-clad tribesmen.

Luckily for Little Bear, just as he trundled up the front porch steps, tripped, and would have been set upon by the shrieking girls, they spotted their brother. Screeching to a halt, they left twin sets of ruts in the ground with the heels of their shoes and made an about-face, heading straight for Walker.

"David!" they screamed in unison.

He let go of Hannah's hand and braced himself as they barreled toward him, wrapping themselves about his waist.

"You're home! You're home!" Olivia, the older of the two, cried.

He laughed. "I haven't been gone that long, sweetpea. We ate breakfast together this morning."

"But it seems like forever," she told him, using her favorite I-can-make-you-feel-guilty-for-anything tone.

"We was afraid you was never comin' back," Emily put in.

He swung the child onto his hip, hugging the other tight to his side. "Of course I came back. I told you before, even though I sometimes go away for a while, I'll always come back."

"Mama says the same thing. Only she worries you'll fall in love with an Indian girl in the Comanche village someday and be so busy with your life there that we'll hardly ever see you. That makes Mama cry."

Hannah watched David's face very carefully after that revelation. Leave it to outspoken, uninhibited Olivia Walker to pass along information her mother probably hadn't meant David to hear. He gave her a wry smile, followed by what she could have sworn was a blush of embarrassed color to his cheeks.

Doing his best to turn the girls' attention away from anything else his mother might have said that he didn't want Hannah to hear, David set Emily back on her feet and pried their fingers loose of his clothing, turning them to face her. "Olivia, Emily, you know Miss Blake, don't you?" he asked.

Olivia straightened immediately, looking ashamed that she'd acted so childish in front of her teacher. "Hello, Miss Blake."

"Hello, Olivia. How have you been?"

"Fine, thank you. Mama says I haven't had to go to school lately because you've been away. Now that you're back, does that mean classes will start again?"

"Bright and early Monday morning," Hannah told her cheerfully. Olivia didn't look quite as enthusiastic.

"And how have you been, Emily?" she addressed the other, younger girl.

"Fine, thank you," she singsonged loudly, mimicking her sister. "You're the schoolteacher from town, the one who teached my sister her letters."

"That's right," Hannah replied, ignoring the child's grammar.

"Mama says I'll be old enough to go to school next year and that you'll teach me my letters, too."

"I sure will. Your letters, and numbers, and everything else. Would you like that?"

"I suppose," the girl answered, twisting the toe of one shoe back and forth in the dirt. "Mama says I have to stay at school all day and I've never been away from my mama for that long before."

Hannah's heart twisted as the child's bottom lip began to quiver, and she quickly hunkered down until she was level with Emily's hazel eyes.

"That's true," she told the girl, "but it's not as bad as it sounds, especially since your sister will be there with you. The time goes by very quickly, and we stop lessons a couple of times a day so the younger students can go outside and play. And there's always the midday meal. You can eat your lunch outdoors when the weather is agreeable, and your mama can come by to see you then, if you like. There are lots of other kids around for you to make friends with, too."

Softening her voice conspiratorially, she added, "You'll be so busy, you probably won't miss your mama much at all after the first day. But don't tell her that or it might hurt her feelings."

Emily's vision was no longer damp and she seemed to seriously consider Hannah's words. Glancing at her sister, she waited for Olivia to indicate whether Hannah was telling the truth. When Olivia gave an affirmative nod of her head, Emily in turn inclined her head in understanding at Hannah.

The four of them stood in silence for a moment, and then David's gaze went to the front of the house. "You can come out now, *ara?*. I'm pretty sure the girls are finished chasing you for the time being."

Hannah turned to see the boy standing— or, more probably, hiding—behind the white slatted railing of the porch. He looked at the two girls, who made no move to tackle him again, and started warily down the steps toward his uncle.

"Where's your mother?" David asked.

"Inside. With the lady."

"That lady is my mother," David told his nephew without censure. "My white mother, anyway, and a very nice woman. Besides, I thought she said you could call her Regan or Mrs. Walker."

Little Bear nodded, looking a little sheepish.

"Have you and the girls been getting along?" David wanted to know.

At that, the boy's eyes went wide, and he shook his head emphatically. "They're *mean*, *ara?*," he declared. "They poke fun at me and chase me, and right after you left, they tried to put ribbons in my hair. They wanted to make me look like a girl."

"He has such fine hair, David," Olivia put in. "Long and straight and soft. We don't know anybody who has such straight hair. No

285

boys, at least, 'cept you. We just wanted to play with it a bit."

Hannah chewed hard on the inside of her lip to keep from laughing at Little Bear's horrified expression. Aside from the fact that he'd been an only child for the past seven years, he'd probably never in his entire life encountered two girls quite as exuberant and opinionated as the Walker children. From her experience, they seemed to take after their mother. Which didn't bode well for Little Bear, if they'd set their narrow sights on him already.

"Let's go in the house," David suggested, taking her hand as the children ran off ahead of them. Little Bear hung back, noticeably avoiding getting too close to the spirited girls.

"I want to talk to Ma and Bright Eyes about this new plan of yours to hide them away in one of Wade Mason's line shacks," David continued. "Then I think I'll ride into town and see if Pa wants to go over there with me to see if Mason is amiable to the idea."

As they started up the front porch steps, he leaned close to press a kiss to her cheek. "Will you be all right here with Regan and Bright Eyes and the kids while I take care of the details?"

"I'll be fine." She smiled reassuringly, thinking how sweet it was for him to be concerned about her comfort. "I like your mother and sister. And I happen to have quite a bit of experience dealing with young children for long periods of time. Besides," she added with a wry smile, "it's probably a good idea for me to stick around and see that your sisters don't try to dress up Little Bear like one of their dollies."

He grinned. "From the sound of things, that could be an imminent possibility."

As he held the door open for her and ushered her into the house, she shot over her shoulder in a hushed whisper, "When you get back from your errand, you may just find that you have two new nieces instead of only one."

"And *Ta?ahpʉ* help me if they turn out to be anything like my little sisters."

"Please?"

"No."

"Please?"

"No!"

"Please? Please? *Please?*"

"*No!*"

"Miss Blake, tell Little Bear he has to play with us."

"Tell them to leave me alone, Hannah," the boy put in desperately. "They want to play army and tie me up like a Comanche prisoner."

Hannah dragged her gaze from where she'd been searching the distance to find a deep scowl on Little Bear's face. She couldn't blame him. Ever since they'd all come out on the porch to see David off on his trip to town and then on to the Mason ranch, and the children had decided to stay outside and play, Olivia and Emily had been badgering Little Bear over one thing or another.

He'd apparently learned early on that trying to avoid them didn't work, either. If he stayed indoors with his mother, the girls stayed indoors, too. If he came outside to get away from them, they followed. And no matter which, they tortured him mercilessly, wanting to dress him up, tie him up, or decorate his hair with ribbons and bows.

"Girls, he shouldn't have to play if he doesn't want to," she told them, swaying gently back and forth in a rocking chair on the porch while they stared up at her from the yard below.

"Or perhaps you're just not suggesting the kinds of games he'd like."

Both girls cocked their heads to the side as though they'd never before considered asking Little Bear what he'd like to do.

"I think he'd enjoy something more along the lines of playing Indian raid. Wouldn't you, Little Bear? You could take Olivia and Emily as hostages, tie them to trees, maybe even shoot them with arrows." She added the last with a sly wink to Little Bear, followed by an encouraging nod.

"That doesn't sound as fun as us tying him up," Olivia complained.

But Little Bear seemed to understand Hannah's meaning and turned on the girls. Before he made even a single move in their direction, they both opened their mouths, screamed at the top of their lungs, and started running as fast as their little legs could carry them into the trees near the barn. Tables turned, Little Bear threw Hannah a wide, grateful grin, and then took off after them.

Hannah chuckled, watching them go. She was happy to sit out here with the children and keep them occupied while Regan and Bright Eyes both took a much-needed, child-free rest. But really, she wanted to stay on the porch so she could watch for David's return.

He hadn't been gone that long yet, perhaps an hour or two, but still she felt the need to stand guard, in a manner of speaking, awaiting his return.

For the last little while, she'd been noticing a cool breeze moving in and a blanket of dark clouds floating across the late afternoon sky, and a clap of thunder far overhead confirmed her suspicions. A storm was brewing, and rolling in fast, as was typical of summer weather in Texas. If David didn't get home soon, he was sure to get caught in the downpour and end up soaked to the skin.

As the first raindrops began to fall, Hannah got up from the rocker and made her way down the porch steps. "Kids!" she called, walking in the direction in which the children had disappeared. "Olivia! Emily! Little Bear! It's starting to rain. I think we should go in."

Entering the woods at the far end of the yard, she found the two girls bound and gagged to a wide tree trunk with what appeared to be strips from their own small petticoats. They weren't tied tightly, she noticed, but it was enough to keep them still and quiet. Probably for the first time in their young lives, judging by the amount of energy they normally exuded.

A very smug Little Bear stood a few feet away, smiling broadly. "You were right, Hannah, it's better to play Comanche warrior and his captives."

At that, the girls let out muffled shrieks of indignation.

"All right," she said around a chuckle. "You've had your fun. Untie them so we can get into the house before we get any wetter."

Little Bear did as she asked, dodging slaps and punches and ignoring the girls' outraged tirades. It took several minutes for Hannah to regain order, but finally she had the girls calmed down and everyone headed back to the house.

As they were crossing the yard, Hannah thought she heard hoofbeats. When she paused, quirking an ear to listen, the children stopped with her.

Sure enough, three riders came into view in the far distance. Her heart skipped its rhythm as she realized they must be David, his father, and Wade Mason. If Mr. Mason was along, they must be coming to take Bright Eyes, Little Bear, and the baby to one of the line shacks on his property for safe-keeping.

She smiled, waiting for them to ride closer, a hand over her eyes to protect them from the now hard-falling rain. Her dress was beginning to cling to the curves of her body, her braided hair sagging with the growing weight of its dampness.

But it wasn't a cold rain, and getting wet was a small price to pay to see David safely returned. The children apparently agreed, for they stood at Hannah's side, equally uncaring of the rain.

But the closer the men got, the more the warm, happy feeling in her belly turned cold and dark. She felt suddenly anxious . . . and then downright frightened.

This wasn't David riding into the yard with his father and friend. This was someone else altogether. Someone bad, someone . . . dangerous.

Chapter Twenty-six

"Little Bear. Get in the house, and take the girls with you."

"But—"

"*Now,*" she ordered sharply without bothering to turn in his direction. Her only assurance that they did what she told them was the sound of several small pairs of feet pattering across the damp ground and up the front steps.

The children had no sooner run out of sight than the three strangers rode into the yard, stopping a scant few yards from where she stood.

The man in the middle looked to be tall and rangy, with a thin, dark mustache curving over the top of his sneering lips. Rain splattered off the brim of his hat and fell to the front of the variegated Mexican-style parka he wore to protect himself from the elements. The other two men were similarly dressed.

"Howdy, ma'am," the lead fellow greeted. "You're getting mighty wet standing out here in the rain."

Hannah clenched her teeth to keep them from chattering. The warm summer rain was drenching her clothes and seeping through to her skin, but the chill came entirely from the sinister sensation emanating from the men before her.

"Can I help you?" she asked without preamble, setting hands on hips and standing her ground in the hope that they would realize they weren't welcome and leave.

"As a matter of fact, maybe you can, ma'am. We're looking for some people. An Injun squaw and her bastard son. The woman was breeding, so she may have two bastards with her by now."

Eyes narrowed, Hannah studied the men before her, trying to recognize which of them might have burst into the room where David had hidden his family and had her play the part of a paid companion back at the Devil's Den. She couldn't tell, but felt strongly that these were the same fellows who had been searching Hell for Bright Eyes and Little Bear. She also wondered briefly how they could justify calling anyone else a bastard

293

when they were obviously less than respectable citizens themselves.

"I'm sorry, I don't know who you're talking
about."

The man in the middle, stationed slightly
ahead of the other two, the one she assumed
was the notorious Ambrose Lynch, leaned
forward in his saddle and narrowed his ugly,
beady eyes on her. "You sure, little lady? We
were told the squaw's half-breed brother lives
here with his family." He spat the last word,
making his opinion of a part-Comanche living with whites clear as a windowpane.

Hannah took a deep breath, biting off a
rude retort. Instead, she smiled at the man
who had so mistreated Bright Eyes, her son,
and her unborn child.

"Quite sure, sir. I think I would know if a
half-breed had taken up residence in my
house." It made her physically ill to use those
words, and to lace them with such derision.
But if adopting an attitude similar to his own
got Lynch and his men away from Bright
Eyes, it would be worth suffering through her
nausea and crawling skin.

Obviously doubting her claim, Lynch
glanced around, looking toward the barn, the
paddock, the wooded area at her back. Then
he examined the house, his gaze lingering on
the windows as though he might spot his
quarry.

"If that's all you needed," she interrupted

his study of the property, "I think I'll go inside now. I am getting wet, as you pointed out."

He pulled his gaze back to her and ogled her bosom, where wet fabric no doubt outlined the curve of her breasts. His mouth turned up into what could only be described as a leer.

A shiver of revulsion rolled down Hannah's spine. *Leave*, she silently begged. *Leave, leave, leave*.

Finally, he shifted on his mount and with two fingers tipped his hat down a fraction more over his brow. "Well, we'll be on our way, then. Thanks anyway, ma'am."

The breath rushed from her lungs in relief as the men turned their horses. Then, just as they started away, three more riders came into the yard.

As soon as David saw her standing behind the group of strangers, he kicked Thunder into a gallop and raced to her side. Jumping to the ground, he pulled her against him and raked his concerned eyes over her rain-soaked form.

"Are you all right?" he demanded, shooting Ambrose Lynch a murderous glare. "Did he hurt you? Touch you?"

"No, no, I'm fine." She brushed a strand of wet hair away from her eyes, ignoring the bite of David's fingers as they dug into her upper arm.

Lynch and his men had swung around once

again to face her and David. In response to David's protective stance, David's father and Wade Mason had come around to flank him on either side. They remained in their saddles, offering added protection without a word, and Hannah noticed both men slowly move their hands to rest on the butts of their sidearms.

"And you said you didn't know no half-breeds," Lynch taunted nastily. "Why, there's an Injun right there, missy, and you seem to be awful friendly with him."

"Back off, Lynch," David growled. He stepped forward, putting an arm out to keep her safely behind him. "She's not a part of this."

"No, she's not," Lynch returned. "But you are, ain't you, Walker? Come to my ranch to visit your sister and end up stealing my wife and son away."

"Bright Eyes isn't your wife," David spat, "she's a woman you keep around to abuse. And I wouldn't have had to steal them away if you hadn't been beating them, you bastard."

Swinging his leg over the saddle and hopping to the ground, Lynch was careful not to make any sudden moves that might invite Sheriff Walker or Wade Mason to shoot him. Of course, his men had their hands on their firearms, too, which could create a deadly crossfire.

"They belong to me," Lynch hissed. "I can do anything I like with them."

David's voice grew just as cold, just as dangerous. "The hell you can."

"The hell I can't." In the blink of an eye, Lynch drew his weapon, leveling it at David's midsection.

Hannah gave a squeak of horrified shock, but just as quickly, Clay, Wade, David, and Lynch's two still-mounted men all had their pistols out and aimed at different targets.

Lynch laughed, a rusty, demented sound. "If you're here, my wife is here. Send the squaw out, half-breed, and nobody has to get hurt."

"She isn't your wife, Lynch," David said again. "You never married her; you stole her from her village and her family. You used her like a common trollop, and abused both her and your son. You beat her so badly she almost lost her second baby, and you'll burn in hell before I let you near any of them ever again."

Lynch took a menacing step closer and Hannah's nails curled instinctively into the material at David's waist.

"You can't keep them from me. And if you try, I'd be more than happy to put a bullet between your eyes, Walker." He brought up his gun, pointing it directly at David's forehead.

Hannah's heart stopped and she envisioned

herself screaming, throwing herself in front of David and taking the bullet into her own body instead. But in reality, she merely stood there, rooted to the ground, frozen in absolute terror. The minute Lynch raised his gun, five triggers cocked, ringing in her ears like a dynamite blast.

"You might want to remember where you are, Lynch," Sheriff Walker put in mildly.

Hannah didn't know how he managed to sound so calm when her lungs hadn't expanded once in the last full minute.

"This is my town," he went on, "and that's my son whose head your weapon is pointed at. Not only do I have enough justification right now to drag your ass to jail, but no one would think twice if I shot you where you stand."

Lynch smirked, never taking his eyes off David. "I wouldn't be so sure about that, Sheriff. Make a move against me, and my two boys, here, will testify that you killed me in cold blood. You'll be the one rotting in a prison cell . . . if they don't hang you first."

"Don't threaten my father, Lynch," David growled. "You've done enough damage to my family already."

Lynch lowered his revolver to the area of David's heart but didn't back away. "I'm not leaving without that squaw and her kids."

It was a standoff, and Hannah's pulse raced

as she imagined the only way it could end—with deaths on both sides.

And then a noise from behind caught her attention.

She tilted her head slightly to the right and saw Bright Eyes come out onto the porch, careful to stay out of the rain. The baby was in the cradleboard in her mother's arms, Little Bear following close at her side. His small hand was clutched tightly around the doeskin of Bright Eyes's dress.

A few steps behind, just this side of the doorway, stood Regan Walker. Her curly red hair was pulled away from her face and a forest green gown hugged her womanly curves. And in her arms she held a rifle; there was no question she was ready and willing to protect her family—extended or otherwise—in any way necessary. Her daughters and her mother-in-law, Martha Doyle, crowded around her, craning their necks to see what was going on.

"I won't go back with you, Ambrose."

Bright Eyes's strong voice caused Lynch and his men to whirl in her direction. David and the others kept their eyes and weapons trained on the intruders before them.

"Come down here, woman," Lynch ordered, "and bring those brats with you. I'm taking you all back to the Bar L where you belong."

Turning toward Martha, Bright Eyes handed

over the cradleboard and gently said something to Little Bear to keep him on the porch. Then she straightened, standing tall, and came down the porch steps into the muddy yard. She ignored the rain completely, making her way toward Lynch and halting less than a foot in front of him.

"We don't belong with you and we won't go back," she said firmly. "You treated us very badly, Ambrose. You don't deserve us any longer."

"Who the hell do you think you're talking to, squaw?" His face flushed red with indignation.

He reached out to grab her arm, and David immediately reacted to stop him. But before either of them could make contact, Bright Eyes took a step back, out of Lynch's grasp, and shook her head.

"No. We are through with you, Ambrose Lynch. You do not love us or you would not treat us as you have. We want nothing more to do with you. Ever."

Grinding his teeth, Lynch sputtered, unused to having anyone—let alone a Comanche woman—refuse him.

"Do you think I'll let you get away with this? Even if your *friends* here," he spat the word, "keep me from taking you today, I'll only come back for you later."

"Do not bother," Bright Eyes answered before anyone else had a chance to come to her defense. "We will not go, no matter when you come or where you find us. And do not think that just because my brother has protected us until now that I cannot protect myself. When I leave here, I will take my children back to the Comanche. If you come there, I will have the warriors in the village capture you and stake you naked to the hot ground. They will cut you, many times and all over your body. They will leave you bleeding and in agony . . . and then the animals will come, drawn to the smell of your blood. First the ants, who crawl into the wounds and nibble at your flesh. And then the skunks, raccoons, and coyotes. Finally the buzzards will swoop down to pluck out your eyes and spread your entrails across the land."

Her voice grew stronger as she went on, and Hannah suspected she enjoyed drawing a gruesome picture of torture and suffering for Lynch.

From the look of things, it was working. Lynch swallowed hard, his skin blanching.

"This is what awaits you, should I or mine ever see you again, Ambrose Lynch. I promise your demise will be slow and painful."

Several long heartbeats ticked by in utter silence except for the rain pattering against the ground and the roofs of the house and barn. Lynch's fearful gaze went from his supposed wife to his children on the porch, to David and everyone who stood behind him in support of Bright Eyes. And then his gun arm began to lower and he slowly holstered his revolver.

"You always were more trouble than you were worth. I'd be better off finding me another squaw than wasting any more time on you." Turning his head, he spat less than an inch from Bright Eyes's moccasin-clad feet. "Go where you like, and take those bastard half-breeds with you."

Spinning, he strode to his mount and pulled himself into the saddle. Following their boss's lead, his men replaced their weapons and awaited further orders.

"One more thing, Lynch," Sheriff Walker put in. "You're not welcome in Purgatory. Show your face in my town and I'll toss you in a hole so deep, you'll never see daylight again." He paused, letting a meaningful moment pass. "If I don't shoot you first."

Without another word and only a deep-set glower etching his brow, Ambrose Lynch turned his horse and rode off, his men close behind.

The remaining adults and children all stood stock-still, watching the three riders disappear into the rain-streaked horizon. As soon as they were out of sight, everyone turned around, exchanging glances. And then they grinned. Grins were quickly followed by low chuckles, the chuckles blossoming into full-blown laughter.

David grabbed his sister and hugged her close, then reached for Hannah and did the same, lifting her off the ground. Hannah buried her nose in his neck, still smiling in triumph. Even when he set her on her feet and loosened his arms from her waist, he kept her hand tightly clasped in his own.

More than content to maintain physical contact with him, she leaned her back against his broad chest and pivoted toward Bright Eyes. "You were wonderful," she said. "I'm so proud of you for standing up to him like that."

"I was shaking the whole time," Bright Eyes admitted, her mouth twisting wryly. "But what I said is true . . . I will not allow him to treat us that way any longer. I will not continue to put my children in danger."

Hannah laughed. "I don't think you have to worry. Your description of staking him in the desert for wild animals to eat scared the life out of him. He won't bother you again anytime soon."

"He'd better not," David growled, and she could feel the tension still vibrating through his body.

Turning to Wade Mason, he said, "It seems we won't be needing to borrow one of your line shacks after all. Sorry to have dragged you out here for nothing."

"Are you kidding?" Mason returned with a lopsided grin, pushing the brim of his hat higher on his head, his arms crossed over the saddle pommel. "I wouldn't have missed this for the world. Besides, I owe your father," he added without elaboration.

Nodding to David, Sheriff Walker, Hannah, Bright Eyes, and the ladies on the porch, he straightened, clicked to his horse, and started to leave. "If you need anything else, just give a holler."

"Thanks, Wade. We'll see you soon," Sheriff Walker said with a wave.

As soon as Mason was out of sight, David gave Hannah's arm a tug. "We'd better get you two inside before you catch your death. You're already soaked to the skin." He ran a hand up and down the arm of her dress, where the fabric clung like honey.

"You get them inside," Clay said, reaching for the loose reins of David's abandoned stallion. "I'll get the horses put away, then be right in."

David followed them up the steps and onto the porch, where Bright Eyes took the baby back from Martha. The child fussed in her cradleboard, her tiny pink mouth twisting as she worked herself into a fit.

"This is a good day to give her a name, don't you think?" Bright Eyes asked, looking over her shoulder at her brother.

"I do. What have you decided on?"

"Because of her and Little Bear, today I

304

found the courage to leave Ambrose Lynch forever. To remember this day and mark her as truly free, I think I will call her . . . Laughing Rain."

Chapter Twenty-seven

The mood under the Walker roof the rest of the evening was celebratory, to say the least. Everyone was happy and full of laughter, relieved that the confrontation with Ambrose Lynch had ended well, glad that Bright Eyes and her children were safe.

Regan insisted Hannah stay for dinner, and the three women worked side by side to prepare a feast that made the long dining table creak with its weight. Hannah enjoyed herself immensely, with the children underfoot and Regan trying hard not to pry into Hannah's relationship with her son. Hannah could tell she was dying of curiosity, especially since she and David had come into the yard together, hand in hand, before Lynch's arrival.

But for the most part, Regan managed to hold her tongue. She didn't ask too many pointed questions and only slipped once or twice by implying that Hannah might soon be her daughter-in-law.

Since Hannah was no more certain of her future with David than Regan was, the attention made her slightly uncomfortable, but she tried not to let it show.

The rain let up while they were eating, and even though it was wet and dark outside, and Regan offered her a room for the night, Hannah insisted on going back to her own cabin. The Walkers were wonderful people and she enjoyed their company, but the house was full enough with Bright Eyes and Little Bear staying there. And, she admitted—if only to herself—she was hoping for a bit more time alone with David.

She breathed a sigh of relief when he offered to walk her home. Though if he hadn't, she'd have probably asked him to accompany her.

The threat of Ambrose Lynch coming after or harming Bright Eyes and her children was past, along with David's need for Hannah—as a protective shield for his sister and a place to hide his nephew. She liked to think she meant more to him than that—much more—but unless he said so, she might never know for sure. Once she had him alone, she hoped to ask him straight out what his intentions toward her were . . . if the butterflies in her stomach settled down enough for her to get the words out.

Saying good-bye and waving to the children, they made their way into the darkness toward the path that would lead to her cabin.

Hannah's dress was dry now, thanks to Regan, who had lent her a conservative wrap to wear while they prepared dinner and her wet garments hung near the heat of the cookstove. Even so, the rain had cooled things off and the evening air cut through her clothes to draw gooseflesh on her arms. She rubbed them absentmindedly, trying to think of what to say to David and how to broach the topic of their future together.

"Are you cold?" he asked, breaking the awkward silence that had fallen between them. Cicadas chirped and leaves rustled around them, but they hadn't said a single word to each other since leaving his mother's house.

"I'm all right," she answered.

Wrapping an arm about her shoulders, he pulled her close, nestling her against his side. "You look cold."

She allowed his embrace for a long minute, wondering how she could suddenly be so uncomfortable with the same man who fewer than twelve hours earlier had been in her bed, very creatively making love to her numerous times.

It wasn't David who made her uncomfortable, though. It was the idea that he could touch her so sweetly that she wanted to weep and then walk away. That he could push aside the heat and passion between them because of the prejudices some held toward him, imagined or otherwise.

The truth was, people here in Texas and in the rest of the western states did think badly of Indians, regardless of the tribe or that they might also be part white. But she thought she'd shown him that the citizens of Purgatory felt no animosity toward him, at least not most of them.

David's beliefs were deep-rooted, however, and even the support of the townspeople might not be enough to convince him to give their love a chance.

And what if he didn't love her as much as she loved him? What if he didn't love her at all?

Tears stung the backs of her eyes and her heart thundered against her rib cage at the very thought. And yet that was what had been bothering her all along. What if his Comanche blood was only an excuse not to stay with her?

Heaven help her, if that was the case and he'd seduced her, never truly feeling anything for her, she would take a page from Bright Eyes's book and stake him spread-eagled in the desert for wild animals to devour. She might even stick around to watch.

Red-hot rage replaced the fear and uncertainty that had swamped her earlier. "David, there are a few things we need to discuss," she blurted suddenly, her fists clenching and unclenching at her sides. She felt his chest expand as he took a deep breath, then let it out, never breaking stride.

"I know," he said simply.

She waited, tense, for him to elaborate.

"Bright Eyes wants to return to the Comanche village. Lynch won't be troubling her again, so she and the children will be safe there."

"I'm glad." Hannah wasn't sure what that had to do with her and David, but she was as relieved as everyone else that his sister would no longer be under Ambrose Lynch's heavy, aggressive thumb.

"She's asked me to escort her," he continued, "and I've said I would."

"Of course," she said quickly. "You should take them back. It will give you a chance to visit your family and friends in the village, too."

David's words made sense, as did her response to them, and yet she felt as though she was wading through a knee-deep mire of confusion. There was something else going on, another point to their conversation that she couldn't seem to comprehend.

This wasn't what she'd intended when she

said they had things to discuss . . . and she thought David knew as much.

"I . . . may not be visiting," he said finally, his low, rough voice reluctant.

A surge of dread swept over her body. "What do you mean?"

"I may . . ."

She looked up in time to see his Adam's apple bob as he swallowed.

"I may stay, Hannah."

His declaration stopped her in her tracks. He went another step farther, then turned to face her when he realized she wasn't with him.

"So that's it," she said, her tone cold and unemotional. "You're leaving and you're not coming back."

"I didn't say I was never coming back. I just think it would be best if I stayed away for a while, gave us both some time to think."

Crossing her arms beneath her breasts, she fixed him with an angry glare. "What is there to think about, David? You either love me or you don't. You're either willing to stay and marry me and take whatever comes, or you're not."

She hadn't meant to put it that way, to say quite so much. But now that it was out, she felt better. She was also giving him a chance to fall on his knees and declare his undying love for her.

So far, he wasn't falling, and her chest

hitched painfully at the idea that he might not.

"I love you," she went on, knowing she had to get out everything she had to say now or hold it in forever and watch him walk away. "I'm willing to marry you and take whatever comes. I don't care what anyone thinks or says. I don't care if all your worst nightmares about the two of us being together come to pass. If the citizens of Purgatory band together against us and run us out of town, if I lose my job and we have to live in one of those squalid little shacks in Hell. I don't care, because I love you, David. I want to be your wife and the mother of your children and die in your arms when I'm an old, old woman."

With each word, she saw David's cheeks grow paler in the dappled moonlight. His teeth grated together and a muscle in his jaw spasmed erratically.

"The question is, do you love me?" She waited for a single heartbeat to pass, and then asked again, softly, "Do you love me, David?"

"More than my own life," he answered, his voice ragged, as though the words were being dragged from the very depths of his soul.

Closing the distance between them, he grasped her shoulders, clutching them tightly. "You have no idea, Hannah. It seems like I've loved you forever, since we were kids in that damn orphanage. And in Comanche, I've told you a thousand times. But it's not that simple. I'm a half-breed, Hannah, and no matter where we go, people will only see a man with red skin and long black hair standing beside a woman who couldn't be whiter if she bathed in lye, with her cornsilk hair and blue, blue eyes. People will stare and point and taunt. And even if we were strong enough to ignore all that, our children would suffer even more."

"What others think is more important than us being together? Is that what you're saying, David?" She understood, she really did, even as she wanted to grab him by the ears and shake some sense into him.

"You don't know what it's like to be young and tormented because you're different. Because you're an Indian." Releasing his grip on her arms, he took a step back, a grave look on his face. "I won't do that to you, Hannah, and I won't do that to an innocent child."

"What if it's already done?" she asked quietly. "What if we've already made a baby? We've certainly been together often enough for it to be a possibility. If a child is already on the way, he or she will be part Indian. Everything you've said could very well happen. Will you make that child a bastard as well?"

The tick in his jaw jumped again. "Are you pregnant, Hannah?" he ground out. "Do you know for sure?"

"I don't know. It's too soon to even suspect. But what will you do if I am?"

"If you're pregnant, I'll marry you," he said, as though it was a death sentence.

The fight went out of her suddenly, along with the vehemence in her voice. Her crossed arms fell limply to her sides and she walked past him, continuing toward her cabin. "Don't bother. I don't want you to marry me because I'm in a family way. I want you to marry me because you can't imagine your life without me."

He caught up with her, tugging at her elbow. "But if there's a child . . ."

"Let me make this easy for you, David," she said, both tired and sad. "Even if it does turn out that I'm to have a baby, I won't marry you. Not if you ask, not if you beg, not if you abduct me and take me across the border into Mexico. Go back to your village, David. I wish you and your sister well. Tell Little Bear I'll miss him."

And then she shook off his touch and started away before he saw the tears that streaked her face or heard the wrenching misery in her sobs.

"Son of a bitch." Walker swore twice in every language he knew. And then he started all over again.

He'd really bungled this, hadn't he? And now, in addition to hurting Hannah a hundred times worse than he'd intended, there was the possibility of an impending child to worry about.

Deep down in his gut, he hoped Hannah *was* pregnant. He wanted all of the things she'd spoken of—love, marriage, children, happily ever after. He wanted everything, and he wanted it with her.

The thought of making a baby with her—a tiny little girl with golden hair and robin's egg blue eyes, or a little boy with . . . with black hair and sun-bronzed skin . . .

He pressed the heels of his hands to his eye sockets, trying to obliterate the heart-wrenching yearning that image brought to life. He wanted it, more than he cared to admit. Even if their children all turned out to have dark hair and eyes and red skin. Even if their next twenty years together were miserable because people treated them like outcasts.

But wanting it didn't make it right. Wanting it didn't justify putting her or their children through the kind of torture he'd endured all his life. And regardless of her claims of being willing to put up with whatever hard times might come, she didn't realize just how hard those times could be. How could he tell her he loved her and then consign her to that kind of misery?

With a sigh of resignation, he started after Hannah, keeping well behind her and out of sight. He wouldn't approach her again; there was no sense continuing an argument with no apparent solution. But he did plan to see that she got home all right.

Keeping his distance, he followed silently, waiting until she'd reached her cabin and closed herself safely inside. The dim light of a lantern spilled through the small front windows, and he leaned a shoulder against the rough bark of a tall pine, straining for a last glimpse of Hannah before he had to leave.

And he did have to leave. He couldn't stay in Purgatory, where he would be within spitting distance of the woman he loved and still have to stay away from her. Going back to the Comanche village, at least for a while, was the intelligent thing to do. It would give him time to think without the temptation of sneaking off at all hours of the night to crawl into bed with Hannah.

His parents would keep an eye on her for him, though. If it turned out she was expecting a baby, he would come back. He would see that she and the child were taken care of, no matter what.

The yellow glow inside the cabin flickered a moment before all went dark. Pushing himself away from the wide tree, he straightened and steeled himself for the weeks to come.

"I do love you, Hannah," he whispered into the black night. And he would miss her, more than his own life. "Be happy, *notsa?ka?*."

Chapter Twenty-eight

Hannah stood at the back of the one-room schoolhouse while two of the older students worked through a complicated division problem at the blackboard and the younger children practiced writing their letters at their desks.

She'd done what she considered a remarkable job of hiding the fact that she was abjectly miserable every minute of every day. She was down to only crying into her pillow in the wee hours of the night, when biting the inside of her lip or pinching the flesh of her outer thigh until it was bruised to keep the tears at bay no longer worked. Whenever anyone asked, she blamed the lavender circles

Heidi Betts

under her eyes on staying awake far too late grading papers.

After the first week of startling at the smallest sound, praying it might be David or searching the distance hoping for some sign of him, she'd given up on his ever returning to Purgatory. He was gone and she was alone, and she would just have to come to terms with that, however agonizing the thought might be.

She had loved him since she was a girl and lived twenty-odd years without him. She supposed she could survive the next twenty without him, too.

Of course, now she knew more about him than when they'd been children. She knew what it felt like to be held in his arms. Knew he loved her, too—or at least claimed to, though he didn't seem willing to put his words to the test.

So the next few decades would be harder to pass than the first . . . she would still be all right. She would simply learn to smile as though her heart wasn't cracked in two, and replace her desolation with false happiness.

She rubbed her fingertips on either side of her head, over the throb of a headache that was brewing beneath her temples. One of the students at the blackboard called her name and she looked up, forcing her attention to the mathematical equation she'd given them to decipher.

While she concentrated on mentally putting the numbers in their proper order and following the line of her pupils' thinking, muffled noises from outside drifted into the schoolroom.

Hannah ignored them, used to the sounds of Purgatory during the day. The children were, too, but for some reason they had been distracted today. One at a time, they turned toward the back of the building, craning their necks as though they could see through the wall and closed double doors.

"Children, pay attention," she scolded, approving the two older boys' work at the blackboard with a smile before sending them back to their seats.

"What is that sound, Miss Blake?" one of the girls asked, still straining toward the back of the classroom, even though she'd been told to straighten up.

"I don't know, but I'm sure it's nothing you need to be concerned about."

Smoothing the back of her gray woolen skirt, she sat down at her wide, neatly organized desk at the front of the classroom. "Let's get back to our lessons," she said. "Penelope, would you like to be the first to read your report on George Washington?"

Penelope stood, paper in hand, but before she could make her way to the front of the room to speak, Olivia Walker darted out of her chair and raced to the doors, opening them a crack to peek out.

"Olivia, get back to your seat," Hannah ordered sternly, rising to her feet.

"Miss Blake, I think you should see this."

Rounding her desk, she started down the middle aisle between rows of desks, ready to twist Olivia's ear if necessary to get her back in her chair. "Penelope is about to read her report, Olivia, and I would appreciate it if you would show her the courtesy of sitting still until she's finished."

"But . . ." The girl glanced over her shoulder, her brows knit in a cross between concern at being in trouble with her teacher and an overwhelming curiosity at what was outside the schoolhouse doors. "I *really* think you should come and see this, Miss Blake."

At the plaintive whine of Olivia's voice, the entire class jumped up and raced to the back of the room. Hannah knew she had little chance of getting her students settled again until she found out what was so thoroughly distracting them.

Olivia Walker yanked the door open as Hannah approached. The hot afternoon sun beat down on her as she stood on the top step leading out of the schoolhouse, so bright she raised a hand to shield her eyes from the glare. Behind her, she felt the children brushing past her and barreling down the stairs.

She opened her mouth to call them back,

to assign some harsh punishment for their extraordinary disobedience. And then she noticed what had them in such an uproar. Several yards away, a mob of people was gathered, headed for the school and closing in fast.

At first Hannah thought something was wrong . . . or even that they might be coming for her. What if they'd found out about her time with David? About her—the unmarried, supposed-to-be-beyond-reproach schoolteacher—being alone and intimate with the son of the local sheriff in the outlaw town of Hell?

After a moment, however, she realized no one in the large crowd seemed angry. In fact, they were all smiling rather broadly as the students danced and jumped around, looking for their parents. She saw Clay and Regan Walker, Wade and Callie Mason, old Fergus McGee and his wife Nelda, the couple who owned the local hotel, and a number of other folks she recognized.

And if they were smiling, they couldn't be coming to fire her. *Could they?*

As they drew closer, Hannah's pulse picked up a burst of speed and then trickled off to a sap-slow gurgle.

David was at the front of the crowd, leading the swarming mass. The corners of his mouth lifted in a grin when he spotted her. But Hannah's mind had shut down completely because she couldn't think of a single reason for him to be back in Purgatory, let alone bearing down on her with a parade of townspeople trailing behind him.

Her nails dug into the rough, painted wood of the railing as they marched forward. She felt frozen in place, but if she'd been able to move, she thought she might have run back inside to hide under her desk.

The better part of the crowd halted several feet from the door of the schoolhouse, but David kept coming. Resting one hand on the end of the banister and a booted foot on the bottom step, he stood below her and tilted his head back, smiling.

"Hi there," he said softly.

Taking a deep breath, she steeled herself, trying not to notice how the midday sun turned his glossy black hair midnight blue and glinted off the bronze of his skin. Though it had been only a few weeks since she'd last seen him, she'd forgotten how fathomless his chocolate brown eyes could be, how the twitch of his lips could send shivers down her spine.

She was still angry with him, darn it. Not because he'd taken his sister back to the Comanche village and stayed there longer than necessary, or even because he'd admitted he loved her and walked away. She was angry with him for not being willing to stay with her, fight for her—fight *with* her—when she was more than willing to fight for him.

She cleared her throat, praying her voice wouldn't break when she tried to speak. "What are you doing here, David?"

"Well, I've done some thinking."

She quirked a brow and then ran her glance over the throng of onlookers, eagerly doing their best to eavesdrop, though they were polite enough to hang back a bit.

"What are all these people doing here?" she hissed, feeling awkward and on display.

Twisting around, he threw a look over his shoulder. "I'll get to them in a minute," he said, returning his attention to her. "I took Bright Eyes and the kids back to the village, and then I stayed there a while. Like I said, to think."

"I hope it wasn't too painful for you," she replied dryly.

He studied her for a minute before chuckling. "I'm getting better at it," he told her with a wink. "Although I wasn't getting far on my own until Pa showed up."

"Your father followed you to the Comanche village? Why?"

"I think Ma might have put him up to it, actually, but he came out to make sure I didn't do anything stupid." He lowered his gaze to the ground for a second before bringing it back up to hers. "Like leaving you."

Her heart stuttered in her breast.

"He told me some things about his relationship with Ma when they first met. And he gave me a few facts about women."

Crossing her arms over her chest, she considered him. She wasn't sure what to think of his story and hoped the doubt she felt didn't show in front of all these people.

"One thing he made pretty clear was that if I made you angry and then took off, you'd probably never forgive me." He bowed his head sheepishly. "I'm kind of hoping I didn't stay away so long that you hate me completely." He raised his head again, any sign of teasing gone from his eyes. "Did I?"

"I don't hate you, David," she answered softly. It was the truth. She didn't hate him at all; she loved him. But at the same time, she wasn't sure she could handle the pain of his leaving again.

"Good! That will make this much easier." He slapped his hand down hard on the flat portion of the railing and then took the stairs two at a time until he was only one step below her. With the difference in their heights, he was almost at eye level with her.

Hannah's breathing turned shallow as her gaze met his. He was too close. She could smell the musky scent of his skin and feel the heat emanating from his wide, well-muscled body.

Arms behind his back, he leaned forward on the soles of his boots and pressed his lips near her ear. "Marry me," he whispered.

She jerked back as though she'd been burned. "What?"

"Marry me," he said again, looking her straight in the eye.

"David." She forced his name past a throat clogged with emotion. "I'm not . . . There's no baby, if that's what you're worried about," she told him, lowering her voice so as not to be overheard by the horde of people still milling around the school yard.

He inhaled deeply and then nodded. "Good," he said again. "Don't get me wrong; I'd be happy if there were a child. Ecstatic. But if it's all the same to you, I'd rather any children we have are conceived after we're hitched. That way, you'll never have cause to doubt why I married you. You'll know it's because I love you, and for no other reason."

Hannah opened her mouth, not the least bit sure of what she intended to say, but he grabbed her hand and pulled her down the steps to the ground where everyone else waited.

With his arm at her waist he said, "You told me once that the people of Purgatory didn't think of me as a half-breed. And you must be right, because when I asked them to help me out this morning, every single one of them was eager to oblige."

Taking her hand, he started to lead her through the crowd, pausing in front of each person as he seemed to tick them off a mental list. "Father Ignacio will perform the ceremony at the church, of course. Mrs. Smith will open the Eat 'Em Up Café afterward and has generously offered to prepare a meal for all our guests. Which, by the way, will be the entire town.

"I hope you don't mind," he added as an aside, moving on to the next person, "but when word got out that I planned to propose, everyone wanted to be involved. And everyone wanted to be there—there for the wedding and here for the proposal."

Hannah shook her head, not sure she was absorbing anything at the moment. She wasn't even sure she was awake. David's words and the crowd around her made her feel as though she might still be asleep in her bed and merely dreaming.

"Mr. and Mrs. Potter are gifting us with their best room at the hotel for our honeymoon night. Unless you'd like to spend it somewhere else. It's completely up to you, *notsa?ka?*. And Mr. McGee at the general store has a case of rings in his safe for you to look at. I want you to pick whichever one you like."

He let go of her hand and took a step back. Facing her, he stood with his arms loose at his sides, looking more earnest than she'd ever seen him.

"I've thought about everything you said, Hannah, and you were absolutely right. I'm

not saying there won't be problems. That
there won't be times when people look at us
differently because you're white and I'm part
Indian, or call our children names—especially if we leave Purgatory. But we're safe
here. These people are our friends."

Her eyes were already brimming, her lungs
struggling to take in air. But his next words
sent her completely over the edge.

"I love you, Hannah. Whatever comes, I
know we can handle it. Together. *I* can handle it, with you at my side. All you have to do
is say yes."

His voice softened and he got down on one
knee in the grass in front of her, taking her
now quivering hand in his own. *"Nʉ? kamakʉrʉ mʉi, notsa?ka?.* Will you marry me?"

For several long seconds, she watched him.
His strong jaw and soft lips, the love and sin-
cerity in his eyes. She looked around her, at
all of the townspeople and all of her students
awaiting her answer right along with David.
His mother was bouncing on the balls of her
feet, her high cheekbones flushed with expectation.

Hannah gave a watery laugh, returning her
attention to the still kneeling David. "If I say
no, these folks are likely to string me up from
the nearest tree."

"Don't say no." His already strong grip on
her fingers tightened. "Unless you don't love
me, after all, or can't forgive me for leaving

you the way I did. But . . . for God's sake, forgive me, Hannah, and say you'll marry me. These folks will string *me* up if you don't."

With a small sniffle, she chuckled and then tugged at his arm until he stumbled to his feet. "You're forgiven. And I will marry you, if only to keep you out of trouble for the next forty years."

A great cheer went up behind them, but David pretended they were still alone as he rolled his eyes heavenward. "Thank *Taʔahpʉ*," he breathed before wrapping his arms about her waist and lifting her off her feet.

His mother was hugging Hannah's shoulders from behind, his father was slapping David on the back, and everyone else was crowding in around them. But David merely held her against his chest and grinned down at her.

"You're a good woman, Hannah Blake."

"You're a good man, David Walker. I've been waiting for you all my life and I'm never letting you get away again."

He ran a hand over her hair, his breath fanning her face as he lowered his mouth to kiss her. "Without you, *notsaʔkaʔ*, there's nowhere I want to go."

Epilogue

Hannah dragged the straight-back chair from her desk across the plank floor and lined it up in front of the far wall. Lifting her skirts, she climbed onto the seat and raised her arms high above her head to attach the oversize papers in her hands with tiny tacks. By the time the students came back in from their noonday meal, she wanted to have their artwork projects covering the area around the blackboard.

"What do you think you're doing?"

The sharp voice startled her and she swung about, teetering on the edge of the chair. Before she could either regain her balance or fall, a strong pair of arms reached out and plucked her into the air.

Heidi Betts

"Good lord, David, you scared the life out of me."

"Which is only about half as much as you scared me when I saw you up there," he grumbled, setting her on her feet. "What the hell do you think you're doing?"

"Hanging these pictures," she told him, crouching to pick up the pages that had scattered to the floor when he'd frightened her. "I want to have them up before I call the children in from lunch."

"A woman in your condition shouldn't be climbing around on the furniture."

Shooting him a guileless grin, she arched her back and stroked a hand over the protruding mound of her very large stomach. "Then maybe you should put them up for me."

He scowled but took the pile of youthful drawings from her and stepped up on the seat of the chair.

She settled sideways at one of the students' desks to watch him. He wore a pair of faded dungarees and a blue chambray shirt, covered by a brown leather vest with a silver star over his heart. He was working with his father now, as the deputy sheriff of Purgatory, and Hannah was so proud of him, she nearly burst her buttons on a daily basis.

Of course, if she told him as much, he would likely say that buttons weren't made to withstand the amount of pressure she put on them nowadays, growing as big as Texas itself. If he was lucky, she would merely scowl and remind him of the part he'd played in her current state as a brood mare. If she was feeling particularly sensitive, she would no doubt burst into tears and have him on his knees, begging her forgiveness, promising never to say anything so cruel and inconsiderate again.

These days, poor David never knew when he might hit an unlucky streak.

But he loved his job, and loved working with his father. He also got a mule-sized kick out of being the letter of the law in a town he used to think despised him. His Comanche blood didn't matter one whit when there was a star on his chest, and he still puffed up like a peacock every morning when he pinned it to his shirt.

"What are you doing here, anyway?" she asked, letting her gaze drift to the finely shaped buttocks poured into his denim trousers.

"I came by to tell you that my father has to transport a prisoner to the jail in another town and needs me to be on duty tonight, probably all night," he said over his shoulder as he tacked pictures to the wall.

"That one's crooked," she put in. "Does that mean you won't be home for dinner, then?"

He straightened the drawing, paying more attention to the rest so he wouldn't have to do them all twice. "I'm afraid not. I know you like to stay in the new house, even though it's not finished yet, but I don't want you sleeping there by yourself."

"Are you suggesting I find myself a substitute husband to keep your side of the bed warm while you're away?"

It was his turn to whirl around and rock on his heels to avoid falling on his face. She smiled, letting him know she was teasing.

"You're a dangerous woman, Hannah Walker. Do you want me to break my neck?"

"Not until the nursery in the new house is completed," she replied sweetly, "and you take me to your sister."

That brought the usual frown to his face. She'd been chattering for months about going to the Comanche village for the birth of their baby—a notion David was none too pleased about.

For as long as she'd been trying to convince him to take her, he'd been attempting to talk her out of it. When the time came, he wanted her to be in Purgatory, with a doctor nearby in case she needed one.

And she didn't blame him. But David had taken her to visit Bright Eyes not long after their wedding, and Hannah had fallen in love with the village and its people. She even suspected that might have been where their child had been conceived.

But as alarmed as she'd been at the way

Bright Eyes had given birth to Laughing Rain, Hannah's heart was now absolutely set on having her and David's child in much the same manner. It would create an even stronger bond between David and his Comanche heritage. Bright Eyes had already agreed to assist her, and Little Bear was going to choose the baby's Indian name.

"You're not having the baby in the village," he said, turning back around to continue posting the pictures.

"Yes, I am," she replied simply, and then distracted him by continuing with the earlier thread of their conversation. "What do you propose I do tonight if you're working and don't want me sleeping at the new house by myself? Should I stay at the cabin instead?"

They'd lived there for several months after their marriage, but for the last little while had taken up residence in the new house they were building near his parents. She didn't mind staying at the cabin, though it would be lonely without him and she wasn't even sure what kind of condition the place would be in after standing empty for so long.

Finished tacking up the drawings, he hopped down and dragged the chair back to her desk. "I thought you could stay with Ma for tonight. I'll come by about the time you're ready to dismiss class for the day and walk you out there, then come back to take over for Pa. You don't mind, do you?"

He stood before her now and she held out her arms, letting him drag her bulk out of the child's desk and chair.

"Of course I don't mind. But I will miss you."

Smiling, he pulled her against him, bent past the swell of her belly, and nuzzled her lips. "I'll miss you, too. This is the first night we'll spend apart, you know."

"I know. And whose fault is that?"

"Mine. But I'll make it up to you."

"Oh, goody." She never minded when David committed minor transgressions because he always did such a fine job of apologizing.

He kissed her breathless, and Hannah forgot all about where they were until scampering footsteps and childish groans broke through her consciousness.

"*Eeeew*, that's disgusting."

"They're doing it again."

"Ma says they'll stop someday, but I don't think so. I think they're going to be doing that forever. Yuck!"

Biting back an amused retort, Hannah pulled away from David, who was also fighting hard not to smile. She'd learned long ago that she was no good at playing the part of a staid married schoolmarm. Mostly because no matter where she and David were they couldn't help but show their affection and consequently kept getting caught kissing.

"Hello, girls," she said. "Is there something you need?"

"We've been waiting for you to call us in from lunch. The boys didn't want us to, 'cause they're having fun running around outside, but we thought something might be wrong."

Hannah glanced at the polished mahogany clock case on the far wall and groaned. More time had passed than she'd realized.

"Everything's fine. Why don't you call the other children in and we'll start on our vocabulary words?"

The two girls ran off to ring the bell that alerted the students to return to the classroom as Hannah turned back to David. "I'm sorry," she told him with a frown. "I really do have to get back to work."

"That's all right. You can make it up to me later," he said with a tantalizing grin.

A shiver of longing tripped down her spine and she nodded, swallowing hard.

"I'll be by at the end of the day." As he passed, he put a hand to her taut belly, kissing her once more, lightly on the lips. "Take care of my *ohna?a?* while I'm away."

"I will," she said, understanding him perfectly.

He'd been giving her Comanche lessons and she was becoming rather fluent in the language, if she did say so herself. Of course, she thought that might have something to do with his teaching methods, which took place

335

late, late at night and involved an almost sinful reward system when she did well.

Children began pouring in the door, talking excitedly and scraping chair legs across the floor as they settled at their desks.

With his mouth close to her ear so none of her pupils would hear, he whispered, *"Nʉ? kamakʉrʉ mʉi*. And maybe once school's dismissed for the week, I'll take you out to the Comanche village."

"I love you, too. And I knew you would," she said, the corner of her mouth twitching with mirth.

He narrowed one dark, long-lashed eye at her. "You did, huh? Don't you ever get tired of being right?"

"No. That's how I landed you, after all."

"Uh-huh." He crossed his arms over his chest. "Well, one of these days, I'll get my turn at being right about something."

She slid her hands over his forearms and leaned close. "You already have. When you stopped acting silly and asked me to marry you."

His gaze turned heated, settling on her mouth. "Yeah. I guess that did turn out better than I expected."

Using one of his favorite endearments, she promised softly, "This is only the beginning, *notsa?ka?*. Only the beginning."

And then, ignoring the loud groans of the

two dozen students surrounding them, she stood on tiptoe and gave her husband a silent taste of their future together. It was only the beginning, indeed.

AUTHOR'S NOTE

Dear Reader:

Thank you for taking the time to read Hannah and David's story. After hinting at a future romance for these two orphans in *Walker's Widow*, I hope you enjoyed seeing them all grown up and falling in love. I know I did.

As many of you may be aware from reading my previous books, *Hannah's Half-Breed* is my first foray into the Native American culture, and I'm sure I made mistakes. For this, I sincerely apologize. But please don't hold it against me—I really did do my best.

One of the ways in which I fear I most likely erred is with my use of Comanche terms. During my research for this book, I learned that Comanche is a dying language with few accurate resources left. I was lucky enough, however, to get my hands on a copy of *Comanche Dictionary and Grammar* by Lila Wistrand Robinson and James Armagost, and this is the main source I relied on for almost all of the Comanche spoken in the story. Even so, I take full responsibility for any inaccuracies.

Just for fun, here is a short glossary of some of the Comanche terms used in *Hannah's Half-Breed*.

haa—yes
ke or *kee*—no
ara?—uncle, nephew
pia—mother
ʜotsa?ka?—sweetheart
uʜa or *ahó*—thank-you
nu? kamakuru mui—I love you

Ahó and happy reading!